CAPPADONNA
IF I SAY SHE MINE, SHE MINE

JAHQUEL J.

Copyright © 2024

Published by Jahquel J.
www.Jahquel.com
ALL RIGHTS RESERVED
Any unauthorized reprint or use of the material is prohibited. No part of this book may be reproduced or transmitted in any form or by any means, electronic, or mechanical, including photocopying, recording, or by any information storage without express permission by the publisher. This is an original work of fiction. Names, characters, places, and incidents are either products of the author's imagination or are used fictitiously and any resemblance to actual persons, living or dead is entirely coincidental.
Contains explicit languages and adult themes.
suitable for ages 16+

CONNECT WITH ME:

Join my mailing list here + check out my website for autographed paperbacks:
JOIN HERE!
www.Jahquel.com
Join my official reading group:
Jahquel J's we reading or nah group?
Be sure to bless my page with a LIKE!
CONNECT WITH ME ON SOCIAL MEDIA:
http://www.instagram.com/_Jahquel
http://www.twitter.com/Author_Jahquel
https://www.tiktok.com/@_iamjah
When writing my books, I run off coffee, anxiety + overthinking. Like to contribute to my coffee habit? You can purchase me a coffee hereeee!

JAHQUEL J'S CATALOG:

Brookwood Series
Interconnected Standalone Series
- From Come Over To Come Home
- He's My Next Mistake
- From Replied To Wifey
- Welcome To Brookwood

Lennox Hills Series
Interconnected Standalone Series
- I'm Fine...Thanks
- Yeah... Thanks
- Never Better... Thanks

Mathers Family
- Confessions Of A Hustla's Housekeeper 1-3
- Confessions Of A Hustla's Daughter 1-2 ✶

Davis Family
- Staten Island Love Letter 1-5
- Staten Island Love Affair 1-4✶
- A Brownsville, Harlem & Staten Island Holiday Affair ✶

Vanducci-Cromwell Family
- A Staten Island Love Story 1-3

Harlem King Saga
- In Love With The King Of Harlem 1-5
- In Love With An East Coast Maniac 1-3 ✶
- Rose In Harlem: Harlem King's Princess ✶

BAE Series
- BAE: Before Anyone Else 1-3
- He's Still BAE 1-3✶
- BAE: Holiday ✶

Homies, Lovers & Friends
- Homies, Lovers & Friends 1-5
- Homies, Lovers & Wives ✶

Series:
- Crack Money With Cocaine Dreams 1-2
- Never Wanted To Be Wifey 1-2
- To All The Thugs I Loved That Didn't Love Me Back 1-4
- All The Dope Boys Gon Feel Her 1-2
- Good Girls Love Hustlas 1-3
- I Got Nothing But Love For My Hitta 1-2
- She Ain't Never Met A N*gga Like Me 1-3
- Married To A Brownsville Bully 1-3
- Thugs Need Love 1-3
- What A Wicked Way To Treat The Woman You Love 1-2
- Finessing The Plug 1-2

Standalones:
- My Lover, My Dopeboy
- I Can't Be The One You Love
- I'm Riding With You Forever
- Forever, I'm Ready
- Emotionless
- Blaquehatten
- Ho, Ho, Housewife
- When Can I See You Again?
- What You Know About Love?
- Hearts Won't Break
- Pretty Little Fears
- Save Myself
- Two Occasions
- I Didn't Mean To Fall In Love

✶ Spinoff

www.Jahquel.com | hello@Jahquel.com | @Jahquel

SYNOPSIS:

Alaia:

After my yaya passed away, I didn't have anyone that cared for me. I mean, not even a month after Yaya was in the ground, he sat me down in the living room and sold me to a thirty-year-old man. I was sixteen, and my big brother, the man that was supposed to protect me sold me off like cattle on a farm.
My entire life has been to please Zayne. I'm his fourth wife, and the youngest wife. Nobody has ever protected or cared for me. I was tossed the cards that life handed me and had to make do with them. That is until Cappadonna Delgato and I cross paths-again.

Cappadonna:
All it took was for me to see her one time in that visitation room to know that I needed her. Alaia, her name literally means joy and happiness, and I didn't see anything of the sorts in her eyes when she stared into my eyes that day. As Allah would have it, our paths were meant to cross on the outside, and they did.
I'm a protector, a provider, and a man, and I don't think Alaia has

ever had that in her life. I don't care what I have to do or who I have to see to make her mine. She went years without knowing what protection and true love felt like, and I'm stepping up to make sure she doesn't go another day not knowing how I feel or how I'm coming behind her. If I say she's mine, she's mine, and I've never been afraid to shed blood to prove it.

HEY THERE...

Capone and Cappadonna may be twins, but they are different, and their issues are different. While Erin and Capone's story was their own, I ask that you allow Cappadonna and Alaia's story to be theirs.
Their relationships won't be the same, and the issues are really not the same. You met Alaia at the prison, and you'll read more about her story in this book. Her story isn't as simple as Erin's story. (Although was Erin's even simple?)

Trigger warning: This book has domestic violence scenes, and human trafficking scenes involving minors. As much as I write for your entertainment, please take care of yourself.
The scenes are minimal but very important for the telling of this story.

Here's to more bang- bang shoot 'em up, emergency rooms and kisses on the nose.

Here's the playlist for Cappadonna:
Apple
Spotify

If you enjoy visuals, check out the Pinterest board for this book.
Pinterest

PROLOGUE

ALAIA
10 years ago....

IN ELEMENTARY SCHOOL, me and Raheem had set up a lemonade stand outside of our Yaya's house. I don't know why we thought we would make a lot in the middle of the hood in Wilmington, Delaware. While we were trying to sell lemonade, everyone was either selling drugs or ass. Raheem, my big brother, had always been attracted to the allure of making fast money.

While I was more than happy to sit and wait for someone to offer to buy a fresh cup of Country Time lemonade, he wanted the money quicker. His lack of patience had always been something that bothered me. He could never work hard to get what he wanted, he wanted to skip steps and get the success without actually doing the work or going through the trials and tribulations.

Our yaya ran numbers out the house and that afforded her to always keep a roof over our heads. When our mother was locked up for first degree murder, she was the one that took us in. Well, she never had to take us in because we were always at her house. Ronnie, my mother, was always quick to drop us off for a weekend and return weeks later.

I could never depend on my mother because she always chose someone over her kids. When she was arrested, it wasn't something devastating because she was never there to begin with. Raheem on the other hand took it pretty hard. He idolized my mother and whatever boyfriend she brought around for the week. He saw the money, jewels, and cars and wanted it all. While all us kids were planning on what we wanted to be when we grew up, Raheem wanted to be a hustler.

"You not going to sit around and spend my money. That's not the shit we on, Alaia," he chuckled, while sealing his blunt with his tongue. "You gotta earn your keep around here some way."

I should have run away all the times the thought crossed my mind. Where was I supposed to go at sixteen? My yaya was my entire world and the one who protected me from the world. All she wanted was for me to attend college.

I would have been the only one to attend college in our family. She wanted me to be better than my mother, to make something of myself. Yaya hadn't been in the ground for a month before Raheem had turned her house into a whore house.

Women and men came from all over the state to climb between the legs of one of Raheem's girls. Raheem said fuck being a police officer, handyman, or even a construction worker. He decided drugs weren't quick enough money, so he turned to selling pussy.

"I'm sixteen, Rah," I said barely above a whisper.

He sparked his blunt and then looked at me with malice laced in his eyes. "All you do is walk around with a fucking book in your hand. Judging the very bitches that keep a roof over your fucking head." He eyed my body down, making me uncomfortable. "Yeah, you would be just right... I got the right one for you."

"One for me?" I choked out, tears falling down my eyes as I listened to my brother talk about pimping me out.

He took the longest pull and blew the smoke out in my face. "You should be lucky that I'm not making you work your pussy in those back rooms."

One of the back rooms used to be my yaya's room. Her room had always been right off the kitchen. It was the first place I went whenever I came into the house, and the source of comfort. I would climb under her blankets while listening to the loud fan in the window, and the sound of the news in the background. It was like my own personal sound machine that helped me drift off to sleep.

"I'm going away to college, Raheem. I promise, two more years and I'm out your hair," I pleaded with him.

"That school shit ain't going to get you far, Alaia. I wish you would just give it the fuck up. Look at this money," he pulled out a knot of money and laughed, his mouth filled with gold.

While Raheem was always decked in the newest designer, and spent all his money in the club, his hoes were always scrapping together money for something. I don't know how many times one of them had to borrow a pad or tampon or something from me.

Even though he didn't treat his girls right, they still stuck beside him like glue. It wasn't like I was given a free ride either. My best friend gave me money to get the things that I needed, or food to buy for my room. Raheem acted like me being here cost him money when I never asked him for anything.

"I'm just going to leave... I won't cost you anything if I leave."

He chuckled. "I have custody of you. You think you about to leave and have them sniffing around here for me?"

"Nobody won't say anything, I promise," I pleaded with him, desperate for him to show up as the big brother I had always wanted.

Raheem had never been a big brother that protected me. He always looked out for himself, so I don't know why I expected different from him when Yaya passed on. I thought I could quietly finish out high school and then go to college.

He would never have to hear from me again, and I would be a figment of his imagination. As I stood here, scared of what was to happen next, the plan I had that used to be so vivid, was quickly dwindling away from me.

"Alaia, get the hell on with that bullshit... I don't have time to keep tabs on you. Unlike the rest of these bitches, I actually give a fuck about what happens to you."

He tried to sound convincing, as if he was a big brother looking out for what was best for me. When in reality, all he cared about was the money he made, and the bitches he pimped.

I nearly jumped out of my skin when the doorbell rang. Raheem had this look of satisfaction on his face when he heard it. "Looks like he actually showed the fuck up," one of his flunkies laughed, as he climbed off the couch to get the door.

"Where the hell you going? Stay right there!" Raheem hollered, as I tried to escape back upstairs to my room.

My comfort in this hell hole.

Since Yaya had left me, I found myself struggling while trying to make the best of the cards that life had handed me.

All I had to look forward to was college and that was taken away from me. Raheem put out his freshly lit blunt and sat up when a man walked into the living room.

I stood with my arms crossed, hugging myself in the corner and unsure on what was about to happen. The man had to be no more than 5'8, he was shorter than Raheem for sure. He wore linen white pants and a graphic T-shirt. On his head, he wore a Kufi and a pair of round gold rimmed glasses.

He was handsome, and from the way he licked his lips he knew that he was. The man wasn't skinny by no means; however, he had a meaty physique that some women might admire. Although, he was about two burgers away from being fat.

"Didn't think you would make it... thought you thought I was bluffing or something." Raheem stood up, embracing the man.

"I told you that I would, right? What is this prize that I had to come all the way out here to witness?" He was impatient, barely wanted to sit or accept the glass of water from one of the women.

"Right here... this Alaia." He pointed to me, who held onto myself tighter, as I put together the clues on what Raheem was trying to do.

The man turned, noticing me for the first time. His eyes told me that he liked what he saw. It was a look I had been given way too many times by Raheem's friends. Their eyes glossed over my body, and I could see the nasty and vile thoughts that were probably running through their minds.

From the way this man stared me down, he had the same thoughts, except he was more subtle about it. Looking away, I wanted to be anywhere but in this front room feeling like a slave on the auction block.

I could run away and never return again. That was exactly

what I planned to do, because I would be damned if Raheem made a living off me. It wasn't right, and I had nobody here to step up for me. My mother was gone, Yaya was dead, and I didn't know my father.

"The price still the same or you trying to gas me up for more?" He folded his arms and glared at my brother, who was stroking his goatee.

Raheem sat there with a look of satisfaction on his face as he looked me over, deciding on if the price would remain the same. He kept surveying me like I was a prized poodle in a show. "Add two more racks on top of that. She smart, too... not one of those dumb bitches."

My heart sank hearing those words leave his mouth. The man stood there, looking over at me once more, then he turned to Raheem and extended his hand.

"Slick ass... I knew you were gonna be talking something different. You lucky she beautiful and a virgin."

If my heart couldn't sink anymore, hearing him refer to my virginity nearly caused me to fall to the floor. "I'm not a piece of property, Raheem. You want me out of your hair... then I will leave." I turned to run up the stairs to grab my backpack.

That was all I needed in the moment. Soon as I touched the banister, one of Raheem's flunkies grabbed me. Zoe grabbed me around the waist and brought me back in the front room.

"Fuck this up for me, Alaia, and I can promise the only time your geeky ass will read is in between working that pussy," Raheem snarled in my ear, while pinching my neck.

I stood in my school clothes looking from my brother, who was supposed to protect me, to the man that I was sure I would be sold to. He looked at Raheem and snapped his fingers at him.

"Take your fucking hands off her... leaving bruises is a sure way to knock the price down." I had got excited that he was taking up for me, then all hope faded away when he referred to me like I was an object, and not a person.

A teenage girl who just wanted to live her life.

"Take her upstairs to pack some stuff while we sort out everything," Raheem told Zoe, as he nudged me toward the steps.

I choked on my tears as I slowly took the stairs one by one. My eyes were blurry as I tried to look up the steps. Except, I could barely see anything and was moving on strictly muscle memory. I wanted to run out the house and never return.

By the time I made it past Zoe, I would be slapped and taken back up the steps. I slowly opened my room door and grabbed my things. Who knew when I would see this room again. After Yaya died, it stopped feeling like my room and more like a safe haven away from Raheem and his foolishness.

I put everything that I could into my pink Jan Sport bookbag, collecting my favorite books. Zoe stood by the door watching me.

"I'm sorry, Laia," he whispered, knowing that he shouldn't have even been speaking to me. Had Raheem knew that we had a friendship, he would have kicked Zoe to the curb a long time ago.

"Sorry would have been warning me about this." I sniffled, cutting my eyes at him as I shoved more things into my backpack.

He walked further into the room. "I swear, this is the first time I'm hearing about this... Rah don't tell none of us shit until it's done or about to be done."

I put my bookbag onto my shoulder and looked up into his eyes. "Well, I guess it's about to be done now, right."

Bypassing him, I made my way back downstairs with my heart in my throat. I felt like I was in a bad dream and eventually I would wake up to pee and then go back to sleep. Except, this isn't a bad dream.

I was being sold by my brother to a man that was much older than me, and there wasn't anything that I could do. Protecting his kid sister was the least of Raheem's problems. I prayed that he never had a moments peace and that this life he was so excited to have turned into everything that he never wanted it to be.

Yaya was a praying woman, and I knew that even without her being here, that I would be alright.

"Don't go causing no damn problems, Alaia. I'm doing this for you... you don't have no place here."

I gathered all the spit in my mouth and the back of my throat and hawked a big blob of spit into my brother's face. He started to reach back and slap me, and the man pulled me away from him.

"Go ahead and hit her while I'm standing here," he threatened and Raheem put his hand down, using it to wipe the spit from his face.

All the girls were all gathered around the Mercedes that stuck out like a sore thumb on this desolate street. I followed behind the man, holding onto my bag and scared of what was to come next.

He held the passenger door open for me and then strolled around it with his phone in his hand. I looked up on the porch and saw Ivy standing there. She was the only girl in the house that was close to my age. She was only seventeen and had been brought to the house in the middle of the night.

I never asked questions on how these women ended up here or why. She asked to borrow a tampon a few times, and we had become close. Ivy always looked out for me with money she skimmed off the top from Raheem. I was going to miss her because she had looked out for me more than my own blood brother.

As the car pulled off the block, I fought to hold back the tears that threatened to fall. Everything happened so fast. One second, I was standing in the living room explaining to Raheem why I needed money, and the next I was leaving the only home that I have ever known to an unfamiliar place with an even more unfamiliar man.

I

CAPPADONNA

"Who wakes up this early and works out?" Erin whispered, as she stood in the doorway of the sunroom drinking coffee.

I laughed as I continued to do push-ups with one arm behind my back. "When you got a bunch of pussy muthafuckas running your day, you don't have a choice on when you can wake up and go to sleep." I finished the last one and then rolled my prayer mat up before taking a seat on the couch.

"We're all so happy that you are home. Especially your brother." She took a sip of her coffee and then took a seat on the opposite couch.

I had been home for a couple months and had been living in my brother's house. With me being here, even with the size of the house, it was at capacity. I mean, Capone had a lot of house, and everyone had their space, I just knew it was time for me to get my own space.

"Feels weird being home. I've been trying to adjust to just doing whatever the fuck I want without a fat ass CO on my ass about it."

She smiled. "Oh please. Like you weren't damn near

running that prison... I know it will take a lot for you to mentally adjust. Just know we're not in any rush for you to leave. We love having you here."

I smiled at her. "I gotta get out on my own eventually, E. I can't keep staying with you and Capo... I need my own shit."

"When are you going to tell Kendra that you're home? You've been home for four months and the girl doesn't know you are home."

Kendra had no clue that I was home from prison, and I wanted to keep it like that until I was ready to pop up on her ass. Whenever I talked to her, I told her that I got a burner phone in and told her not to visit because I couldn't have visits. Kendra was never excited to come visit me anyway. Her ass always complained about the ride to the prison, so I was doing her a favor by not having her come visit me.

"I don't know. Got to be the perfect time."

Me and Ken were like water and vinegar and only I could say that shit. Whenever Capone called himself being knowledgeable on my relationship, I always shut his ass down. Maybe I knew he was right about Ken, and there was a part of me that felt like I had to continue to hold her ass down.

Then again, I wanted to wring her fucking neck because she hid that I had a son from me. It had been hard being on the outside and not popping up at her crib and choking her ass out. I laid in bed plenty of nights wondering why she chose to keep that away from me. Even with me not having money like I had now, I would have still stepped up to the plate and raised my son.

"There's no such thing as the perfect time... and there's no reason to rush out the house. We're not rushing you out, Capp." She stood up, just as her big-headed ass husband stood in the doorway.

I watched as he kissed the top of her bald head, and then

dropped a few kisses on her lips. Capone had never loved like the way he loved Erin. There was no other woman put on this earth for my brother. I had to admit, being around the both of them for the past few months reminded me what love looked like.

It was patient.

Kind.

I sounded corny as hell, but that was what love was for me. Love was finding that one that I could take down my walls for. Someone that was patient because I've been behind the wall for years. I'm guarded as fuck and know that I'm a handful. When I thought about that person, I knew that it couldn't have been Kendra.

Kendra was selfish as hell, and she wanted everything to be about her. The real reason I hadn't popped up on her was to see how hard she would go to see me. Would she call the prison to even inquire why I couldn't have any visits? I set my self-up because she didn't do any of that shit. Instead, she used the direct line to ask me for more money or to upgrade her whip.

We've both grown apart while I was in prison, and I was avoiding the truth because it was easier to just have someone on the outside. I wasn't the same man that I was before I went in. Yeah, I would still set some shit off, but I wasn't the same guy that wanted to dip in and out of different women.

"Damn, you just woke up next to her... pipe the fuck down," I brought my twin back to reality, as he watched his wife switch out the sunroom.

He turned his attention back to me and broke out in laughter. "Fuck you. You mad because your hood rat somewhere getting her nails done."

"Fuck you."

"I'm saying... why the fuck you sitting back and waiting on

popping up on her." He pulled his phone out and scrolled down his screen. "She hit me up last night to ask me for some money."

"The fuck do she need all this money for?"

"I don't know, but she be fucking blowing through it like her last name Delgato. Mrs. Delgato don't even spend that kind of cash."

"Cause your wife frugal as hell... I saw her clipping fucking coupons last week, Capo." I couldn't help but to laugh.

Erin took her role as Capone's wife seriously, and she ran this house just like it. I watched as she took care of the kids and my brother and knew that was exactly what I wanted in a woman. I was a traditional nigga. I wanted my woman barefoot and pregnant while I brought home the bacon – beef of course.

Even though Erin could have anything that she wanted, she still shopped at regular stores and cut fucking coupons. She was grounded and hadn't let her name change her, not even a little bit.

"Chill on my wife. If she wanna save me money, then who am I to stop her."

"She probably barked on you about complaining."

Capone sunk down in the chair with his feet kicked up. "She fucking stubborn, bro'."

I laughed. "She def give you a run for your damn money. Erin and Ella are like night and day. While she saving you money, Ella spending money like it's going out of style."

"Ain't my money though... she fucking with some football player she met. Damn near kissed the nigga in his mouth when I met him... finally she got somebody to take her mind off us."

Capone wanted to step away from everything because for the first time in his life, everything was at peace in his life. He had been holding the torch and running it up while I was locked up. Through everything, he has held this family together and provided.

Even though I wanted my brother by my side, I respected that he needed to be present with his new wife, daughter, and son. I wasn't that sad because I knew if I needed him, he was lacing his boots and coming to kill some shit behind me.

"How much she need?"

He looked down at his phone. "Like ten bands.... Talking about she need it for a trip she going on."

Not that I expected for Ken's life to stop when mine did, I guess I expected her ass to be down more for me. Instead, she was living her best life on my dime and didn't have time to at least write me a damn letter.

"Hmm."

"When the fuck you going to bring up the Chubs situation? He been running errands for you, and he your whole ass son."

Chubs had been around, and I hadn't let him know that I knew he was my son. The shit was clear that he was my son. He looked like me, and I couldn't deny him if I wanted to. I guess I was scared to approach the subject because I hadn't been there.

How could I call myself a father when I had never been there, and only found about him last year? I was always the type of man that stood behind anything that I was responsible for, and Chubs wasn't one of the things I could say I stood behind because I didn't know about him.

It wasn't like I had a clue that Kendra had a kid. I mean, shit, she had gained some weight when she came back, but I didn't think anything of it. Honestly, I loved a thicker woman, so I was turned on by the extra weight she had gained.

"Capo, nineteen years."

"Not your fault, Capp. Stop fucking beating yourself up about something that was out of your control. Nobody knows her reasons for keeping you out the loop. Clearly, he wanna be a part of your life because he found you... feel me?"

"I'll never be able to get that time back... I wouldn't have wanted this life for him. I've been sitting back for the past few months because I don't want to put her head through a window, Capo."

Capone messed with his beard, the same time that I reached up to touch mine. It was creepy how much we were in sync, even after being apart all of these years. "All I can say is make those memories and build the relationship. Chubs is one of the realest niggas on the team... he was made for this shit. He's grown so ain't much you can do about that but focus on being his pops. Leave that other shit alone right now."

"I hear you."

"Yo, I'm leaving," Jaiden popped his head into the sunroom and spoke to Capone.

"What up, Kid?" I nodded my head.

"Oh, we speaking... 'cause you called me soft for fouling you yesterday while we was playing ball."

I went from hearing how Jaiden couldn't play like he used to play, to playing him last night and him dusting my old ass. I may have got in my feelings and called his ass soft when he fouled me.

"Water under the bridge, pussy," I joked.

"Man, don't be mad because you both old as hell... Hit me if you need something."

Capone raised his brow. "Still tricking on shorty?"

Jaiden smiled sheepishly. "You fronting like you ain't the biggest trick for E."

"Difference is she is my wife."

Jaiden put his finger to his chin. "She wasn't when you bought that mini cooper... I'm out," he called as he made his way down the hall.

"He got you there." I laughed.

"Fuck up. You need to figure your own shit out so you can get you a wife... or wives." Capone stood up and headed out the sunroom.

I leaned back on the couch and closed my eyes thinking about the day when I would find a wife. Over the years, I would sit on the phone and promise Kendra that I was going to marry her when I came home. As the years went on, I stopped making her that promise because I wasn't sure I wanted her to be my wife.

The Ken I left behind wasn't the same Ken that sat across from me. She checked her watch more than she locked in with me during the visit. When she spoke, all I heard was what she wanted and never about me – us.

She never put herself in my shoes to see what I wanted. I was locked up and having to live through her and whoever came to visit me. Even knowing how much she had changed, I still wanted to be with her when I got out.

Now, I wasn't sure what I wanted from her. She hid a son from me and never said anything to me. I think what made everything worse was the fact that she didn't raise our son. While I was shelling out money to buy her whatever she wanted, she didn't have the decency to even raise our kid.

It showed me the kind of woman she was, and that wasn't the kind of woman I wanted as a wife. With me approaching thirty-nine soon, I had a clear view of what I wanted for my life. I had years in a cell to think about what I wanted for my life when I was released.

I wanted an easy and peaceful life when I walked through the doors of my home. In the streets, there was no peace, especially with me running them. However, the moment I crossed my threshold, I wanted my woman to greet me and be my peace.

Know that I was out there getting to the money, and she was under our roof making our house a home. Kendra's ass was so busy running those same streets that I knew she could never be that kind of woman.

As a man, one who has grown, I didn't want her to be someone that she wasn't. I stood up and stretched before going to change and go on my four-mile run around the neighborhood. Routine was important to me, so for the past few months I continued with my same routine.

It was a nice change to eat cleaner. In prison, no matter how much money you had, you had to eat all that processed bullshit. I enjoyed being able to have fresh fruits and vegetables that didn't come from a fucking can.

"Your green juice is in the fridge, Cappadonna," Jo called from the kitchen table, enjoying her tea with a newspaper in her hand.

"Appreciate you, Jo. I'm fasting... remember?" I smiled as I headed out the kitchen to get my run in.

2

ALAIA

I HELD my swollen stomach as I watched them carefully lower my husband's body into the grave. In our religion, we didn't bury in a casket. Your body was placed on top of a wood topper to prevent the body from touching the soil, and positioned to face Mecca. Zayne was murdered on Sunday and here we were on a Tuesday burying him.

My thoughts hadn't fully processed that he was no longer alive, and that I didn't have him anymore. When he was released from prison, I thought that he would finally get himself together. He gave me every sign that he would never get his act together, even while in prison. All he did was make false promises and gain weight while behind bars.

The only thing he had accomplished was me getting pregnant. As I stood here with my very swollen eight-month stomach, I didn't know what to do. Zayne had three other wives, and they all had children and had come before me.

If that wasn't enough, each wife couldn't stand me. Especially when it came to Fatima. She hated me from the day I stepped into her house at sixteen years old. Zayne drove me to his house, that he shared with Fatima, and told her that I was his fourth wife.

He didn't offer any other explanation other than I was to be taught how to do things. Fatima stared at me, a younger woman who was tossed into her home and told to teach the way of her world.

A younger girl who would be pleasing her husband.

I could understand why she hated me. Hell, I hated my own self and my brother because he was the reason I was in this situation. Fatima taught me everything while I lived in her home. Zayne was hardly ever there. He would stay between his other two wives' houses, and then come over whenever he felt like it.

When Raheem sold me to Zayne, he was thirty years old, and I was sixteen. A sixteen-year-old girl being sold to a damn thirty-year-old was so wrong, and my brother did it like I was a pair of sneakers.

Fatima walked over toward me, looking down at my stomach. "Hmph, seems like he accomplished something."

You would think after damn near raising me and showing me how to be a woman that she would have grown a soft spot for me. It wasn't like I had willingly chose to be with her husband. I was sixteen years old when I lost my virginity to Zayne.

When Zayne moved me out of Fatima's house into a small apartment in Brooklyn, I was always alone. Always having to fend for myself and care for me. Zayne was never around unless it came to having sex.

Years of unwanted sex, abuse and miscarriages is what I had to endure because I had been sold. It wasn't like I could run away and get away from him. Where would I have gone? He always told me that he would find me, and when he did it wouldn't be good for me.

I converted to Islam, and covered my hair because that was what Zayne wanted. As the years went on, he preached so much about the Quran and why we had to follow the teachings that I wasn't sure about anything. Zayne was a big fraud and used religion as a way to cover up his bullshit. Any real Muslim didn't believe or do half the shit that he did.

I don't know how many times I saw him have a drink, and that wasn't allowed. It was hard to connect with a religion that was forced onto you, especially when it was by a fraud. Out of all of his wives, I was the only one that made the trips to visit him.

When he was released, it was the other wives he ran to and made sure had everything they needed. I was the last stop he made, and by then he was empty handed. Before he was killed, he had been talking about moving to Delaware to be closer to his family.

Money was tight and he said he couldn't keep up paying for the apartment that we had, along with all of the other houses his other wives owned. I had a small rental apartment with one bedroom, had to walk up six flights of stairs, and *I* was the one that had to give up my home?

When Taz told me that Zayne was killed, I sobbed for an hour after I got off the phone. Not because he was dead, but because I was finally free. Zayne was a horrible man that had done horrible things to me for years.

"Taz is going to take care of us now that Zayne isn't with us," Fatima explained, and I looked at her like she was crazy.

"As his wives?."

"It's what Zayne wanted. Has he never told you what would happen if he ever passed on?" She looked at me skeptical, as if Zayne told me everything.

She's his first wife, so their relationship had always been

stronger. Zayne told me what he wanted me to know, which was barely anything. "No."

I was ready to go home because my back was killing me. Plus, I didn't want to be here anymore. I refused to sit here and cry like Zayne was a good man. He was a man that took a teenage girl across state lines and made her his fourth wife.

It was a miracle that I had been able to carry this pregnancy this long. After all the pregnancies that I had lost, I was starting to believe that I was broken.

"Well," she looked over at Taz, who was talking to other people. "He should be coming to visit you to explain everything soon. You know, Taz has way more money than his brother ever did."

If I didn't know any better, Fatima seemed like she was excited that her damn husband was gone. I knew why I was happy that Zayne was gone, but what the hell was her reason? He treated her like gold.

I skipped out on going to dinner at the mosque and went home. There was so much that was unclear on what happened to Zayne. All I knew is that he was shot and killed. Taz refused to give any of us anymore information.

I slowly climbed all the steps, taking a break between landings, until I was in front of my door. My apartment wasn't much, and our landlord was a creep, but it was still home. It had been home for the past three years, and I appreciated every piece of secondhand furniture I had sourced.

Zayne wasn't much help when it came to turning this into a home. He barely gave me money and whenever I asked, he accused me of being greedy and only wanting money. I believed he tried to use something from the Quran to guilt me.

He always did that.

I carefully unpinned my hijab and then snatched it off, tossing it onto the couch. Covering my hair had never been something I wanted, it was forced onto me. All of this was forced onto me, and I had no other choice but to oblige.

It pained me to say that I hated my religion, and this wasn't something I would have chosen. I remember there was a time when I sat and read the Quran. I started to love the faith and identified as a Muslim woman.

Then Zayne would do something and use the Quran to guilt me. That was when I started to hate everything about it.

Sitting on the couch, I rubbed my stomach and took a few deep breaths. I didn't know what was next for me and this little one. It wasn't like I had family to fall back onto. Raheem was still running bitches out of Delaware, but I heard a rumor he was paralyzed because of a bad shoot out that went down, killing most of his people and damaging our yaya's house. I wasn't sure how true it was.

I wasn't sure how lucrative his business was with him being in a wheelchair, and Yaya's house not being very wheelchair accessible. I hadn't spoken to my brother since the day that I left that house.

He called and checked in with Zayne because they had business together. I was never part of those conversations, so I never knew if he cared enough to ask about me. I lost my childhood and was forced to become a woman quicker than I was ready to be.

My only hope for this baby I was carrying was to give them a life that they didn't have to hide from.

∼

As I carried the bags of groceries from the Key Food, I spotted Taz in his brand new BMW. Zayne always envied his younger brother because he had more money. He always laughed at how his life was easier because he didn't have any wives.

Taz always gave me the creeps because he looked at me like he wanted to devour me whole. Even modestly dressed, he eyed me down like he could see me through my clothes. He hopped out the car and quickly took the bags from my hands.

"Why didn't you call and tell me that you need groceries? I would have made sure that they were brought to you." He followed behind me as I let us into the building.

He was full of shit like his brother.

Taz wouldn't have sent anybody over here, and I would have had to lug these groceries down the block and up these damn stairs. For the sake of not having to carry the groceries upstairs, I was going to humor him and his fake concern.

"I know you're busy tying up all the loose ends with your brother." I huffed while damn near crawling up all the steps.

When we finally made it to the top, I almost passed out from trying to get the key in the damn lock. Taz put the groceries in the kitchen while I sat down on the couch trying to catch my breath. The summer hadn't even come in yet, and I was about to die from the little bit of heat we were getting with spring.

"You need some water or something?"

I held up the water bottle that I kept on the coffee table. "I'm good. What brings you on my side of town?"

"I'm about to head back to Delaware but wanted to come check in on you. Fatima told me that she let you know the arrangement that Zayne wanted."

Of course, she would take it upon herself to say that I was aware. What if I wanted to pretend that I didn't know. "Taz, I'm not in the space to play wife to you after losing my husband."

He cocked his head to the side and looked at me. "*Play* wife? You will be my wife, Alaia... Zayne has told you; I'm fucking sure of it."

Why were they all assuming that Zayne told me things? The big bitch barely told me the shit that I should have known. "Why does it sound like I don't have a choice?"

"What other choice do you have? How you gonna afford this place?"

I looked around my small, but quaint apartment and knew he was right. I mean, I could get a job, but who was going to hire me at eight months pregnant? I've never worked a job in my life, so I didn't know the first thing about going out and getting one. I never finished high school, so my job prospects were already limited.

"I don't want to move to Delaware, Taz."

"Not asking you to. You can stay here and I'm going to take care of you and the others… just need to make sure you know what this is."

The banging from next door made him grab his gun. "It's my next door neighbor. Her boyfriend knocks her around."

It was normal to me because we both took turns getting knocked against the wall. We both minded our business and never got involved with each other's shit. I knew when I saw her man staggering up the stairs that the night would be a long one, and she would leave out the next morning with dark shades and caked on makeup.

The shit was wicked, and we both went on about life like it was a normal occurrence. In reality, it wasn't normal, and both our men deserved to be dealt with for the abuse they provided. At least mine was now in a grave.

"Oh shit."

"Yeah."

His phone buzzed and he looked at me. "Fatima need me to stop by the house before I leave. You need anything?"

I needed him to get the hell out of my face, but I couldn't say that. "Just some money for laundry."

Taz dug into his pockets, peeled off some money and handed it to me. "Don't hesitate to let me know when you need something, Alaia. I'm slowly getting my feet wet out here, so I'm looking for houses. I want you to move into the house with me."

"I'm good here."

Taz stopped looking at a picture on the wall and looked at me. "I don't think I fucking asked you, Alaia."

Just like that, the switch occurred. His brother had the same switch, and it was scary never knowing what actions or words would flip it on. I had been on this very end of Zayne's flip switch many times, and I wouldn't wish it on my worst enemy. They could be the nicest people and then with one word or sentence they switched like a whole different person.

"Okay."

My neighbor was already being knocked around and I refused to be the one being knocked around next. "I'll be back out here next week. Call me if you need something."

"Alright."

As I waddled to the door, he stood there looking down at me. He forced a kiss on my lips, and I wanted to push him away from me. "You wife number one for me." He gave me another kiss and I felt sick to my stomach. His brother wasn't even fully in the grave, and he had already moved in on his wife.

As I slowly closed the door behind him, I felt like I was never going to escape this family. If Zayne told me that he would always find me, then Taz finding me would be ten times easier. He had the money and the pull to find me wherever I went. Not to mention, where was I going to run away to? I had no money, education, or job.

I was stuck.

Raheem truly fucked me over for a couple grand.

3

CAPPADONNA

THE TRAPS WERE ALL UP and running like that fat bitch Trilla never existed. Money was good and business was even better. Nobody was stupid enough to try something with the way that Trilla had been taken out. With the way Capone had cleared house, I had to admit it was quiet in New York.

Almost too damn quiet.

Naheim was on his phone, staring at the damn nanny cams he had installed all over his house. "Come take a ride with me."

"She do know that he doesn't like avocado," he spoke more to himself than me, because I didn't give a fuck that his son didn't like avocado.

Soon as we hopped in the whip, I sped off the block. It was freeing getting in my truck and speeding down the streets that I had grew up in. Everything had changed so much since I had been away. There was a fucking Apple store and Whole Foods downtown Brooklyn. I never thought I would see the day when I would see a Crown Fried Chicken in the middle of gentrification.

It was easy to maneuver in and out the hood because I was always in and out. All you saw was a black-on-black Hell Cat Durango with the darkest tints speeding on and off the block. Naheim was still with his head in his phone as I made my way through the different blocks.

When I was released, it was hard for me not to want to whip his ass all up and through Capone's crib. I had given him my baby sister on a platter, and he fumbled that shit horribly. How the fuck do you lose a woman like Capri?

Now all he did was pour into his son and probably pray that Capri would take him back. Capri was too good of a person because she helped him with his son. When his nanny couldn't make it, she would step in and be there. They were damn near co-parenting a child that wasn't hers. I saw how Capri was with the baby, and I could tell that she loved him because he was a piece of Naheim.

Their shit was complicated, and with her and Kincaid serious, I wanted no parts in whatever the fuck they had going on.

"You pay her a shit ton of money for you to watch the cameras when you're not there." I snorted, looking over at him moving the camera angles on the screen.

He finally put his phone away. "He's teething...I don't like leaving him when he has a slight fever."

"What's going on with the nurse chick you was smashing?"

Even though Naheim fucked up, he was like a little brother. I had practically raised his ass when we were on the inside. I would always choose my sister first, but that would have been hard because he was part of me, too.

If I had known this was how they would have ended, I would have denied them both from getting together. I thought Capri would go for one of those guys in her law school. A square that I didn't have to worry about.

Not my baby doll, she always had to have things her way.

"I'm not smashing her, Capp." Naheim laughed. "We went out on a few dates, but other than that, I ain't really on that."

"Cause you think you got a chance with Capri."

"Nah."

"I think R. Kelly has more of a chance running an all-girls group home than you have getting back with Capri... you gotta move on, son."

Naheim busted out laughing and shaking his head at me. He needed to give up hope that he and Capri would reunite. I wasn't saying it could never happen, but while it wasn't he needed to get on with his life.

"A man can dream... right?"

"Dreaming and being delusional is different. Son, you already had her and fucked that shit up. Focus on yourself so you never make the same mistake twice, feel me?"

He nodded his head in agreement. "I hear you."

"When the fuck you going to pull up on Kendra?" He switched the subject, like I knew his ass would. "You been home cruising the same streets as her and ain't slid up in her yet."

"Sex ain't everything."

"You ain't had no buns in years and it ain't everything? When I got out, I couldn't wait—"

"Before you finish that sentence, make sure it's worth getting your head put through the windshield. That's my baby sister you talking about," I warned.

It was hard enough getting out of prison and seeing how much Capri has grown as not only a person but a woman. It was easy to keep her in the box that I had put her in while I was in prison. She was always my baby sister, and even though I knew all the shit she was going through, it never registered to me that she was a woman.

The shit was weird.

Now that I was home and saw my sister often, it was hard seeing her as an adult. As a woman that could hold her own. Capone put me onto how Capri knew how to hold her own. I was so proud of both Capone and Capri because they held shit down while I was away. As the oldest, it was hard sitting back not knowing how things would play out with our family.

Capone made sure that he kept Capri away from the life and made sure that she wasn't completely clueless. When he told me how she let off shots out an eagle with one arm, I knew my sister wasn't shit to mess with.

"Alright... but getting some pussy has to be on your list of shit to accomplish. That's probably why your ass been working out so much."

I chuckled. "I work out because it brings me peace. Just because I'm free doesn't mean that it was something that I was going to give up."

"What the hell is your plan?" Naheim was about to bust a blood vessel trying to see what my plan was when it came to Kendra.

He was acting like I was plotting on killing her ass or something. "I'm good with not letting her know that I'm home right now." I slowed the car as I looked out the window.

"What the fuck..." Naheim's words were cut off when I busted a U-turn right in the middle of Nostrand avenue.

I doubled parked and put the car in park. "Hold up."

I hopped out the car and walked a little bit down the block before I came up on someone familiar. "Why you out here pushing this big ass shopping cart with all this laundry?"

The woman froze, her small hand on the handlebar, and slowly turned around. When she turned, her eyes instantly recognized me. While her eyes recognized me, mine didn't recognize her swollen belly she was toting along with the heavy shopping cart.

When I spotted her in front of the fish spot, all I saw was her face. You didn't see beauty like hers often, and I never forgot about her. "Mr. Cappadonna Delgato," she smiled up at me, her dimples as deep as a damn ocean.

The fuck was going on with my heart? Soon as she smiled up at me, my heart did some weird shit in my chest. It felt like it was flipping around or some weird shit.

"I didn't think you would remember me."

She pulled on her hijab slightly. "It's not every day you receive a free ride from a stranger. I make it a point to never forget the people that help me. I never got the chance to say thank you to you... so thank you. I'm happy that you're finally on the outside... let's make sure you stay out here, too."

"Where you heading?"

She touched the laundry bag. "To the laundromat to wash all these clothes. I've been putting it off for too long, and I need to start getting prepared for this baby."

My mind went crazy thinking about that bitch nigga putting his hands all over my baby. Not only did he touch her, but he also went ahead and put his seed inside of her. If that wasn't enough, he had the nerve to get her pregnant and then have her out here pushing a fucking shopping cart while pregnant. I wanted to punch him in the chest and pistol whip his ass because he had her out here like this.

"Let me walk with you," I took over the shopping cart, and she was hesitant at first, then she tried to take the cart back over.

"I'm good, I promise." I saw hints of fear in her eyes as she quickly scanned our surroundings, then looked up at me. "I just don't want to make trouble for you."

I didn't mean to laugh in her face the way that I did, but it was funny that she thought she could make trouble for me. "You crazy if you think you could ever make any trouble for me... you pregnant pushing this heavy cart on one of the hottest days... I'm fucking helping you." Even though it was still spring, today happened to be one of the hotter days in New York.

Reluctantly, she allowed me to take over and I pushed the shopping cart slowly as she walked beside me. To Alaia, the shopping cart came up a little below her chest. For me, it looked like I was pushing one of those kid shopping carts around.

"How long have you been home?" she made small talk, still taking in her surroundings. I knew a little bit about Alaia and knew the nigga she was with wasn't about no pressure. I didn't even have to know her like that to know that he didn't deserve her.

"A few months."

"How has it been? Zayne struggled for a bit when he came home," she sighed.

I laughed. "Yeah, his ass struggled on the inside, too."

I never got his name because I was too busy herbing him like he was a little nigga. The one thing I couldn't stand was when a man acted like he was like that in front of his woman. Meanwhile, behind closed doors, he was a fucking herb.

"He passed away a few weeks ago," she looked up at me.

If I didn't know any better, she didn't seem broken up or even sad about it. "My condolences."

"You can keep them. Zayne was a horrible person and I'm at peace knowing that he's going where he deserves to go." She sighed, then stopped before putting her hand on top of her stomach.

I could see the small beads of sweat accumulate on her forehead. "You good?"

"I think I've overdone it with carrying all these bags downstairs, then walking here," she made light of it, and I didn't find it funny.

I waved for Naheim to pull my whip up closer to her, and he did quickly. "You pregnant, Ma... why would you be doing all of this?"

"I don't have anybody else to help me. Mr. Delgato, I don't have much of an option. My daughter is going to be born either way, and I have to be prepared for her." She winced, touching another side of her stomach.

Leaving the shopping cart on the curb, I gently guided her over toward my truck where the air was already blasting. Naheim had gotten into the back, and I helped her get into the passenger seat. "Laundromat right there... I'm gonna bring your clothes. Chill here."

"I have to do my laundry. I don't know if you know, but I can't just leave my clothes there and it will magically get done."

I grinned as I pulled out my credit card. "I ain't been locked up that long. Ma, I know how laundromats work. My moms used to work in one for years."

She rummaged in her purse and tried to hand me a crinkled hundred-dollar bill. "I cannot ask you to pay for my laundry..." I gently closed the door before she could finish her sentence.

Alaia must have realized that she wasn't going to get through to me. I walked her clothes to the laundromat and paid for them to wash and fold them for her. I gave them my number to call when it was done.

Before heading back to the car, I dipped into the corner store and grabbed some water and then jogged back to the car. When I got in the car, I turned my wheel and then sped off the block.

"Drink some water." I handed her the water, while she put the seatbelt around her. "Dropping you back to the spot." Naheim nodded when I looked at him through the rearview mirror.

It took less than ten minutes to drop Naheim off at the corner store, and then speeding back off the block. "Thank you for saving me once again."

I looked over at her, and then my heart went all haywire again. Her olive complexion, light brown eyes and two beauty marks that graced the opposite sides of her face made me go stupid in the chest.

Not even mentioning when she smiled. Alaia didn't even realize that she could get whatever she wanted out of me with those dimples. "You don't ever gotta mention or thank me."

"Where are we going?"

"I was hoping that you would tell me your address so I could drop you home."

She told me her address as she continued to take small sips of her water. "I can tell that you're one of the good ones. You came home and can promise that you not going back."

"Nah. My family already lost years with me being away, I'm never going back." I switched lanes, and then looked over at her. "What about you?"

"What you mean?"

"How the fuck you even get mixed up with a nigga like your *husband*."

Alaia laughed. "Um, excuse you. Why you saying husband like that?"

"Cause that man had more than you coming to see him... not much of a husband," I pointed out.

"He has more than one wife... look at you assuming."

The chicks he had coming to visit him weren't other wives.

If Alaia was wearing a hijab, more than likely he had his other wives doing the same. The women that came to visit him wore some of the skimpiest shit that they were allowed to get away with for his visits.

"I never assume. If I'm speaking on something I already know. If he was so horrible, how did you get mixed up with his ass?"

She looked out the window, becoming quiet. "A long story."

"A story that I'm going to learn one day."

Her head snapped in my direction. "Are you always this cocky? How do you assume that I would want to share my story with you."

I licked my lips. "You going to share it."

She turned to look back out the window. "Maybe."

The first time that I saw Alaia, she took my breath away. Every time she would come up for a visit with her *husband*, I always watched how she moved. She was so quiet and graceful at the same time. On the occasion he made her laugh, I watched how she would toss her head back and expose those dimples.

Since I was always across the room, I never knew the affect that those dimples could have on someone.

Especially me.

I damn sure didn't plan on running into Alaia today, or else I would have been taking her somewhere else to chill with her longer. It was funny how I would always think of her in my cell, and now that she was right here next to me, I couldn't dedicate the time I wanted to getting to know her.

For the remainder of the ride, she rubbed her stomach, and stared out the window. I looked down at my phone at the text from Capone. He hit me with the address where Kendra sent him. Instead of him showing up, it was going to be me popping up on her. I needed to see what was up with her ass anyway.

When we pulled onto her block, she leaned up and closed her eyes when she saw a car parked in front of her building. "Everything good?"

"That's Zayne's little brother. He's going to flip out because I'm getting out of your car." I could hear a slight panic in her voice.

"That nigga be putting his hands on you?" I immediately asked because I was gonna go shove my size fifteen sneaker up his ass.

She took a deep breath with a shaky voice, she explained. "No. Zayne had it arranged that if something ever happened then Taz would take on the role as my new husband... I'm basically property to him and his brother."

Alaia unbuckled her seatbelt as she looked back at me. "The fuck kind of shit they on... you want him to be your new husband?"

"Of course not. I don't have much of a choice because he controls the money and pays the bills. Thank you for helping me, Cappadonna. I truly appreciate you."

I started to get out the truck and she stopped me, climbing out. Soon as homie saw her, he hopped out his car and rushed over to her with anger in his eyes.

"Who the fuck whip is this?"

"He...he just helped me with a ride. I felt like I was about to pass out," Alaia stammered, and I didn't like hearing her having to explain herself to this short muthafucka.

This little bitch looked like the old school rapper, Lil Zane, and had the nerve to be trying to strong-arm Alaia. I rolled the window down and leaned on the arm rest. "Mine... the fuck is the problem?"

Taz nearly ripped his neck off with how fast he turned to face my window. "Yeah, I got a problem when my woman is getting out of strange men cars."

"Ain't shit strange but you and your brother sharing women... the fuck kind of shit is that... weirdo ass nigga."

Alaia was silently pleading with me behind him. "Yo, who the fuck is you?" He raised his shirt, showing me a gun, like I gave a fuck.

"Aye, baby boy, let me tell you something... if the next time I see her, and I will see her again, she has a mark on her, or tells me you put your hands on her, we gonna have a problem, ight?"

"Who the fuck are you to tell me what I can and cannot do with my fucking woman?" I've met plenty of men like Taz in my life.

All bark with little to no bite, or he always had someone do the biting for him. "Alaia, I'll see you again, Beautiful."

She gave me a quick smile before she turned it off and headed toward her building. "This nigga must not know who he fucking with."

I revved my engine and stared his little ass right in the eyes. "Nah, you don't know who you fucking with. Ain't gonna be too much my woman shit before she eventually becomes mine... I'll be seeing you around if you go ahead and put your hands on her."

As much as I didn't want to leave her with this nigga, I knew that I couldn't force her back into my truck. I wouldn't be no better than her fake ass husband or his little brother. Alaia was willingly going, so there wasn't much I could do until I saw her again.

Taz was at a loss for words while I sped off the block and headed toward the address that Capone sent me. I put it into my GPS, turned my music up, and thought of the next time I would be seeing *my* woman. There wasn't no way that I was going to allow her to slip through my fingers after the way I thought of her when I was locked up, and the way my heart acted out of control when she was near me.

Alaia ain't even know it yet, but she was mine.

4

KENDRA

"Girl, you know whenever you call, I will throw whoever I need to out the chair for you," Sassy, my hairstylist said, as she ran her hand through my natural hair. "Who footing the bill this week?"

"This hustler that I'm fucking with from Delaware. I met him a few months ago when I was out there for my nephew's birthday party." I laughed, knowing that if there was one thing I knew how to do, it was to find a nigga with money.

Sassy was always clued into the mess that I was into because she barely had a life. Her life revolved around this salon, so she never really did anything for herself. We had been friends since kids, so we were thick as thieves.

She held my skeletons just like I had held hers. We were more like sisters than best friends, and it had always been like that from the first day she asked to borrow a crayon from my sixty-four count.

"What exactly are you going to do when Cappadonna comes home? The freedom that you have now isn't anything compared to what he's letting you slide with when he's home."

I sucked my teeth and allowed her to massage my scalp before she got to work. Cappadonna was my entire heart, and we had been through everything together. When he got knocked and sent upstate, I promised I would hold him down, and I have been holding him down.

Whenever he wanted to see me, I was taking that long ass drive up to the prison to visit him. He called; I answered before the phone could reach the second ring. I've been down with him and holding him down for so long that I needed to have my fun too. Capp was possessive and in the worst way. It was the reason we had broken up so many times when we were younger. He didn't even like the next nigga looking at you. He and Capone may have been twins, but they were different in *some* ways.

Capone wasn't as crazy as his damn brother, and from what I knew he wasn't as possessive. Then again, he didn't really like me so it wasn't like I could observe him much. The only time we saw each other was when he came to drop me money off.

Like today, he was supposed to be coming to the shop and dropping some money off to me. Cappadonna may have had his shit with him, but he made sure that I was paid. I never had to pay for anything since Capp has been in prison.

He made sure I had everything I could ever want. All I had to do was complain and he made it happen.

He was *Mr. Make It Happen*.

"Capp is going to have to realize that I'm not that same twenty-one-year-old girl he left when he was locked up. I have a life now, and he has to respect that I have one."

All the chicks in the salon were all oohing and ahhing as I was getting my scalp massaged. When Sassy stopped, I turned around to tell her to continue, and Cappadonna Delgato was standing right in the middle of the salon.

All six feet, six inches of him with muscles just standing there staring at me. I could see his tattoos coming up his neck. All my senses tingled when I looked at his ass, and I wanted to climb him. My short ass looked like a kid compared to him.

"Oh yeah?"

"Baby!" I ran right into his arms, and he picked me up. I kissed him on the neck and wrapped my arms around him, but for some reason something felt off with him.

"Let me holla at you outside real quick," he spoke lowly in my ear as he continued to hold me.

"I just know he talks her through it... dear God, it's me," I overheard one of the women in the shop say as he walked by her while he carried me out the salon.

Capp put me back on the ground when we got outside the salon. I looked up at him, still shocked that he was even standing in front of me. Even in his prison jumpsuit Capp always stood out and looked good. So, it was no surprise as he stood in front of me dressed in a pair of jeans, Timbs, and white fitted designer T-shirt that he looked even better outside of his prison greens. His hair was freshly lined up, and his beard was combed out and glistening from the sheen he used.

"Baby, when the hell did you get out and why didn't you call me?" I tossed my arms around him, staring up at him.

My pussy jumped thinking about when he would have me to himself later on today. It didn't matter where I got dick from while he was locked up, none of them could ever compare to what Cappadonna carried around in his pants.

He had always been the one that could make me squirt across a damn room from just looking at me. I had waited years for this exact moment, and he was acting all dry with me. I shook him and he didn't move while staring down at me.

It felt like he was taking me in and analyzing me or something. His ass was making me nervous with that look he was giving me. "You not the same twenty-one-year-old, right?"

I laughed while reaching up and touching his chest. "I was just talking my shit... you know how I am."

"Tell Sassy you 'bout to dip."

I reached up and touched my hair. "Not with my hair like this. Let me get my hair done and I'll meet up with you later...I can't believe you're home. We need to go to the club tonight, baby," I suggested.

I was excited to be on my man's arms when everybody saw that he was home. It was one thing for everyone to know that I was Capp's girl and another for them to actually see me with him. Everyone thought I was crazy waiting all these years for him, and now they were about to see. With Capp being home, my life was about to be upgraded.

With the way Capone had his wife driving around in a Bentley truck and living in a mansion, I was sure I was about to be next. Capp would give me whatever I wanted because I had been loyal to him and held him down while he sat down to do his time.

He wrapped his arms around me and kissed me on the forehead. I couldn't help but feel like something was off with him. "I'm not going to the club, Ken. The fuck wrong with you?"

"We used to love going to the club together, babe," I pouted while crossing my arms. "We can get drunk, and you know I'm always nasty when I drink."

He screwed his face up. "I don't drink, Kendra... do you even listen to half the shit I talk to you about."

"I mean, I thought you didn't drink because you were locked up. There ain't liquor flowing in and out of there anyway. Unless you was drinking out the toilet."

His jaw tensed as he leaned back on the hood of his truck.

"I'm Muslim. Told you that when I converted. I figured we could go out to dinner and chill for the night."

He was finally out of prison, and he wanted to do a boring dinner and chill for the night? I thought when he came home, we would be ripping the streets and in every party that was going on. With the weather getting nicer, everybody was throwing a kickback and I wanted to show up on his arm.

"How long have you been out?"

"Is that important?"

I stepped back and stared at him. "Yes. You don't look like somebody that was just released. A new whip, clothes and you look pretty comfortable."

"I'm comfortable everywhere I am... being free don't change shit, Ken. Get your hair done and I'm gonna see you later."

I stepped back into his arms and stood on my toes while puckering up my lips. He dropped a few kisses onto my lips and grabbed my ass in the process. The roughness from his grab had me ready to abandon this appointment and go back to my place.

He didn't know how much I wanted him in this moment, or how much I counted down until I could climb back on top of him and ride the fuck out of him. "I'm happy you're home, baby."

"Yeah, me too." He slapped my ass, as I walked back into the salon.

I watched from the doorway as he swaggered around the truck, getting in and peeling away from the curb.

Fuck!

I had been so damn surprised that he was home that I forgot to ask him for the money Capone was supposed to drop off to me. Not once did Capone's ass even tell me that he was home. I should have known he would have kept it a secret because that was how they both always moved.

Sassy slapped the back of her chair and I quickly sat down. "Girl, when the hell did he come home?"

"I'm not clear on that, but he's been home for a hot second because he don't seem like he's freshly out," I pondered while I felt Sassy get to work on my hair.

I've loved Cappadonna Delgato since the first day that I had met him. Even without a pot to piss in or a window to throw it out of, he always had this cocky bravado. He moved like the world owed him something and that always turned me on.

The Delgato twins moved like they were God's gift to earth, and being completely honest, they were. It didn't matter how many niggas I messed with, none of them compared to Capp. Even though it was two of them, he had managed to become one of one.

I hated that I had hid the fact that we shared a son together. When I got pregnant, Capp didn't have money like he had now. He was still trying to get on and worked ten times harder. There were some weeks that I didn't see him because he was so deep in the streets that he hardly came up for air.

When I say that man didn't have time for me, he never had time for me. I thought by moving to Jacksonville with my grandmother that it would change his mind. He would stop running the streets and pay attention to me. That nigga looked me in the face and told me to have a safe flight. I couldn't back down on what I told him I was doing, so I packed my things and left to live with my grandmother.

Even when I boarded that flight, my heart had always been with Capp. Despite what people loved to believe, I loved him when he didn't have a dollar to his name. I was heartbroken when I left him behind and moved. His ass never checked on me and didn't give a damn that I had picked my life up and moved away.

A couple weeks after I got there and settled in, I found out that I was pregnant. I didn't know what the hell I was going to do. Spite brewed within my veins, and I refused to tell Capp that I was pregnant with his baby. It wasn't like his ass was checking for me, anyway, so why should I tell him that I was carrying his baby.

Say what you want about the Delgato men, they were good men. Cappadonna would have stepped up to the plate and raised our baby. I was too bitter and didn't want him to be involved. I was determined to raise this baby on my own and not reach out for any help.

When I was a couple months pregnant, I met a dealer from around my grandma's way. Back then, I just knew he was doing a lot because he had a nice car and flashy jewelry. Even when he found out that I was pregnant, he still wanted to be there for me. I would have been a fool to walk away and not accept the help.

By the time I was about to give birth, Dax had moved me out of my grandmother's house into his condo. He set up a nursery for the baby and everything. I stopped thinking about Capp and started focusing on a man that clearly wanted me.

When Capella was a month old, Dax was murdered in front of our condo building. They didn't care that he was on his way home with diapers and formula, they shot him in cold blood, and I witnessed it.

I was in the window rocking Capella and saw when they ran up on him and shot him. The formula fell to the floor along with the diapers, and I stood there stuck with tears falling down my face. Dax had been the only person that gave a damn about me and wanted to help me raise this child.

There were no wills or estates when it came to the streets,

so I had to pack as much as I could and move back in with my grandmother. I tried to be a mother for a few months, and I couldn't do it. Capella was such a fussy baby, and motherhood was so hard. If it wasn't for my grandmother, I don't know what I would have done.

I told her I was going to New York to visit and would be back, and I left Capella with her and never looked back. Motherhood wasn't for me, and I had worked ten times harder not to end up with another baby inside of me.

So, when Capp always spoke about becoming a father, there was a part of me that felt guilty. I robbed him of the chance to be a father to our son. Prison didn't matter either because he would have been present in our son's life.

A secret like this could end us and even end up with him wanting me dead. There was a lot of things that he didn't do, and being lied to was one of them. Especially with a lie this big.

∼

CAPPADONNA HELD the door open for me as I stepped out and he closed it behind me. He took my hand in his as he led us up the steps into a fancy steakhouse in Jersey. I held onto his hand tightly as he told the hostess that we had reservations.

The restaurant screamed opulence. The array of foreign sports cars parked by valet told me that before we made it inside of the restaurant. It was on a cliff with a beautiful view of the beach and water below us. Depending on the table you were assigned, you could view the waves crashing onto the rocks below.

Capp gently pull me in front of him and kept his hand on the small of my back as the hostess led us to our table. I felt super sexy in the mint green slip dress that hugged all my curves. I didn't pay nearly a car note every month on Pilates for nothing. My lifestyle was very much due to how well my man took care of me.

Were there others that filled the gap while he was away? Yes. None of them meant anything to me and I never kept them around long enough to feel anything for them. I used to feel guilty about sleeping around behind Capp's back, and then changed how I was looking at the situation. If the roles were reversed, I knew he wouldn't have been able to be faithful to me.

Now that he was home, I wasn't worried about anything besides him. It was time for us to start our life and put all the years behind us.

"Thank you, baby," I thanked him as he held my chair out and pushed me in.

He walked around the table, wearing a pair of dress pants and fitted white shirt that had his muscles damn near busting out the seams. He complimented the outfit with a simple gold chain. God, he looked so good that I wanted to skip dinner and head back to my place.

"Welcome to *Meso*. We're so happy to have you joining us for dinner, Mr. Delgato. Can I recommend some wines that might pair best with your evening."

I have never heard of someone recommending a wine that would pair best with your evening. With the way I was ready to gobble this man down, I needed something stronger than wine.

Capp looked up from the digital menu that was handed to us. "Water is good."

The waiter looked at me, then back to Capp. "We have a delicious house lemonade if you would like to try it."

He was trying to impress Cappadonna because so far, he didn't seem impressed. It wasn't anything to do with the restaurant or the waiter, he normally looked like that. He wasn't a man of many emotions and that was before he was locked up, so I knew it would be ten times harder pulling them out now.

"We'll take the lemonade. I'll do a vodka sour as well."

He clasped his hands together. "Very well. I will leave you to look over the menu while I get your drinks. Please don't hesitate to wave your hand if you need anything from me."

"Thank you," Capp finally spoke without looking up from the menu. I looked over the menu and there were a few things that I wanted to try. "You still drinking?"

I groaned inwardly because I had promised him that I would stop drinking. "I told you that I would try and stop. I don't drink nearly as much as I used to."

"Then why lie and tell me one thing when you're going to do the other?"

I put the menu down and looked across the table. He was staring right at me with this intense scowl on his face. "It's not like I didn't try to *not* drink. I stopped drinking for a few months."

"Ight."

Ight? What was that supposed to mean. I envisioned the day that Capp came home to me for years and this wasn't what I had in mind.

"Now that you're home, we need to focus on our future. The lease on the condo is going to be up soon, so I think we should start looking for houses. We should also move your stuff into the condo, too."

"I'm staying with Capone and Erin right now." He swiped through the menu, and then sat it down to stare at me.

"You don't want to move in with me?"

"You just said the lease is about to be up. Why the fuck would I waste time moving in with you to just move out in a few months."

"What area do you want to live in? I saw some nice brownstones in Brooklyn. We can be right in the middle of everything. Brooklyn isn't the same as it was before you left, babe."

"I don't want to be in the middle of everything, Ken. The fuck I look like being in the mix after just getting out. I want to be tucked away from everything when I come home at night."

Before he could say it, I knew he wanted to live near his brother out in New Jersey. I didn't have anything against Jersey, I just didn't want to live there. I liked being in Brooklyn where everything was right here. If my girls called me to have brunch last minute, I didn't have to pay a bunch of tolls and drive an hour to get to them. I could order me an Uber and be with them in minutes.

My life was situated in Brooklyn, and I didn't want to pick up and leave because that was what Cappadonna wanted. People spoke, and I heard that Erin did whatever Capone wanted, including moving into that big ass mansion out in Jersey.

Just because we were both with brothers didn't mean I had to follow her lead and move like she did. I was my own woman, and I didn't want to be some housewife tucked away in a mansion. If Capp wanted, we could find a mansion right here in the city and live perfectly well. We could have dinners every night at different restaurants and live life with just the two of us.

"Well, I don't want to live out in Jersey."

"I never asked you to move out there with me," he nonchalantly replied, hurting my feelings in the process.

"What do you mean? The whole plan had always been us moving in together, getting married and having a life together."

"You forgot having kids."

Capp wanted kids and he told me this on more than one

occasion. He was adamant about having them and wanted a bunch of them. I had one kid, and the experience was so traumatic that I didn't want to have another.

I wished people understood that just because we were women that not every woman wanted to be a mother. I learned early on in my son's life that I didn't want to be a mother, and that I should have gotten rid of him.

Hell, I was more a rich auntie than a mother. When it came to my nieces and nephews, I showed up and out for them. Capella had always been taken care of, even if it wasn't by me. He had a great life, and he knew me as his mother.

He called my aunt his mother because she was the one who raised him. It wasn't like he was kept in the dark about who I was. I was the mom who pulled up on him and took him to get whatever sneakers he wanted.

Capella called me when there was something that he wanted, and my aunt told him no. I was the fun parent that popped in and out but made sure that he had everything that he needed. Nobody could ever make me feel guilty about the relationship me and my son had.

We weren't the closest mother and son; however, he knew if he needed me that I would be there. Capella was a lot like his father and moved on his own. The older he became the less he needed me or anybody.

I hadn't spoken to him in a full year because whenever I reached out, he never returned my phone call. He moved out of my aunt's house, and she only sees him when he pops up on Sunday to have dinner with her. At least she could call and get through to him. The little nigga didn't bother to call or answer the phone for me.

"I told you that I don't want to have any kids and you told me that you respected that."

He messed with his beard and stared at me. "You love to

rewrite history, Ken. I told you that if you didn't want to have kids then I would find someone that would."

"And I told you that I wish you would. Just because I don't want to have kids doesn't mean you can toss me away like I'm trash. I've been the one here holding you down and you're gonna do me like that."

He laughed.

This nigga laughed in my face like I wasn't on the verge of tears. The thought of having kids sent me into an emotional spiral. Nobody understood the toll having babies had on your physical and mental health, and I didn't want any more kids.

"Chill out with all that."

"You have some nerve to tell me to chill out when you're the reason that I'm about to cry." I dabbed the corner of my eyes and looked away from him.

The waiter came back with our drinks and was prepared to take our food orders. I ordered their steakhouse macaroni and cheese with bacon, while Capp looked at me disgusted. He wanted me to swear off everything that he didn't associate with, and I didn't want to.

I loved a good drink now and again, and a greasy burger with extra bacon. Just because we were together didn't mean I had to give up the things that I loved. "Very well. I will get those orders in."

"Still on that swine."

"Yes. I would appreciate it if you didn't look at me like I disgust you." I folded my arms, on the defense because this dinner wasn't turning out like I thought it would have.

"You good."

I needed to change the subject. "I was thinking we could go out to brunch tomorrow morning and then do some shopping. I'm sure there's some stuff you will need."

"I'm fasting."

"Why?"

"It's Ramadan, Kendra. Why the fuck do you think I asked the waiter to bring me a date." I heard when he asked, I just didn't think anything into it.

"Oh. So, we can't go out to brunch?"

He shook his head as the waiter brought him the date, and he peeled it while saying something before eating it. I sat there looking at him like he was a stranger, because essentially, he was a stranger to me.

5
KENDRA

My eyes fluttered open when I smelled Pine Sol and bleach in the air. Last I checked the cleaning lady didn't come until next week. My senses fully kicked in because then I heard the music playing and Cappadonna singing along to the music. We had gone to bed not even four hours ago and he was up like that was normal. I usually didn't drag my ass out the bed until after noon and here it was seven in the morning, and he was cleaning like he didn't pay for a cleaning service weekly.

Last night didn't go the way that I thought it would have. I thought the minute we hit the house that we would have been ripping each other's clothes off and fucking on the couch. It was something that I missed about him. Capp would get it on anywhere when it came to me, and I desperately missed that.

After he forced me to brush my teeth, he then allowed me to kiss him all over him while rubbing his body. I was practically throwing this ass on him, and he was just sitting there like I was a statue.

Other than me giving him head and him directing my head, we didn't spend the night having sex with each other. I was practically begging him because I was so wet, and he told me to be patient. Why the hell did I need to be patient with dick that was supposed to be mine? I had been patient for years and now that it was right in front of me, I wanted to do more than suck on it until I choked. I wanted to feel it inside of me and climb him like a jungle gym. So much for wishful thinking because his ass got his nut off, and then we went to sleep.

When I entered the living area, he was wearing a pair of briefs, singing "Joy" by Blackstreet while mopping the floors. He turned and realized that I was standing there and smiled.

"Bout time you woke up. I made some breakfast and put it in the microwave for you." He finished up mopping the floors.

I rubbed my eyes and sat at the counter. "We pay someone to come clean the condo. Why are you cleaning this early in the morning."

He sat the mop bucket against the wall and came to wash his hands. "I'm always up early. You need to start getting up early. I thought you would eventually grow out of sleeping in."

"Now you know that I would be sleep if I could." I giggled and accepted his version of breakfast.

It was scrambled eggs and cut up apples. "Why the fuck your fridge so bare? You don't cook?"

I hated cooking and I never stocked my fridge because I was always out with my girls. If it happened to be a night that I stayed in, I didn't mind utilizing the Doordash app to get me food within minutes.

"I don't food shop often because I'm barely here and I almost never eat when I am here." From the way he looked at me, I could tell that he didn't approve of the way that I lived my life.

"I'm supposed to eat junk food or go out to eat all the time. That's not logical."

"You have the money to eat out as much as you want. Why are you complaining because I don't cook. Capp, this isn't the 1940s, women don't sit home and cook for their men anymore."

He wanted an old school woman and that was the furthest thing from who I was. As he was about to say something, his phone started to ring from across the room. Ignoring me, he went and picked it up.

"Um, hey, Alaia?" he mocked the other person and then took his conversation into the next room.

Who the hell was Alaia and why was she calling my man, and why was he more lighthearted with her than he had been with me for the past twenty-four hours. Abandoning my food, I went ahead to the room to listen to his conversation.

When I entered the room, he was pulling on a pair of sweatpants with the phone cradled between his shoulder and ear. "Sit tight... I'm not too far from you."

He tossed the phone onto the bed and put his chain on, before slipping his feet into his sneakers. Before we met back up for dinner last night, I had stopped and got him a few things he would need at my place.

I figured we could have brunch and then continue shopping for him today. As he got dressed, I realized that he was about to leave, and the plans I had for us would no longer happen.

"Who was that?"

"I be clocking who call your phone?"

I folded my arms. "Nobody has called my phone, Cappadonna. I heard a woman's name and now you're getting dressed to go to her."

I was jealous.

He had been giving me the third degree about everything in my life, and within seconds this woman had gotten him to smile and joke with her, and now he was being secretive about who she was.

"I'm going to help a friend out real quick. Why the fuck you beefing?"

"What about our day? I thought we could spend the day together." My phone pulled us both from the conversation we were trying to have.

I went to grab my phone and saw it was Sassy calling me. Ignoring the call, I focused my attention back onto Capp.

He kissed me on the cheek. "I got something that I need to handle."

The little kisses on the cheeks were pissing me off. I wanted him to shove his damn tongue down my throat, toss me onto the bed and pound my insides out until I screamed that I was about to cum.

Capp was acting like he was scared of the pussy or something and that was pissing me off more than him leaving to go meet up with another chick. Who the hell was this chick and why could she just call him once and he came running?

I never checked his visitation logs because I assumed that it was only his family. Capp was loyal and if he gave you his word that he was with you, you didn't need anything other than his word.

There was a small nagging feeling that told me that I should have been checking his damn visitation log, because who the hell was Alaia, and why the hell was he so quick to go running for her?

"Is that something more important than me?" I batted my eyelashes as I looked up at him with my sad puppy dog face.

He cocked his head to the side and smirked. "I always wondered what that look liked when we were on the phone."

"What?"

"Nothing. Ken, I don't need to go shopping because Erin and Capri made sure to handle all of that for me. I'm good... go shopping and chill with your girls."

"Why didn't you tell me that you were getting released? I could have gotten everything ready for you... I am your girlfriend."

He shrugged. "They were already on top of it. What the fuck you want me to do? Burn the clothes and have you rebuy everything?"

"That's a thought." I folded my arms.

"You can't be fucking jealous of my sister and my sister-in-law, Kendra." He was making it seem like I had no reason to feel jealous or even be offended that neither of them called to tell me that he was released.

"I should have been told that you were coming home. Capri has my number and not once had she reached out to me to let me know. I don't know Erin, but even she could have reached out if she wanted to. I'm kept in the dark like I haven't been out here holding you down."

"Ask yourself how many times you have reached out to Capri since I been locked up?"

He had me there.

I didn't reach out to anyone except for Capone and with the way he acted, he made me not want to reach out to anyone else. It wasn't like I was invited into the folds of the family when Capp went away.

"Doesn't matter. They should have reached out to me."

He shook his head and looked at his phone. "I'm 'bout to head out... I'll call you later."

Capp didn't even give me a chance to sulk or say something because he was out the door. I texted Sassy to meet me at our favorite spot so we could get some real food.

The only thing that I had gotten from last night was a sore throat and cleaned floors.

∽

"You mean to tell me that he didn't give you no dick? I expected him to fuck you when he carried you up out the salon." Sassy looked at me like she didn't believe what I had told her.

I was three lemon drops in at our favorite brunch spot. Cappadonna had left my condo over two hours ago and I hadn't heard shit from him. Not a text message or anything.

"All he let me do is give his ass head. Then I woke up to him mopping my floors this morning."

Sassy broke out into laughter. "Do you think he messes with somebody else and probably got some from her?"

"It's been weird, Sass. He comes home and it's not some big ass celebration of us being up under each other. I expected when he came home that I would be up under him for at least a month."

"Like you said, you both have changed through the years. I told you that it would be unrealistic of you to keep the old version of him in your head. He's a different man, and a much older one."

Leave it to Sassy to always be the voice of reason when it came to me. She had played that position for all of our friendship, and I honestly wouldn't be who I was if it weren't for her always being the voice of reason.

I don't know how many times I had broken up with Capp, and it was Sassy that told me that I was in the wrong and I needed to fix things.

"The energy is weird between us. I guess I didn't expect for it to feel that way."

I couldn't shake that there was something off between me

and Capp. We spent a long time apart, so it was normal for things to feel different. This didn't feel different though, it felt like something was off between us. Clearly, it was only with me because when he was on the phone with *Alaia*, he seemed fine.

"Give him some time and space. Feeling crowded isn't the best thing for him." She paused. "When do you think you're going to tell him about Capella?"

"Never." I swigged the rest of my drink and signaled for another.

I don't know why she even brought Capella up. What Capp didn't know wouldn't kill him. He didn't need to know about him because then it would just be a big ass mess between us.

"You cannot keep his son away from him forever. I never agreed with the situation in the first place."

Sassy thought telling Cappadonna that he had a son that I hid from him would be a simple conversation. She only knew what I told her or the small interactions she had with him before he was sent away.

There was a dark side to Cappadonna, and I feared being put on that side. He always told me that he would never hurt me, and I believed him. If I told him something like this, he would fucking choke me until there was no more life in my body.

"Capella is fine without knowing his father. Do you see him complaining about never having a father?"

"How the hell would you know how he feels, Kendra? You barely have a relationship with your own son." She called me out, like I needed this bullshit right now.

Sassy was the only person that could pull my card and I never got angry with her. As much as she was always down for me, she had no problem checking me and telling me when I was wrong.

"Is it my fault that he never calls or picks up the phone for me."

Sassy narrowed her eyes with a confused look on her face. "Um, yeah. Kendra, you dumped him with your grandmother, then you went ahead and had him shipped to your aunt. I'm pretty sure all of this is your fault and there is a reason he doesn't pick up the phone for you."

"What the fuck bitch? Why you have to be on my case like this? Capella has always had anything that he wanted. He's never gone without and you're acting like I'm some deadbeat mama that dropped him off at foster care."

"He's had everything he wanted except his mother and father. That messes with kids well into adulthood. You think he gives a fuck about any of those sneakers you bought him?"

I pulled my phone out and called Capella. With all the drinks I had consumed, maybe I should have waited to call him. I was about to pull my phone away from my ear when he answered the phone.

"Yo."

God, his voice sounded just like his father's it wasn't even funny. "Boy, this is your mama, you know better than to answer the phone like that."

"What up, Kendra?"

I pulled the phone from my ear and looked at my phone. "Kendra? Boy, you know better than that."

Capella always called me mom when he was growing up. It was understood that I was his mother, and he would call me that. Even my aunt referred to me as his mom because he called her mama.

"I'm in the middle of some shit, Kendra... you good?"

I felt so low when he spoke to me like I was some random chick that called him. It was his tone when he said my name. I carried his ass for nine months and fucking tore because he was a big ass baby.

"I don't give a shit if you're in the middle of something. I'm your mother and I'm calling to talk to you."

Capella laughed. "Kendra, I'll hit you back."

He didn't even wait for me to respond before my phone made that beeping sound. I tossed my phone into my purse and looked at Sassy who didn't seemed surprised.

"I was there for him. Even if you don't believe I was there enough, I showed up for him," I pointed my finger at her and guzzled down my fresh lemon drop.

I could have dumped his ass with family and never came around. Instead, I stayed in his life and was at every birthday party. Well, not every birthday party. I still sent money and gave him whatever he wanted.

"Whatever helps you sleep at night. I'm your girl, and I'm riding for you always. However, we have to realize when we fell short as parents and acknowledge that."

Sassy had two teenage daughters, and she was a very present mother. I've watched this woman stay late at the salon and then still make it early to a dance competition. She was born to be a mother and I loved that for her.

She needed to realize that people parented differently, and I shouldn't be made to feel like shit because I chose to raise my son a certain way. I felt it was best not to keep Capp in his life because what could he have done from behind bars?

His ass couldn't offer anything but financial support like I've been doing. It was bad enough making those visits and seeing him like that. I refused to have Capella see his father that way.

Call me wrong, I felt like I did what was best for *my* son.

6
ALAIA

"What do you mean you can't give me my clothes? These are my clothes," I argued with the Chinese lady behind the counter.

I didn't give a shit about my clothes; I was more concerned with my daughter's clothes. This was all the clothes I had for her, and this woman was telling me that she couldn't give me the clothes.

"These not your clothes... A man came and pay for these," she waved the receipt in my face, then turned her attention to the next customer who needed to buy her overpriced laundry detergent that was kept behind the counter.

"He was a friend of mine that dropped them off for me. See, those are baby clothes... I'm pregnant," I showed her my stomach thinking that would make her change her mind. Instead, she looked at me, and then went back to folding clothes behind the counter.

"No ticket, no clothes." She shoved the receipt across the counter. "Call friend and tell him to bring you ticket."

I snatched the receipt and looked it over, noticing that he

had left his phone number. Quickly, I punched the numbers in and paced the small space in front of the counter hoping he was the kind that answered strange numbers.

It was early in the morning, and I hated to even interrupt him with this. He had already paid three hundred dollars to get my clothes washed, so the last thing I wanted to do was to bug him about a stupid ticket she really didn't even need.

"Yo." He didn't even sound like he was asleep or had been woken up out of his sleep. Cappadonna sounded like he was bright eyed and bushy tailed.

"Um, hey, Cappadonna?"

"Um, hey, Alaia?" he mocked me with his deep voice, and I smiled. How did he even know it was me?

"How did you know it was me?"

"I recognize my future wife's voice anywhere... what up with you?"

"Um, so I need to pick up my laundry and she's refusing to give it to me without a ticket. Do you think you can talk to her and tell her to give me the laundry?"

"No."

"Excuse me?"

"I'm on my way."

"Cappadonna, that is not necessary. I can manage on my own, you've done enough." He laughed and remained quiet, but he was still on the line.

"A real man could never do enough for his woman... don't forget that, *Alaia*." It was the way he said my name, like it rolled off his tongue.

He didn't need help pronouncing it because it just came natural to him. "You don't need to come and do this... I promise I can handle it."

"Aye chill out... you stressing my baby out."

"Your baby?" I choked out and looked at the phone.

It was clear that he had been drinking or hitting the good weed because how the hell did my baby become his? "Sit tight... I'm not too far from you."

He ended the call, and I rolled my eyes at the lady at the front while I sat down to wait for him. When I first met Cappadonna at the prison, I could tell he was different from the usual men. He had a look in his eyes that I couldn't shake.

What other man would pay for a car service for a woman he didn't even know? Even when I saw him after that, and tried to discreetly thank him, he acted like it was no sweat off his back. I didn't know what he did because I was clueless when it came to what was going on around me.

I never had a life or friends because Zayne kept me in the house. As much as I wanted to be friends with his other wives, they all hated me for whatever reason. I mean, I didn't want to be his wife so I figured we could have each other's backs. Except, none of them liked me or tried to get to know me. They acted like I swooped in and stole their damn husband away from them.

Having a grown man shoving himself inside of you when you were a sixteen-year-old virgin wasn't something I wanted. I didn't want to be forced to perform sexual acts on a man that swore he was so religious. Zayne used his religion to get away with having multiple wives and doing whatever the fuck he wanted. Taz was the same way, except he decided to take on his brother's wives.

My skin crawled.

When Cappadonna dropped me home the other day, I just knew Taz was going to come behind me and knock my head between the stove and the fridge. He was so fired up about their confrontation that he never came upstairs. I waited in the living room for him to come upstairs, and he never did. After an hour, I locked the door and showered before going to lay down.

Since then, I hadn't heard from Taz, and I didn't know if I should have been scared or what. With the way that Cappadonna came at him, I could tell he was bothered. What tickled me was how fired up Taz was and how nonchalant Cappadonna was. If he would have stepped out his truck, he would have towered over Taz.

Capp was a big guy and towered over most people. Not only was he tall, but he was muscular, too, nice, and thick. I could tell from his shoe size that the man was more than blessed between his legs. I could probably fit both of my feet inside of his shoe and still have room. His tattoos covered up his body like a second skin.

The bell connected to the door chimed when it opened. Cappadonna stepped in dressed in a pair of gray sweatpants, tank top, and pair of Nike AirMax sneakers. He swaggered over toward where I was seated.

"I told you that you didn't have to come all the way over here." He helped me stand up, dropping a soft kiss on my head.

I don't know why that small gesture made me feel so whole. I've never had this feeling in my entire life and within five seconds he had made me feel that way. "And I told you that I was close by. How you going to get all these clothes home by yourself?"

He slid the ticket to the lady who was showing all her damn teeth in her mouth. I guess he did have that aura about him. She pushed the cart around the counter and looked at me. "See your boyfriend help you."

"He's not my boyfriend," I corrected her.

"Yeah... the fuck wrong with you? I look like a boy to you. I'm her man." He looked at her, and then held the door for me while pushing the cart out the laundromat.

"Now why in the world would you tell that woman that?"

He ignored me while holding the door open for me to get inside. I knew by now that there was no need to argue with him. Climbing up into his truck, I got comfortable while I watched him toss the laundry bags and shopping cart into his trunk like it was nothing.

When he hit the button to close the trunk, he jumped into the driver seat and headed in the direction of my house. I stared at him and noticed the love bites on his neck and felt jealous. Why in the world would I even get jealous when he wasn't my man, and I was sure he was just being nice by helping me. I was thinking too much into the little comments he made. He was joking with me.

Those damn Braxton Hicks started up again and I rubbed my stomach while trying to breathe through them. They weren't intense like regular labor pains; they were just uncomfortable. I always considered them a reminder that I was going to be this baby's mama soon.

How could I give this girl the world when I depended on every damn body. I had nothing to give her. What could I teach her when I hadn't been taught anything but to lay on my back and obey a man that didn't give a shit about me.

"Aye, what's the matter?" Cappadonna looked over at me, then quickly pulled over in front of a bus stop.

It wasn't until he put the truck in park that I realized that I had tears coming down my face. I've always been a person that got so deep into my head that I blocked everything around me out. It was something that I had developed when I was sold to Zayne and had to live in his world. I guess as I became older that it stuck with me. Life was easier when you could block out the shitty parts.

"I'm alright... I'm sorry. I was thinking about something."

He got out and came around to the passenger side, opening

it and kneeling down until he was staring in my face. "What's the matter? You missing your *husband?*"

Hearing how he said the word husband caused me to laugh. "I'm not missing that man, I promise. You don't need to say husband like that every time you speak about him, either." He took both his hands and wiped my face.

"Then why you crying silently. I don't like that shit, Joy."

"Joy?"

Each time a tear slid down my face, he reached up and wiped it away. "Your name means joyful and happiness."

"That's funny because I've never felt those emotions in my life. How do you know what my name means? I don't even know what my name means."

"You will." He grabbed my hand as he looked around him, his gun sitting right to his left. "You hungry?"

I perked up at the sound of food. "We sure could eat."

He smiled. "Bet... let me feed you before you start crying again."

Cappadonna made sure that I was alright before he got back in and sped off the block toward our destination. I tried not to retreat inside of my head as I watched him maneuver through the streets with ease.

One hand was on the wheel and the other was leaned on the arm rest with him settled back. His seat was so far that he was nearly in the backseat. I mean, he was very tall so that was to be expected.

"You had a good night? I hope I didn't ruin anything by calling you this morning." I felt bad that I had to call him to come pick the laundry up.

He took his eyes off the road and looked over at me. "You didn't ruin nothing... 'cause nothing happened."

"Your neck says differently." Even with all the tattoos on his neck I could spot a passion mark with my eyes closed.

Whoever left them must have damn near made their lips sore trying to get them so dark. Cappadonna wasn't light by any means, and I could still see them.

"She extra as shit."

"I hope that she doesn't have a problem with you helping me. Make sure to tell her that I have a husband," the words tasted bitter even saying them.

Taz stepping in as my husband felt wrong on many levels. No matter how wrong it felt, it was my reality and I had to deal with it. I've been giving the short end of the stick my entire life, so this was something small to a giant.

"You don't have a husband," he sternly replied, looking like he was pissed off that I even said the word.

His jaw twitched as he drove through the Holland tunnel. It was crazy how I didn't question it. My ass was just sitting in the front seat going along with wherever he was taking me.

"Actually, I do," I whispered.

"Yeah, we gonna see about that." He laughed to himself, and it wasn't a normal laugh like he had told a joke.

My phone pulled me from analyzing it too deeply and I sighed when I saw it was the Lamaze studio that I had been attending the past few months.

"Hey Blaire... I've been meaning to call you," I answered the phone, turning to look out the window.

"Girl, I was worried when you didn't show up last week. Is everything all good over there. Baby didn't come early, did she?"

"Oh, no. She's still in here." I laughed lightly. "My... um... my husband passed away, so I was dealing with that."

"Oh God, I am so sorry, Alaia. Here I was calling about your payment not going through for this month and you're dealing with this."

"No, don't feel sorry... La'Bloom Lamaze has been amazing

for me and my body. I plan on coming in soon, so I will make the payment then."

"No, the next class is on us. Consider it some flowers or a pan of lasagna." She laughed, causing me to genuinely laugh.

I enjoyed people who didn't get all weird whenever death entered the chat. "Oh, really? I appreciate that. I will see you next week."

"Alright, Alaia... please take it easy."

"Will do." I ended the call and slipped my phone back into my purse, enjoying the ride.

Fatima showed me to the guest bedroom where I would be staying. I looked around the pale gray room with a full-size bed in the middle of the room. Nightstands adorned each side, and there was a small flat screen Tv on the dresser. The room was nicer than my room that I had back at Yaya's house, so I wasn't complaining about the accommodations.

Zayne had dropped me off and then left out to do something. He never gave an explanation and Fatima never asked for one. She kind of just accepted what he told her and that was what it was. Aside from a few items of clothing that I had packed, I didn't have many clothes.

"We get up and pray every morning. Even if Zayne is not here, we still get up and pray," she explained, and then pulled out a mat. "Your new mat."

"I'm not really religious."

She gave me a crooked smile. "Not religious but you thought to marry my husband."

I was confused on if she was really this dumb, or had he truly brainwashed her ass. How did any of what was going on look like I was a willing participant in any of this? How the hell was I supposed to respond to her? I wasn't religious, and she expected me to get up early and pray.

"I...I don't know how to respond."

She sucked her teeth. "You need to read this and understand your new life. You're not going to sit around and sleep with my husband without contributing to this house."

She handed me the Quran and then turned to leave out the room.

My eyes fluttered open when I felt someone gently shaking me. When I opened my eyes fully, we were parked in front of a diner. I jumped up slightly and Capp held onto my arm, while staring at me.

"You always twitch in your sleep?"

"I wasn't aware that I did it in the first place," I replied, as I unbuckled my seatbelt.

He came around the car and helped me out the front seat. It was hard to do a lot these days with this belly. When we entered the small diner, we took a seat toward the back. Cappadonna made sure I could fit in the booth and sat across from me where he could see who came in and out the diner.

I looked over the menu while the waitress made small talk between me and Cappadonna. She took my order and then went behind the counter to put it in with the cook. My mouth watered at the pancake combo that I had ordered.

"Sorry for eating in front of you when you're fasting," I apologized. I overheard him explaining to the waitress that he was fasting.

Because I was pregnant, I didn't have to participate because I needed all the food and water for the baby. "I'm good. I want you to eat so you can feed the baby."

"Here's your grits, hun. Your food will be out shortly." She turned toward Capp. "Hun, are you sure there's nothing that I can get you... it's on the house." She winked.

I don't know why the hell she did that because I could see how irritated he had become. She was insinuating that he wasn't eating because he couldn't afford both our meals when he just explained why he wasn't eating. "Beloved, if I wanted to buy this bitch I could. I don't need your charity, and I said I'm fasting. Bring her food out and worry about her."

The woman was shocked as she backed away from the table. In his defense, he told her that he was fasting, and she still continued to pry about him having some food. Even though he was calm when he spoke to her, I could tell that he was upset.

I reached my hand across the table and placed my hand on top of his. "Hey, breathe...she's stupid. Long as we know the reason you're not eating, that is all that matters."

"I had people like her ass always make smart comments disguised like they want to help when my parents were raising us. We grew up with nothing, and they always fucking had some shit to say. Pook the only man that always gave my father respect. He'd put extra pieces of fish on our plates because he knew his fish was a treat for us."

"He sounds like a sweet man."

"A good man... when I found out that he was about to lose his market, I couldn't have that happen." I could tell those small memories of when he was a child meant the most to him.

They were probably what molded him into the man that he was. "Is his market still around?"

"Yeah, up in Harlem... why?"

"I don't know... maybe I might want to visit and try his fish... sheesh, you nosey."

His crooked smirk appeared on his face while he looked over at me. "How the fuck did you become associated with a slime ball like the man you were with."

"My husband."

"Alaia, call that man your husband one more time." His body tensed up and I laughed, finding his anger funny.

"Why does it bother you when I call him my husband? You

sitting across from me with passion marks and you got the nerve to be getting angry with me." I tasted the grits, and they could be better. "By the way, that's not very good of you to be having sex during Ramadan. Might as well eat some food."

People often thought Ramadan was about us Muslims fasting from food. You fasted from all different things, sex being one of them. It was the time for us to grow spiritually and become closer to Allah.

As much as I was shoved into this religion, I had fell in love with certain aspects of it. Before I had become pregnant, I participated in Ramadan every year. I always looked forward to becoming closer to Allah. Praying that he would guide me and release me from the personal hell I had been sold into.

Zayne never fasted and I could tell from the receipts in his car during the hours he was supposed to be fasting. He was such a joke to the religion that I felt embarrassed to be his wife at times.

"I didn't fuck... just got some head," he bluntly explained, and I raised my eyebrow, not surprised by any of what came out his mouth.

"Still the same...you ejaculated... no?"

"Yeah, and I'm about to again with the way you looking at me with your cute ass." I looked away from him and had to contain myself again.

"You seemed like someone who is very strict and in control."

He leaned back in the booth. "Not the easiest thing when it's being tossed at you. I fucked up and I'm not going to do it again."

"Hmm."

"What about you? Your parents Muslim or did you convert for a fuck nigga?"

"I was actually forced into it. Wasn't on my to do list for

life, you know?"

He looked at me curiously. "By who?"

"Does it matter? I do love my religion; I just don't agree with everything that I have been forced to do. Like covering my hair, it was never a conversation. Just something I was expected to do."

"There are a lot of women who are devout Muslims that don't cover their hair. Nobody will think less of you if you decide to take your hijab off."

"Would you want your wife to wear one?"

He messed in his beard. "I would want my future wife to do whatever she was comfortable with doing. The only thing I require is for her to dress modest."

Even before Raheem forced me to go with Zayne, I had never been one of those teens who liked to wear short skirts and show my body. I had always been comfortable with baggier clothes, and not showing too much. I believed there was a way that you could still be sexy without exposing your body.

"She's going to be a lucky woman... ouch." I touched my stomach where my daughter kicked me.

This little girl kicked me in my ribs all day long. I couldn't wait until she was born so we could square up. "Yeah, I'm already knowing she will be.... You alright?"

"She kicks me all day long."

The waitress must have been too embarrassed to come back over, so she sent someone else to bring me my food. "It hurt like that?"

"Imagine someone being inside you and kicking you in the ribs... yes it hurts," I giggled, as I cut into my pancakes.

"I ain't got no problem imagining being inside of you." He looked me in the eyes, his stare giving me chills as I quickly broke our eye contact.

"Anyway."

"You excited to be a mother?"

I paused and thought of the loaded question before I responded. When I first found out that I was pregnant, I cried. For days, I cried and prayed for Allah to take this baby away from me. I never wanted to bring children into this mess that I had with Zayne. I spent the majority of my time alone, and he would disappear for days at a time.

Not to mention that he had just got out of prison. Who knew when he would go back because he didn't know how to act right. No matter how much I prayed her away, she stayed, and I had no choice but to acknowledge that she was a blessing.

My daughter was my only family that I had, and she wasn't even born yet. I hadn't spoken to my mother or brother in years. He made money off the backs of innocent women and girls and put that money on her books. She wasn't a fool to his dealings and encouraged them when I still lived in Yaya's house.

I'm sure he probably went to visit her, and they spoke about how they would sell me off, and then split the money. My mother, if I could call her that, was never a parent to me. She never showed me how to be a woman or took the time to raise me. She pawned us off to our grandmother and never looked back.

So, neither my mother nor brother were my family. I was out in this big world alone with no source of family or support. Despite not having any, I was going to make sure that my daughter had everything.

"Not at first." I took a bite of my pancakes. "I don't have family and her father wasn't worth the skin he was in. Some days, I'm not ready and want to keep her inside of me. Then, there's the other days when I think of how nice it would feel to have some family... you know?"

"Nah, I don't know. I can imagine it feels lonely not to have family. I'd give everything up for my family." I could tell he meant every word.

"Some people aren't that blessed. I always envisioned what it would feel like to have a mother and father. I've managed as best as I could without them." I leaned back in the booth and rubbed my stomach. "I don't have much to give her, and I don't even know what our future looks like. I can promise that I'm going to try to give her the world and be the mother that I never had. Nobody ever tried to give me the world, so I'm going to give it to my little girl."

I don't know why I had become so emotional. It was the stupid hormones because I hardly cried. When I moved into Fatima's house, I cried every day for six months. When I realized nobody was coming to save me, I learned to get on with it.

Cappadonna reached for my hands and put them into his as he rubbed my hand with his thumb. "When my sister-in-law introduced you to me, I remembered your name. I had one of the guards look up your name. Next day during chow, he told me what your name meant... sounds crazy as shit, but I couldn't forget you from that day. No bullshit either."

"Why though?"

"When I looked into your eyes, I saw how lost you were. How in pain you were, and I didn't even know your story. I still don't know your story, but something is telling me that when I learn it, that I'm going to want to paint the city red."

"Then it's settled... you won't be knowing my story." I tried to make the moment lighter because it had become heavy. "Ouch... goodness."

His phone started to ring, and he looked at the name on the screen then back at me. I tried to remove my hands from his so he could answer the phone and he kept them there. "I don't need to get that call right now."

"I promise you can answer your phone... It's alright."

He made no attempts to answer the phone and continued to caress my hand with his thumbs. "You going to tell me your story, Joy?"

"Um, no. You just told me that it might make you want to paint the city red." I didn't bother to correct him because it seemed like he was settled on calling me Joy and had been waiting to call me it since he learned the definition of my name.

Cappadonna gave me a crooked grin. "Tell me your story and I'll decide... can't make you any promises."

"Why do you care so much? I'm just a stranger you met in a prison visitation room... I promise I'm not that special."

His expression became stoic as he continued to hold my hands. The same back and forth motion his thumb made against the back of my hand never stopped. "I've watched you, Joy. Every visit, how you would be so stressed if you forgot something his big ass wanted. I've felt protective of you since we've been in that prison visitation room. Now, I'm not only protective of you, but I'm also protective of *y'all*."

"Y'all?"

He eyed my stomach. "You full?"

I noticed he switched the subject often. Instead of answering my questions, he would skip to the next thing that was on his mind.

"The food isn't all that great," I admitted.

"Shit, there wasn't many options since we both up early. I'll make it up to you," he promised me, and I never was the type that believed in men making promises.

For some reason my gut told me that Cappadonna wasn't the kind of man that broke his promises to people.

7
CAPPADONNA

As we drove back to Alaia's apartment, I kept looking at her snoring peacefully in the passenger seat. I watched as her chest rose and fell while she slightly twitched in her sleep. I wanted to know her story so bad that I could taste the shit. I could sense it was some crazy shit from the way she avoided talking about it. She didn't come from a perfect family with the white picket fence and ugly ass dog. Alaia had experienced pain and I knew it the moment our eyes met in that visitation room.

Capone always joked that I had this weird thing with people. I could always read somebody within five minutes of meeting them. I knew if you were full of shit, or you were solid. When I met Alaia, I felt pain in my chest that I had never experienced before. I've had my share of pain, yet the pain I felt when I stared into her eyes was a different kind of pain. One that I had never experienced. Her eyes told a story that I knew would make me want to turn the country upside down. It was crazy that her name literally meant joyful and happiness, and that wasn't the first emotion I experienced from her when we met.

Even when I held her hand, I could tell she wasn't used to affection. It was something that was foreign to both of us. I hadn't been affectionate with a woman in years, and here I was holding this stranger's hand, never wanting to let go.

I felt more connected to Alaia than I did my own conniving ass girlfriend. How the fuck could I have years under the belt when it came to Kendra, and not have any of these feelings for her?

"I know, I know... I was snoring." She sat up, holding her stomach. "Were we in the middle of a conversation?"

"We were."

"I'm sorry." She snorted while she laughed.

We pulled up to her building and I double parked, while helping her out. Alaia waddled to the back of the car and tried to grab a laundry bag. "Don't piss me off, Joy."

"How are you going to get all these bags up there?"

"You seriously asking me that when yo crazy ass tried to bring them home alone? Start your ass on all those steps you were complaining about before I carry you up next."

She turned her ass around and made her way up the steps, stopping between each landing. Meanwhile, I had made four trips, and I was done before she finally made it up the stairs. This apartment building wasn't good for a pregnant woman. It made me mad thinking of her carrying all those laundry bags down by herself.

Alaia unlocked the door and flipped the switch on the wall. The lights didn't come on, so she flipped the switch a few more times and the lights didn't even pretend to flicker. She waddled over toward the couch and plopped down defeated.

"I texted him and reminded him to pay the stupid electricity bill... I hate this shit," she complained, scrolling through her phone.

I brought the rest of the laundry in and looked around her

small ass apartment. It was bigger than my cell, so I couldn't speak much on it. I guess it was big enough for just her and the baby. You could tell she really tried to make it home.

"It's hot as shit in here... and you need lights."

"Yeah." Her phone started to ring, as she waited for whoever to answer. I leaned on the wall, continuing to survey the room.

There were no pictures anywhere around the apartment. This could have been anyone's apartment, and I wouldn't have known because there was no personalization anywhere. Pictures, art, or even fridge art.

The Chinese menu was the only thing that was clipped to the ivory fridge. I say ivory because at some point in its life, it used to be a white fridge.

"What the fuck do you want?" that familiar voice snarled when he finally picked up the phone, and Alaia looked at me, silently pleading for me not to say anything.

"Hey Taz... um, the electricity is off." She nervously fiddled with the end of her hijab, while focusing on a permanent stain on the linoleum floors.

"What the fuck do you want me to do about it? Maybe you should have thought about that before you brought some random nigga to my crib that I'm now paying for."

The day that Allah decided to make corny niggas, I wished I could have had a conversation with him. Instead of taking it out on me, he was taking it out on an innocent pregnant woman. My chest was hot with fire as I walked closer to her.

Alaia quickly put the phone on mute. "Please, Cappadonna... you don't have to live with or deal with him. If he knows you are here, he will make it worse for me," she pleaded with me, and I hated that shit.

I paced the small area from the TV back to the kitchen

while she spoke to him. "He was giving me a ride home... nothing happened between us."

"You think that shit is appropriate? Your fucking husband just passed and you out here accepting rides from random men."

"I'm sorry, Taz. I... I don't want the food to spoil."

"I'm sorry, Taz... oh now you sorry," he mocked her. "I'll be back to the city in a few days... I'll handle it then. You need to be packing because you moving into my crib anyway. Maybe some time in the dark will make you realize your priorities and this family... and Zayne bragged that you were the easy wife." His little ass had the nerve to scoff.

Alaia swallowed her spit and pride before she spoke. "I am so sorry, Taz. I promise I will never dis—"

Her conversation was cut short when I snatched the phone and ended the call. "If you think I'm about to sit here and listen to you beg that bitch to turn on the lights... you got the wrong fucking nigga, Joy."

"Cappadonna, I need him... *we* need him," she had tears in her eyes as she held her stomach. I slipped her phone into my pocket and looked at her, my heart beating out of control within my chest. "You don't understand... I can't survive without him."

"I don't give a fuck what you think you can't do without him. Pack a few things and come the fuck on. I'm not leaving you in this hell hole until he decides to bring his ass back to the city."

"My house is nice," she argued, offended that I called this little piece of shit a hell hole. Between the junkie that passed me on my third trip up with the laundry, the broken downstairs door, and the lack of lighting and fucking elevators, this shit was a damn community trap house.

"Do all that talking while you grab your shit, Joy."

She folded her arms, calling herself challenging me. Alaia had to be around 5'4, I may even go 5'5, and was no threat to me. In fact, she was actually cute when she called herself being sassy.

"Where am I going?"

"We're going to a hotel," I told her and waited by the door.

I've never prayed so hard for something in my life. I was praying that this nigga decided to pop up here and puff his chest out. I wanted to pick him up by the neck and slam his ass into the fucking fridge until he was in the freezer without me even having to open the doors.

Alaia sat there debating on whether she wanted to pack some things, then went to the room off the kitchen. If she thought she was staying in this hot ass apartment with no air, she had me fucked up.

I was fucking sweating in here, so I couldn't imagine how hot she felt carrying another person inside of her. When she had everything she was bringing, we headed downstairs, and I helped her into the car. Before getting in the car, I checked my surroundings before we headed off her block.

"You don't have to get a hotel room. I could have made do for the three days... I've lasted seven before. It's not a big deal."

I turned to look at her. "You even hear yourself? Why the fuck are you putting up with that shit? Make me a promise right now." She refused to look me in the eyes. "Alaia, look me in the eyes."

Her gaze slowly left the window and landed on me. "What's the promise?"

"I want you to make me two promises."

She huffed. "What are the promises?"

"Look me in my eyes when I'm talking to you... give me that respect, and I promise you'll never want for nothing."

"Second one?"

"You will never open your mouth to beg a nigga for anything. I don't like that shit, it's beneath you and as long as I have breath in my body you won't ever have to."

I didn't take the look in her eyes personal. She wanted to trust me, she desperately wanted to believe that what I was saying was true.

"You're asking me to go against the only person I have, Cappadonna. That's not something that I can do right now. I have to think about my daughter."

I gripped the steering wheel as we drove through Brooklyn to head to the Brooklyn bridge. "You moving in with him?"

"I don't have any other choice. I'd rather move in with him than sit in a dark apartment with no food. He already told me what it was, and I don't need your acts of kindness messing up that plan."

I bit the inside of my cheek and then made a sharp U-turn and headed back to her building. "I'm not about to make you walk up those stairs again. Where's your important stuff? Passports, birth certificate, etc."

"I don't have any of those things. Zayne always kept those things from me."

I turned and faced her, studying her face. "Alaia don't fight me on this because I'm trying not to rip this fucking roof off the truck. A lot of shit isn't making sense right now and I promise you don't want me to start drawing my own conclusions."

"What do you expect? For me to ride off into the sunset with you? This is my life, and only I have to deal with that."

We sat in front of her building, and I stared straight ahead while trying to calm myself and get my thoughts together at the same time. "I ain't got enough food in my system for this shit."

"I can manage. You don't need to save me, Cappadonna. As

much as I appreciate the help... I don't need you taking on my shit."

As she reached for the door handle, I kept my focus straight ahead. "Get out this whip if you want to."

Alaia paused, never pulling the handle to exit the car. "Why do you want to help me? You barely even know me."

"You're not going to sit up in that hot ass apartment. How the fuck am I supposed to sleep tonight knowing you in the crib with no lights on." I pulled away from the building for the second time, abandoning my current thought – for now.

We both were silent as we drove to the city to the hotel. I checked us into a presidential suite at the Willshire hotel. Alaia put her bags down on the couch and looked around the massive suite. The shit was costing me a couple grand a night, but nothing was too much for her.

I wanted her to be comfortable for a couple days. Alaia wasn't trying to let me help her, and I couldn't just force her to do what I wanted. I wouldn't be no better than the nigga she was so called married to.

She walked slowly over toward the panel of floor to ceiling windows. "I don't think I've ever seen the city like this before. People actually live a life where they can stay in places like this."

I leaned on the pillar in the living room and watched as she took all of this in. "You don't think of views and shit when you're in survival mode. I've been there before, and now I find myself caught up in even the smallest sunset. You don't realize how important watching the sunrise and set are until they're taken away from you."

She turned around slowly. "I'm sorry for being ungrateful earlier. You just wouldn't understand my life and I don't want you getting involved."

"I'm grown enough to make my own decisions on what I

choose to get involved with, Alaia." I looked at her, and she looked away from me nervously. "Your room is on the left end... if you need something let me know."

"Okay," I heard her whisper as she took her bags to the other side of the suite, and I went into my room to take a quick nap.

Kendra had been hitting my phone since I ran out the condo earlier, and I didn't have any plans on calling her back. Alaia had me ready to fight the fucking bell man with the way she was acting about this Taz muthafucka.

What the fuck did he have over her? And why was she staying in something that she clearly didn't want to be involved in? I stripped down to my briefs and got under the covers before my eye lids grew heavy and I was knocked out seconds later.

My phone vibrating on the nightstand woke me up, and I was pissed. I hated when my sleep was disturbed. I tossed a fucking guard out my cell the one time his ass came in there slamming shit around. I sat in the hole for a good month and didn't regret shit about it.

As I felt around for my phone without opening my eyes, I located my phone and grabbed it, opening my eyes to see Kendra's name on the screen. I slid my finger across the screen and put the phone to my ear.

"Yo."

"Yo? I've been calling you since you ran the hell out of my condo, and you got the nerve to answer the phone with *yo*. You and... never mind. Where are you and are you coming over tonight?"

"Nah. I'm chilling tonight."

I didn't have no plans on leaving this hotel suite unless I had to, and Kendra wasn't a reason to leave. From the way she was sucking her teeth, I could hear the argument brewing and I wasn't in the mood. It was hard enough even being around her knowing that she had kept my son away from me.

"What the fuck is really going on with us, Cappadonna? You show up to the salon after not telling me you were released. Then we don't fuck, and you run out my condo to go be with the next bitch. Is that bitch who you want to be with? Let me know cause I'm going crazy," she whined into the phone.

My feelings toward Kendra were all screwed up. One minute I wanted to choke the hell out of her, then the next I tried to see things her way. Even though I didn't agree with her decision, I was trying to give her grace and understand why she may have kept him away from me. It was hard keeping that grace when she was on my fucking nerves about shit that wasn't her business.

"Ken, I just woke up and I ain't trying to hear you flapping your fucking gums because I didn't fuck you... I told you I would hit you up, why the fuck you blowing my phone up?"

"Cause I'm your girlfriend, Cappadonna. Who is this chick? Is she somebody you're fucking?"

"I'm not currently fucking anybody this month, Ken. When I decide to stick my dick in some pussy, I promise I got you with a picture."

Kendra gasped so loud I thought she had lost her voice for a second. "Why do you insist on trying to hurt me? I bet you just finish fucking that bitch you ran out of here for."

"If you weren't so fucking selfish you would know why I haven't been in no pussy...except, you too focused on shit that has nothing to do with you!"

"Fuck you, Cappadonna! I'm so fucking done with you!"

she screamed through the phone like I hadn't heard that before.

The only difference was that I was on the outside and I could do more about it than I could before. Whenever Kendra couldn't get her way, she would break up with me and then refused to answer my calls. I usually had Capone check in on her and make her ass call or visit me. I didn't need my twin this time and could pop up on her ass whenever I wanted and there wasn't shit she could do about it.

"You think that this is a game and I'm serious. I've wasted enough time with you, and I refuse to waste another minute on you!" she screamed like a fucking lunatic into the phone. "I'm going to date and fuck whoever I want."

"Go ahead and see and I bet I shoot at you both," I calmly informed her, as I settled back into the bed like I hadn't just been yelling with spit flying from my mouth. Kendra wasn't stupid and should have known how I got down.

If she thought she was going to be fucking other niggas in my face, she had another thing coming. Kendra wasn't done with me until I told her she was done with me. I could easily talk to her and ask her about our son, but since she played in my face for the past nineteen years, I was going to have my fun playing in her face.

Before she could even reply, I ended the call and went to take a piss. I stretched as I came out the room and saw Alaia sitting on the couch. She had on the hotel robe and her hair was tied up in a regular silk scarf.

Her beauty was undeniable. I was so damn attracted to this woman that I didn't think I could leave her alone. I've spent a lot of time thinking about her. Whenever I saw her nigga, I would slap his ass in the back of the head because he had what I wanted.

It wasn't often that another nigga had something that I

wanted. Zayne had someone that I wanted and then he had the nerve to not treat her like the precious jewel that she was. He stepped on her like she was yesterday's trash.

"You tend to wake up screaming all the time?" She had this sly smirk on her face while she rested her hands onto her stomach.

I plopped down on the couch beside her. "How did you sleep?"

"Sleep? I've been sitting here since I got out the shower. This view... I don't know... I just never imagined feeling like this about a stupid view."

"What you feeling, Joy?" I leaned my head back on the couch and watched her try to figure out her emotions.

"Since I moved to New York City, the only times I've been in Manhattan was when I was catching the bus to head upstate. I've never seen it like this... your version of New York." She winced, as she rubbed her stomach.

The robe didn't fit her all the way, and her protruding stomach hung slightly out the robe. "Can I?"

"Really?"

"Only if you comfortable. Don't do no shit you're not comfortable with," I explained, comfortable enough to accept a no, if she was uncomfortable with me touching her stomach.

"I'm not uncomfortable." She untied the robe, and her stomach was just there. The purple and blue stretch marks climbed up her swollen belly like vines growing on a house. Her stomach was a home for her baby girl. Alaia took my hand, and she placed it on the side where I could feel her baby.

"Oh shit...feels like she's trying to high five me or something." I smiled, as I continued to move my hands around her stomach.

Her stomach was so hard that it couldn't have been comfortable to sleep. The baby was active as hell, as she moved around her stomach and pushed up in different spots. "She waits until it's time for bed to get active."

"She's a night owl."

"She better not. I'm already scared about what happens when she comes, and I have to do the midnight feedings."

"Aside from late night feedings... you scared?"

She looked down. "So scared. I've never done this before... what if I get this wrong?"

"Can I tell you a secret?"

"Of course."

"No mother has ever done it before... that's the thing about parenthood. You can figure out what works for you as you go. I watch my brother as a father, and I see how he parents and then think about how our parents were with us. He didn't have a clue how to be a father when his son was born... guess what?"

"What?"

"He figured that shit out and now he's one of the best fathers that I know. You'll figure it out, and I'm gonna be right here to help you."

"It sounds nice saying it, huh?"

"What you mean?" I kept my focus on her stomach, as I poked around, her baby poking back at me.

"Promising me that you're going to be there. It sounds nice when saying it, but we both know that's not either of our reality. You have a relationship and I have my situation."

"Is your situation worth bringing her into?" I looked over at her, while she tried to avoid eye contact with me. "Eye contact, Joy... told you that."

She dragged her eyes from her stomach to meet my eyes. "That's a cheap shot."

"Nah, that's a real question."

Alaia pushed up off the couch and walked back over

toward the windows. "It's a question that I refuse to answer right now."

"Fair."

She came back to sit on the couch. "Thank you for this... I don't think I will ever forget this view."

"How long have you been in New York?"

"Ten years... I was born and raised in Delaware... came here when I was sixteen." As she spoke about where she was born and when she came to New York, I could see her disassociating as the words left her mouth.

Alaia was only twenty-six and she had the spirit of someone much older. She had seen a lot and been through even more. "How long have you been wearing the hijab?"

I decided to change the subject. "Just as long as I've been here."

"So, you moved here when you were sixteen years old. Where the fuck were your parents?" I gathered that she didn't move here alone, but she also didn't move here with her parents.

"My mother is in prison and my father is somewhere in his skin. Never really knew him," she shrugged it off like it was nothing.

My parents were my fucking heart. I couldn't imagine getting through all those years away without them and my siblings. When I felt like I was going crazy, it was my father that got on the phone and prayed with me. Whenever he could, he was up at the prison to visit me and keep me in good spirits.

People assumed because me and Capone were raised by both our parents that we wouldn't have gravitated toward the streets. We had two immigrant parents that were busting their asses to take care of us. None of that shit ever sat right with me, so naturally, I went to the streets to find a solution for the problem.

It brought me complete joy knowing that my parents never had to work again. They could sit back and enjoy the life provided to them by their boys. When Capone told me he was stepping back, I respected that because he had been running for so long that he deserved it. He deserved to sit back and be a husband and a father, while knowing that I had everything under control.

"Then who did you come out here with?"

She turned to look out the window. "You know I don't always wear my hijab. I've only wore it when it came to visiting Zayne when he was locked up. Soon as I was back home, I would snatch it off and wear my hair out. Whenever I would take it off, I felt like I was rebelling and sticking it to him... even though he never knew."

"Stop switching the subject."

"The man at the corner store near my house didn't even recognize me until after a week the last time I didn't wear it." She continued talking like she hadn't heard me ask her a damn question. I quietly and patiently allowed her to finish talking.

"Alaia."

"I wore this for so long because Zayne told me that I had to. Muslim women wore this to respect their husbands." She turned to look me in the eyes. "You're not the only one that can switch subjects whenever you want."

I chuckled. "Oh, you think you're funny."

"I used to be funny... I lost it a long time ago." She sighed.

"He's dead, you don't have to wear a hijab if you don't want to," I replied. "Despite what people think, it's the woman's choice if she wants to wear one or not... bet his ass didn't say that."

"Never. Always made me feel like I had no other choice, or I was disrespecting him. So much of what I so called did disrespected him... I never knew what was right or wrong. Nobody ever sat me down and taught me how to be a good Muslim." She snickered. "I probably sound crazy as hell saying that."

I took her hand into mine. "You don't sound crazy at all. That bitch was weaponizing our religion to control you. This has to be something that you want, not because it was forced on you."

"I struggle so much with my faith in Allah." She continued to look down at her stomach. "When I was younger, I hated this religion so bad. Blamed it for the reason my life was the way it was now."

"Don't tell me you be eating pork on the low, too." I smiled.

She cut her eyes at me before that smile graced her face. "No, I haven't gone that far."

"What about now? You still hate it?"

"I don't hate it anymore. I...I just struggle so much with what's right and what's wrong." She wiped away a tear that had escaped.

There was so much to unpack with her relationship with Allah and tonight wasn't the night. Alaia had to travel her own path and if that meant that she didn't want to be Muslim anymore, that was her decision to make.

"You don't have to figure everything out tonight or even tomorrow... whatever you choose with you and your daughter's life is your decision."

She turned to meet my eyes. "Would you marry a woman that wasn't Muslim?"

I had no plans on marrying Kendra after the shit that I had found out. Before any of that, I did have plans on coming home and marrying her. I always told her that I would hope she would convert for me.

"I would hope that the woman I love would want to

convert and share my religion with me. Have her own relationship with our faith so we could come together as one."

She smiled. "I hope you find that, Cappadonna."

I wanted to tell her ass that I had already found it, but she was too busy playing games. If Alaia told me what was going on with her right now and let me know she didn't want to move in with shorty duwop, I would buy her and the baby a house right now.

She wouldn't have to ask or beg, because it would already be done because that's how much I was on her.

"You hungry?"

She nodded yes. "Very hungry. I wanted to wait for you to wake up and ask if we could get room service."

"Whenever you with me you never have to ask for something. If you were hungry, order as much food as you want, Alaia." I held her chin gently and stared into her eyes. "I mean that shit, too."

"Okay."

She didn't hesitate to grab the cordless phone and put in an order for food. I noticed how she ordered two of the things she thought I might enjoy. I kicked my feet up, and turned the TV on while listening to her stress that we didn't want any bacon on our burgers or the bacon cheese fries.

40: Heard you out... need to link soon.

I looked down at my phone and saw Forty's text message. I've been so lowkey that not even Forty knew that I was out. Forty was always off the grid and resurfaced whenever he needed to. I was assuming he found out that I was out and wanted to see me.

Me: Let me know the place and time... I'm there.

8
CHUBS

I REMEMBER the day I realized that my great-aunt wasn't my mother and was in fact my great-aunt. For a seven-year-old, that changed a lot in my life and none of the adults in my life realized it. Kendra always came around and I always called her mom out of respect, never knowing the reason.

Francie, my great-aunt, always told me it was a respect thing and that I should call her that whenever she came around, which was never often. Kendra popped out for birthdays and important life events and even then, her ass was always fucking late.

My aunt and cousin, Jasmine, always said that Kendra loved to be the center of attention. She was too into herself to be a mother. I always overheard these things, but the older I became the more I realized how true it was. I couldn't count on one hand one thing my mother taught me, other than to be about myself and make sure I keep some money in my pocket.

If it was one thing that Kendra had, she always had some money and made sure everyone around her knew it. I stopped craving that motherly love and started using her for what I needed from her. I had all the newest sneakers and fresh clothes because that was all she was good for. When it came to spending time together, she was there to slide a credit card or peel off money out her wallet.

The older I became, the more my aunt tried to keep me sheltered from everything. She told lies that she thought were helping me when in reality all they were doing was confusing the fuck out of me.

If it hadn't been for my cousin Jasmine, I wouldn't know who my father was or the fact that I had a whole family that knew nothing about me. She was the one that told me about my father and where he was.

I used to be so angry with him because why wasn't he around? Until I realized that he was in prison and as far as he knew, I didn't exist. When I learned that he was a twin and who his brother was, I really needed to be put on. Kincaid grew up on our block and he and Jasmine dated for a little while.

When Jasmine went away to college, they broke up. She wanted more and to get away from the city, and Kincaid was so drawn to the streets that he would never leave them. I always fucked with him and told him that Jasmine was the one that got away from him.

If his ass knew that she was back in New York for good, I think his relationship with Capri would be threatened. Kincaid was crazy about my cousin, and I saw some of the shit he did to make sure she was always protected.

When I found out that Kincaid was running for Capone, I begged his ass to put me on. I wanted to be close to my family, even if that meant that I would be doing shit my aunt wouldn't be proud of.

Kincaid put me through his own host of test before he set the meet up with Capone. I remember when Capone walked into the room. His presence was so damn big that the room felt smaller than it actually was. He carried himself like he knew he was better than everybody he met. The same aura I could only imagine my father had, too.

I worked my way up until I was running right beside him and still hadn't worked up the courage to tell him that I was his nephew. Every time I was about to say something, I always chickened out like a pussy.

"You going to play or keep staring at the screen like you confused?" Jaiden's voice reminded me that I was in his room playing Madden.

"Fuck up. You be cheating any damn way."

When Jaiden caught his first body, it was only natural for us to become close. It wasn't every day that you caught a body. Since we were the closest in age, we naturally clicked and had become close.

"What's on your mind, Gang?"

"*Gang?* You hanging around those prep school kids too much." I chuckled, tossing the controller on the bed, and taking a seat in the chair near his window.

"Shut up. Is this about your father, who is in the kitchen right now... you can just go and tell him the truth."

"And look crazy as shit. Some random nigga that been running errands for him for the past few months is telling him that he's his son... come on, Jai."

It was hard being around the man that was responsible for creating me. Like I expected, Cappadonna's presence was very much like his brother's. The Delgato twins just had this aura about them that made you wanna yell *that nigga got that shit on*. That was how large it was, and if you weren't a secure man, then you were going to feel fucking weak around them.

"You don't think you look crazy running errands and being around without him knowing? What happens when he finds out?"

"I ain't ask for this shit... why the fuck do I have to be the one to tell him?"

Jaiden checked his phone before getting up and stretching. "Life is filled with decisions. Which one are you going to choose?"

"Like you trying to decide when you gonna stop wasting Elliot's time?" I quickly switched the subject.

"I'm not wasting her time... we enjoy hanging out. Is it a crime to hang out with a girl now?"

Jaiden was doing everything except calling this girl his girlfriend. "You just like fucking without having to give her a commitment."

"I ain't ready for all of that. Just because we're going to the same college doesn't mean we need to be together... shit, I feel guilty even fucking with her."

Joie was the reason he was scared to move on. He felt like he was betraying her by moving on with his life and his reason was valid. It felt like some kind of betrayal to keep on breathing while the person you love wasn't given the same opportunity as you.

"Eventually, she's going to ask for more and those are the decisions that *you* are going to have to make." I checked my phone and stood up to dap Jaiden before having to bounce.

"Whatever. You coming to Jo's birthday dinner?"

"Already know. She ran down on me before I came in here," I laughed.

Whenever I crossed the threshold into this house, I felt the warmth and love this family had for everybody. They treated me exactly like family, and none of them knew how much that meant to me. I already struggled with mama issues, so having the women in this family look out for me the way they did made me appreciate them.

Capone trusted me to protect his family and I didn't take it lightly. Even with things having died down, I still looked out for every person and would put my life on the line if it came between mine and their lives.

"Be safe, bro'." Jaiden dapped me up. "Don't be laid up with shorty either... get back to work, bitch," he joked, and I flipped the middle finger up at him, as I left the room to head to Brooklyn.

On my way out, Capp was sitting in the sunroom and peeped me from afar. "Heading out?"

"Yeah, back to the money... you good?"

"I'm straight. Be safe," he replied.

This would have been the perfect moment to tell him. Instead, I allowed it to slip through my fingers. I don't know how many more chances I would get, but I needed to stop being a pussy and let him know that I was his son.

9
KENDRA

When Cappadonna called me and told me he was taking me out today, I almost broke my knee trying to get out the bed. One thing about Capp, if he told you when he was coming, you better be ready. I knew I was always running behind, so my ass was up early this morning with my eye patches on, spiral curling my hair and doing my makeup.

After our argument a couple days ago, I wanted to put all the hostility behind us and start over fresh. This was a new chapter for us, and we couldn't keep repeating the same shit that we did when we were younger. The only way I was going to get that ring was if my ass stopped eating pork and acted right.

When I heard the front door open, I spritzed some perfume on my neck, and headed to the front. I almost had a damn aneurysm when I saw Ace standing in my kitchen. I tried to breathe, but I couldn't because I couldn't believe that he was actually standing here.

"What the...what the fuck are you doing here?" I whispered, as if Capp was actually in my condo.

If he knew another man was here, he would have killed the both of us and then took a nap. I've seen Capp in action, and he was about that action. That was why it always surprised me when I played in his face the way that I did.

I had convinced myself that he had a soft spot for me, however, the more I saw him since he'd been home, I was starting to believe that I made that up all on my own and this man would kill my ass if he had to.

"I came to the city early and figured I would surprise you with a date." Ace looked around confused. "Why the fuck are we whispering?"

"Ace, you should have called me and told me."

"It wouldn't have been a surprise then, Kendra. Why the fuck are you acting all weird?" He continued to look around.

Me and Ace met when I went to my nephew's birthday party in Delaware a few months ago. He was on me hard, even when I told him that I had a man. With it being closer to Capp's release date, I was trying hard to clean up my act.

Ace didn't give a damn when I told him that my man was locked up. He wanted me, and I wanted his money, so I finally gave in and allowed him to take me out. One date turned into a bunch, and he was peeling me off money every week.

He made trips back and forth from Delaware to New York to take me shopping and spoil me. I had become so caught up in what we were developing that I forgot about Capp for a while. I broke all my rules, giving Ace a key to my condo, and acting like a girlfriend when this was supposed to be temporary.

"My man is home," I revealed.

I was shaking in my heels because I didn't want to be on the news being wheeled out in a body bag. I was too damn cute and young to be dead because I couldn't keep my men away from each other and in check.

"I don't give a fuck... I'm supposed to disappear because he home." He puffed out his chest, and I leaned on the counter knowing that we were both going to die.

Ace walked over toward me, kissing me on my neck and I removed myself from his arms. Not because I didn't want him, but because I knew that I would want some dick and I couldn't have none. Capp had been depriving me of some, so I would take it from anywhere.

"Stop, Ace," I moaned, trying to move away from him, and he held me in place near the kitchen island. "He's on his way to pick me up now."

"Kendra, I told you that I was on you, and I wasn't going to let up. Baby, I fucking love you... I told you that shit." He picked my hand up and looked at my hand. "Where's your engagement ring?"

I knew the minute he picked my hand up he was going to ask about the ring. Nobody, not even Sassy knew that I was engaged to Ace. It was a secret that I had planned on taking to my grave. Seeing as though I might be meeting my grave sooner than later, I didn't know what to do.

When Ace took me to the Bahamas and proposed to me, I was so in the moment that I accepted. A bitch wasn't thinking about her man locked up in America. All I was thinking about was the fat ass cushion cut diamond engagement ring, and the beautiful suite that he booked for us.

It wasn't until Ace started talking about children, moving to Delaware, and actually getting married that I realized that I had fucked up. Don't get me wrong, I did love Ace and had fell for him. Maybe I was more in love with the way he spent money than the actual emotion that love was.

What I did know is that Ace needed to leave now or I was going to end up at the bottom of the Hudson River, and he was going to end up chopped up on someone's front lawn. The city had finally relaxed from the mayhem that Capone had inflicted on it.

Even I knew not to call or text for some money because his ass wasn't well in the head in that moment. It didn't take a rocket scientist to know that he was the reason NYPD was working around the clock to figure out all the murders that were going on.

"Do you really think I can wear that around him, Ace? Seriously?"

My phone chimed from across the room. "I don't give a fuck what you think you can't do around him. Kendra, you told me that you were going to end it with him... what the fuck is going on?"

"I promise, baby. I'm waiting for the right moment to do it," I lied, knowing damn well that I would rather pick every piece of hair out my scalp one by one before I ever looked up in Cappadonna's eyes and told him about some shit like that.

He kissed me on the lips once more before he released me from the counter. I rushed over to check my phone and Capp had sent me a text letting me know he was pulling up in five minutes, which happened to be four minutes ago.

"He's here." My heart felt like it was about to come out my chest and sit at the counter to witness what was about to go on.

Ace shrugged. "Guess we can get what you need to get out right now."

"Fuck no... I mean, no. Not the time or place, Ace. A lot of men live in this building, so you can just leave and act regular." I stopped to look at him. "Do you trust me?"

"You know I do."

"Then trust that I'm going to handle this without your assistance."

He walked over to kiss me once more before heading

toward the door. "Date night whenever you're done. I want to take you to some fly place my homie owns."

"I'm excited." I stared straight at the door praying that when he opened that door Cappadonna wasn't standing there.

My chest settled when he wasn't there once Ace opened the door. He blew me a kiss before he left, and I finished getting ready before heading down behind him. Capp's truck was parked in front of the building when I got downstairs, and he was eyeing Ace leaned on his Mercedes.

This is why I could never marry this nigga. He didn't fucking listen and felt like he had some shit to prove. Capp got out his truck and strolled around to the passenger side and hugged me.

He grabbed my ass and kissed me on the lips. This was the most action I had gotten from him since he popped up at Sassy's shop, and I was going to take it before he went back to being all cold and mean.

Ace looked more hurt than pissed as he stared at us. When Capp opened the door and waited for me to step in, he turned over toward Ace. "The fuck you looking at? You wanna see me fuck her, too? Damn."

"Nigga, suck my—"

"Before you invite me to your dick... decide if that's what you want your last words to be," Capp lifted his shirt, showing his gun.

Ace looked away before he turned back around. "You heard what the fuck I said."

Capp was about to stroll his ass over there and I hopped out the car. "Cappadonna, can we please go. That is my neighbor's son, and you don't need to be bickering with him."

He looked from me to Ace like he already knew something and was waiting for me to blurt the truth out. I got back in the car with my fucking heart in my ass while Capp took his sweet ass time walking back to the truck.

"God, if you get me out of this, I will be better," I whispered before he finally got his ass back in the car.

"You fucking that nigga?"

"What?" I asked in a high-pitched voice.

"You heard what the fuck I said." His hand touched my bare thigh, and he gave it a squeeze. "You gave that nigga *my* pussy, Kendra?"

"Why would you even assume something like that? He helps me if he sees me with bags, but I don't pay that man no mind... He probably has a crush on me or something."

He kept his hand on my thigh, applying slight pressure and sped out of the spot, slowing down enough to look Ace in the eyes before continuing on.

"Erin's aunt is having a birthday dinner at their crib," he informed me on where we were going, and suddenly, I would have rather sit between both Ace and Capp in the middle of a fight.

Capone hated my ass with a passion and never hid the shit either. He acted like he smelled something bad whenever I came around. Capri was nicer, but I could tell I wasn't her favorite person either.

"Your parents going to be there?"

"Yeah."

I inwardly groaned because being at a dinner with people who disliked me didn't sound like a good use of my Saturday. For Capp, I was going to swallow my pride and be the best girlfriend today.

We didn't speak much on the ride over. Every so often he would send a text message while driving with his knees or turn the music up. Was this how it was going to be with us now? I missed when all we used to do was talk and joke around with each other. It felt like that side of us had faded away and wasn't coming back anytime soon.

Cappadonna put the code into the gates, and then pulled through soon as they opened. There were a few cars in the front, and I said a silent prayer that everything would be cool. I thought he would give me a pep talk before we got out, but his ass was out the car and opening my door before I could even speak.

I grabbed his hand for support, and we walked into the house. I've never been to Capone's house, and now I understood why. This home was like a piece of art, something that was out of a home magazine.

"This is your brother's house?" I whispered stunned by what I was witnessing.

The cars displayed in the foyer were all color coordinated. Even the mini cooper had a place within the array of different exotic sports cars. I continued to hold onto his hand while taking in everything. The big wedding picture in the foyer was beautiful, and Capone truly looked happy as he stared down into his wife's eyes.

I can say that I had never saw the side of Capone since I had known him. Not even when he was with Ella. This side of him was gentle, caring, and in love. His wife looked up into his eyes like he was her entire world.

The picture made me feel all sappy and guilty because I had betrayed Cappadonna. Would he ever look at me like this, or would we be ruined before we could get to this phase of our relationship?

"Oh, my baby," Jean came out the kitchen and hugged her son, reaching up to touch his face.

When it came to Jean, her boys were her entire world. She treated them like her babies, even though they were grown men that nearly towered over everyone.

"What you in there cooking, Ma?" Capp kissed his mother on the head, and gave her a tight squeeze, dropping my hand immediately.

I knew one of the hardest things for him was to be away from his mother while he was locked up. Cappadonna could deny it all he wanted, but that boy was a mama's boy and had always been.

"Josephine has me in there making all her favorites. She has really milked the *I'll do anything for you* card for this dinner," she smiled, and then turned her attention over toward me. "How are you, Kendra?"

While Capp was on the inside, I had the least contact with his family. I felt weird coming around and being with them when he wasn't here. Before he was arrested, we weren't that close, either.

His mother always accused me of using him. I was with Cappadonna when he was pushing that busted ass Nissan Altima with the broken back window. How could I be using him for money when he barely had any? She always seemed to forget the fact that I actually broke up with him and moved away.

"Hey Jean. It smells amazing in here," I complimented her, not wanting to have any issues because Jean Delgato could be petty as she wanted to be.

"Hmph. Everybody is outside in the back. CJ convinced his father to open the pool earlier this year," she snickered, clearly smitten by her grandson.

Capone Jr. would be able to get away with murder in his grandmother's eyes. Her boys were so perfect, and nobody could tell Jean anything different. I latched back onto Capp's arms, as we headed toward the back.

I took a deep breath when we exited out the back door. Everyone was in the back chilling and having a good time.

Capri was in the pool with CJ, while Kincaid sat on the edge of the pool watching them.

Capone was sitting on one of the couches with his wife on his lap. She was laughing about something, and he kept rubbing her thighs while he spoke. I was taken back that she was bald. I'm not talking short cut fade, I'm talking sun glistening off her head bald. I've never formally met Erin or spoke two words to her.

She had come with Capone a few times when he dropped money off to me, but we never spoke because Capone acted like I was poison or something. He didn't even allow me to get close to the damn car to acknowledge the damn girl.

"Capp, you made it!" Erin noticed us and came over to hug him. He pulled her into his arms, dropping a soft kiss on top of her head.

"I told you that I was going to come... why you surprised?"

She smiled. "I don't know why I get surprised anymore. When you and your brother say something, you both always come through." She stopped and looked over in my direction with a smile. "Hey Kendra! It's finally nice to meet you."

She was so warm, as she hugged me and then pulled me over toward where everyone was sitting. How the hell did a grinch like Capone end up with such a nice wife?

"Thank you for inviting me." I smiled, allowing her to pull me where everyone was. Capp followed closely behind us, taking a seat next to his brother.

They exchanged some words that only the two of them could hear while Erin was introducing me to everybody. My heart was caught in my chest when I saw Capella sitting on the couch next to Erin's cousin.

My hands started to sweat, and my vision started to go blurry. I stood there trying to keep myself calm while Capella sat there coolly. As if he wasn't sitting across from his damn father that had no clue he even existed.

"Hey everyone." I smiled, looking at all of them. "Um, where's the bathroom?"

Erin took me in the house and showed me where the bathroom was. I didn't give a hell that I just spent an hour applying all this makeup, I splashed water on my face soon as I locked the bathroom door behind me.

How in the world did Capella end up running with Capone and Cappadonna? I wasn't that involved in his day-to-day life, but I damn sure didn't think he was running with them, or involved in the streets at all.

When he turned eighteen, I didn't send as much money as I used to because I told my aunt that he needed to learn how to get a job to care for himself. She didn't agree and we butted heads on the subject.

If I continued to send him money, it would be enabling him to sit on his ass and do nothing with his life. When I said that he needed to get a job, I wasn't thinking about selling damn drugs with his father.

After a few minutes, I finally calmed down enough to fix my makeup and exit out the bathroom. "Everything all good with you?"

I jumped when I heard Capp's voice. He was leaned on the wall near the bathroom, and I hadn't noticed that he was even standing there. Ever since seeing my son on the couch, my vision was clearly blurred, and I needed to lay down.

"I think I ate something bad... I don't feel too good," I quickly lied.

This man was like a blood hound when it came to the truth. He looked at me sideways and then took my hand. "You wanna lay in my bed?"

"No, I'm good... I don't want to ruin the party... I splashed some water on my face and I'm feeling better."

The sound of hiding in his room sounded better than going out there and pretending I didn't know my own son. Capp took me back outside, and I sat down on the individual seat right between the two couches.

"You all good, Kendra?" Capone asked with this snarky ass tone.

Capp needed to understand that his damn brother was a fucking jerk, especially when it came to me. "I'm good, Capo."

"You don't need no money or nothing, right?"

Erin pinched her husband. "You better behave, Winston."

He kissed her on the lips, pulling her closer to him. I don't know how much closer he wanted her on him, because she was already on top of him. "Michael says he is on his way." Ryai looked up from her phone.

"Man, call him Big Mike. We don't know a Michael," Jaiden, Erin's brother, joked with his cousin.

"Look at her... all grinning in her phone for Big Mike," Capp started to laugh while teasing Ryai about her relationship.

I knew Big Mike from around the way and I always assumed his ass was broken. He's never been connected to any woman. Shit, some people in the hood were starting to believe his ass was a robot or something.

The man didn't smile, and his entire life revolved around Capone. If it was one man that would take a bullet for Capone besides his twin, it would have been Big Mike.

"You and Big Mike are together? How did that happen? All that man does is breathe Capone," I joked.

Nobody laughed and I felt stupid for even trying to blend in.

"You be breathing in a lot of shit... see me saying something?" Capone calmly stated, while Erin just stared at me.

Ryai put her phone away. "We are together, and that's my baby... not too much on him."

I realized that I was going to just shut my damn mouth going forward and try to blend in as best as I could. Capp was in his phone, like he had been on the ride over here. He showed Capone and Erin something, and they both smiled.

What the fuck was he showing them? There was so much unanswered when it came to Capp and this mystery girl that he refused to even acknowledge or explain to me. I felt like a stranger sitting here. Everyone was all connected, like a tight knit family, and then it was just me.

"Look at the birthday girl," Capone clapped his hands while everyone turned to look at the brown skinned woman coming down the steps from the house.

She wore a long white Kaftan style dress and accessorized it with gold accessories. Her heels were even gold, as she flipped her copper hair over her shoulder and spun around.

"That's my mama... fifty-five where?" Ryai stood up and embraced her mother. She kissed her daughter back and sat on the edge of the couch.

"We could have flown to a private island for your birthday... you know that, right?" Capone looked at her.

Jaiden came over and kissed his aunt on the cheek, hugging her while standing beside her. "Which is why I wanted a simple dinner with you guys. The trip that you are sending me, Walt, and your parents on is more than enough."

Erin came over toward her aunt and smiled. "You look beautiful, Jo... I love you so much." She hugged her.

I could tell that they were super close as a family. I didn't know Erin's story; however, I could tell that her aunt meant the world to her.

"Oh, hey... how are you? I'm Jo," she introduced herself to

me once she noticed me sitting there. Probably sticking out like a sore thumb.

Capp sat there with his legs crossed at the ankle, watching the exchange between me and Jo. He didn't bother to step in and introduce me, instead he sat there messing with his beard like he was in deep thought.

"Hey, I'm Kendra… Capp's girlfriend."

"Oh, *the* Kendra." Her eyes widened. "Well, it's finally nice to meet you. I hope we'll see a lot more of you around here."

I giggled. "Yes. I hope to be invited to more functions."

Capp didn't look like he wanted to invite me anywhere but to hell. I sat there feeling more alone than I had when he was away. My chest was hurting while trying to hold my composure. My son sat to the left of me and his father to the right of me.

"Hey Kendra," Capri greeted, keeping it short as she embraced her brother and then went to shower so she could change.

"Unc, what up?" CJ walked over to his uncle.

"Ain't shit but the sky."

"Smooth cat," CJ looked to his father, and smirked before Jean called him to come shower and get ready for dinner.

I just knew when CJ was older that he was going to break hearts like his father and uncle. He idolized them both so much. Capp's relationship with his nephew never wavered, even when he told everyone not to bring him to visit him.

As the sun started to set, Capp had disappeared from the crowd, leaving me to sit there. Erin had went to get she and Capone's daughter, and everyone was fawning over her. She was a beautiful chocolate baby.

"Look at Daddy's lil' gorgeous," he kissed his daughter's face, and then handed her back to her mother.

"What's her name?" I decided to try once more to make

small talk and try to win over my future brother-in-law. If me and Capp were to ever make it to where marriage was a possibility, Capone was the key to that. Capp trusted his brother's word, so I needed to make nice with his jerk ass if I wanted to be the next Mrs. Delgato.

"Capri. We call her Cee-cee," Erin answered because her husband just stared at me blankly like I hadn't asked his ass a question.

"She's beautiful. Look at that thick curly hair."

"The heartburn was awful when I was pregnant with her. She got the same hair that I used to have." Erin kissed her baby.

You could tell being that little girl's mama was her greatest joy. Just the way she looked down into her eyes told me she would do whatever for her child. It made me emotional to think of the love a mother had for their child.

It must have skipped me because although I loved my boy, I never got that feeling of just stopping everything to be his mother. I understood I was selfish, and maybe there may have been some disconnect within my brain that caused me to think like this.

My own mother wasn't the best role model, either. She dropped us off constantly with my grandmother, or we spent school nights at my aunt's house all the time. Me and my sister never had a stable place to stay growing up.

We were always being evicted out of some apartment we had only been in for a few months. Even when I would run to hug or love on my mother, she would always push me away. I can't recall one time when my mother kissed or told me that she loved me. Her famous words were, "I'm not about to put my life on hold for you girls." The maternal gene must have skipped us both and went straight to my sister.

Kalisa was the best mother to her daughter and son. I

admired how she gave up her life to raise her kids as a single mother. You didn't see my sister without her kids trailing behind her. It was the reason her ass was single and always crying about never finding the one. The bitch never liked to leave her crumb snatchers to find some forever dick.

"Kendra?"

I realized that my stupid ass had went into a damn daze over my mother. "Huh? Sorry."

"You got kids, Kendra?" Capone asked, picking in his beard. As far as his ass knew, I didn't have any kids and he was acting like he hadn't known me for years. "I don't got no little nephews or nieces running around, right?"

It was at this moment I was glad that Capp had went off to do whatever he did. Capone was acting like he knew more than he was letting on and I was nervous. "You know damn well I don't have any children... I'm going to find your brother." I quickly excused myself, looking over at Chubs who didn't have any reaction.

I expected his feelings to be hurt. Did he even know that Cappadonna was his father? Maybe I was thinking too deeply into this, and he had no clue that his father was Capp. He just worked for the Delgato's and had become close with them.

Softly opening the door, I caught Capp on his knees praying. I silently stood in the corner of the room and gave him his space. When he finished, he rested on his knees, and looked behind him.

"You are always free to learn and join in with me whenever you want."

Capp and I had discussed me converting and at the time I promised that I would. It was easy to make promises when the man had years to go before he was actually free. Now that he was on the outside and serious about his religion, I couldn't keep running from it.

He was acting like he was the most devout Muslim to begin with. I wasn't trying to cover my hair, give up good bacon, and whole list of other things. I couldn't starve myself all damn day and give up drinking. That would send me over the fucking edge, and Cappadonna wasn't trying to hear me.

"I'm good watching you. Did you have a good pray?"

He stood up, rolling his mat up. "Good pray?" He snickered to himself and sat the mat over in the corner.

I walked over toward him and put my arms around his neck. Silly of me to expect him to pick me up and kiss me on the lips. "We can have a quickie right here. Nobody would even notice that we are gone."

Only God knew how bad I craved this man, and he was over here withholding like he didn't want me just as bad. He picked me up and moved me out of his path and went to the bathroom. I was right behind him as he let that big muthafucka out his pants to take a piss.

My mouth watered at the sight of it, and I wanted to drop down to my knees and please him. "Homie was staring at you like he knew you like that."

"Huh?"

"The nigga that was posted in front of your building."

How did the conversation end up back to Ace in front of the building? I wanted to punch Ace in the face for showing up to my house unannounced. It was my fault because I made it alright for him to pop up and surprise me.

That was then, this was now, and I couldn't have him using the damn key and Capone was sleep in the bed. I pushed a lot of buttons and knew how to get my way, but there was no number of head, kisses, or pouting that would get me out of another man having the key to the condo that Capp paid for.

"Baby, seriously? I told you that he's my neighbor's son. He knows me because we say hi and bye, and he helps me. I told you that."

"Helps you how, Kendra? The nigga was heated when he saw you get in my whip." Capp wasn't as stupid as Ace.

I could beat Ace over the head with some bullshit and we would be straight. Cappadonna wasn't going to accept any damn explanation from me. He was an overthinker and had always been. Added with the fact that he was possessive, that didn't make a good mixture.

Especially when I was out here giving his pussy away to whoever made me blush. I was ashamed of the way I had been acting out here. Maybe I should convert, I needed a blessing or something.

"Dammit, babe... are you serious right now?"

He washed his hand and turned to look at me. "Dead fucking serious. I find out you giving that pussy away, I'm snatching it from between your legs. Now, what the fuck he be helping you with?"

I don't know what his brother had told him. There had been a few times throughout the years that Capone had run into me out with another guy. I always played it off like we were friends, but I knew he never believed me.

"With bags and stuff when he sees me coming from the grocery store. You're thinking too deep into it." I continued to gaslight him, unsure if he was falling for it, or if I should throw in some tears too.

He eyed me down before walking past me, leaving me in the bathroom. It wasn't that easy when it came to me and Ace. We were engaged and he wanted to be with me, but I was also the reason that he was now moving to New York to set up operations out here.

I may have given him money that Capone had given me to help him with his re-up. It was small amounts at first, then he needed more. Once his money got straight and he secured a connect, that was when he started tricking on me and had given me that money back and then some.

If Cappadonna ever found out that I had used money he gave to me for another man. A man whose main goal was to be the top dog in New York, he would kill me with his bare hands.

As I was leaving the room, I ran into Capella coming out the bathroom. "Oh, what up, Kendra?"

I wanted to slap the sly smirk on his damn face with him calling me Kendra, but being as we were supposed to be strangers, I was going to accept it. "What are you doing here? Does Auntie know what you're doing?"

"Boss man invited me, so I'm here chilling. Why... you know something about them?" He eyed me down.

I took a deep breath, so he didn't know that Cappadonna was his father. "You need to be worried about school or something... what happened to football?"

"I stopped playing football when I was ten, Kendra."

It was the way he said my damn name that made me upset. He said it like I was some stranger on the street instead of his damn mother. As much as I wanted to address everything, this wasn't the place to do it.

"We need to talk soon, Capella."

"Chubs," he corrected me.

"I named you Capella."

He smirked; the same smirk was damn near identical to his fathers. Capella was only a few shades lighter than his father and had locs. Besides that, he had his father's entire face. I remember holding Capella when he was a baby and would stare at him and pray that I felt a connection.

I never felt a connection to him or motherhood. A part of me used to feel bad about it, and now I just accepted reality. My aunt loved the hell out of Capella and took great care of him. Even though me and his father wasn't around, he still got the love he needed from her.

"I don't go by Capella... I go by Chubs. Excuse me, the food ready and I'm ready to grub." He quickly excused himself and went down the hall.

I left the subject alone for now and went to join everybody in the massive formal dining room. Even though I was right beside Capp, something I had longed for, for years, I felt sick to my stomach knowing the way I had lived while he was away.

10
ALAIA

When I signed up for this Lamaze studio, I was interested because it specialized in classes for solo parenting. If you had a partner, you were more than welcomed to bring them along. For the most part, the studio focused on single mothers and women whose partners couldn't attend.

I wasn't stupid and knew that Zayne wouldn't give a damn about taking a class with me. When he found out that I was pregnant he wasn't all that excited. I guess when you already had six children, what was one more?

I didn't know what to expect when it came to pregnancy, so I researched everything to be sure. Lamaze classes were at the top of the recommendations along with a doula. We met with a doula and Zayne shut it down right away because he said he didn't like the way she was looking at him.

His compromise was that he would pay for my class to keep me happy. It did bring me some joy to be around other women going through the same changes that my body was going through. I didn't have friends, so just having forty-five minutes to chat and pretend my life was normal felt nice.

I got out the Uber, and quickly entered the studio. Blair was at the front desk and smiled when she saw me rush in. "Look at that belly. I swear it has doubled in size since I saw you."

I giggled, my entire body shaking in the process. "I feel like she won't have any more space to last one more month."

Blair hugged me. "Sorry about your husband. I hope you are taking care of you during all of this."

She was so sincere and caring every time we spoke, and never knew how much it meant to me. I wasn't used to women being like that with me at all.

"Thanks, Blair. I'm taking it day by day."

I would be a liar if I said that I didn't miss Zayne at all. There were some days that I found myself missing him. It was weird because I didn't shed any tears when I was told he passed away. Some days I thought about the times that we did laugh. It wasn't always bad with Zayne, there were times when we laughed together, or he showed that he may have cared for me more than he let on.

There was a time when I told him that I had become interested in art, and he bought me a book from the bookstore with a bunch of contemporary art. It was the sweetest thing he had ever done for me, and I appreciated him for it.

She returned back around the counter so she could continue welcoming everyone in. I walked over to the counter, digging into my purse for my wallet. "Oh, no. You are fine... you've been paid up. Someone called in and paid for your next classes, and even enrolled you in the postpartum class I have."

"Excuse me?"

"Yeah, they went ahead and booked you right on up. I guess you have some special people surrounding you." She winked.

I slowly waddled into the studio area and found my place in the back. There were a few husbands present, since not every mom that attended this class was a single mom. Some of the women had husbands in the service, so when they came alone that meant their husbands were deployed.

Like I always did, I stopped and spoke to a few of the moms that I always chatted with. One of them introduced me to her husband, who then helped me get down onto my mat.

"Thanks so much... Don't disappear when it comes time for me to get up," I joked, appreciative that he helped me down here.

This little girl was growing so fast, and I wasn't sure I would have any more room for her. Labor was the biggest thing that scared me. Being alone in the delivery room was a huge fear for me. I didn't have anyone there to hold my hand and tell me everything would be alright.

My nerves forced me to confide in my emotional water bottle. Why I drank water before this class puzzled even me. I pissed like a racehorse and seemed to be up at that damn bathroom every five minutes.

"Had enough water?"

My head had a mind of its own as it nearly snapped in the direction of the familiar voice. Cappadonna, all six foot whatever of him, was kneeling down to get on the mat sitting beside mine. I had been so busy gulping water and secretly stressing about birth that I didn't feel or even hear him come beside me.

"How...how did you even know where I was?"

He licked his lips, specks of gold in his mouth peeking through. "I observe my surroundings and who I'm sharing them with, Joy."

Blair clapped her hands as she entered the studio, ready to start her class. The lights lowered a bit, and everyone got comfortable for the small speech that Blair always gave us before we got into stretches or whatever we would be doing today.

"Were you the one that paid for all of my classes?" I whispered, still not over the fact that he was sitting beside me.

"Shh," he shushed me, and started paying attention to whatever Blair was chatting about. I couldn't even focus because he was here.

Taz eventually paid to turn the lights back on, even though he didn't show up at my apartment. I was just grateful to have my lights back on, and to not have to inconvenience Cappadonna anymore. The suite that we stayed in had to have cost him a lot of money, and I didn't want him spending that much on me.

Cappadonna had to handle some business, so he left me in the suite. Taz sent me the confirmation that the lights were back on, so I quickly packed and left, leaving a note on the coffee table.

Our conversation that day had become too heavy for me, and I was scared. He wanted to know too much about my life, and I was afraid to be honest and tell him. A story about a girl being sold by her brother wasn't exactly a crowd pleaser, and I hated for anybody to feel bad for me.

I felt bad leaving without telling him that I was, but Cappadonna was the kind of man that would gladly take on your problems. The problems that would come out of this if he and Taz had any reason to beef would cause me guilt.

Taz wasn't like his brother at all, and he would go far to prove a point. Zayne had his limits, while his brother didn't have any, and if I brought drama to Cappadonna's front door, I could never forgive myself.

"In that head of yours again, huh?"

It was only after I shook my thoughts away that I noticed everyone was standing waiting on me. Capp offered his hand

and helped me to my feet. I didn't even know what we were doing because I had been zoned out.

"What are we doing?"

Cappadonna came behind me, like the other men in the class, and reached down below my stomach. Like Blair demonstrated, he lifted my belly slowly, taking away the weight and pressure that I carried.

"Oh my," I moaned because it felt that good.

"Feel good, huh?" His cool breath tickled my ear lobe, as he had to bend to fully hold my stomach up since I was much shorter than him.

"Now, whenever your partner is ready you can slowly put it back down," Blair coached, while she used one of the women for demonstration.

"You ready?"

"Not yet." I rested my head against his chest, as he patiently held my stomach. I had forgotten how it felt not to carry around nearly seven pounds of baby on your pelvis.

"I'm on your time, Alaia."

I smiled while enjoying the temporary pleasure. When everyone else started to let down their partner's stomach, I figured we should do the same. "Okay, now."

Just as gentle as he was upon pick up, he slowly let my stomach down. The rest of the class was refreshers on how birth will be, and reminders for us to do certain things, and pick up raspberry teas and all the remedies to help the baby come out when it was time.

Capp helped me off the floor when class was over and I grabbed my bag, swinging it over my arm. Blair said her goodbyes as we left out the studio and I stood out front looking up at him.

"I am sure you had a million better things to do than to come to this class." I rubbed my stomach while looking at him.

"Never matters what I have going on, as long as I made you a priority."

I smiled. "I appreciate you coming today. It felt nice not being alone today." I switched my bag onto my other arm.

"Let me give you a ride home," he offered. Since I spent the little money I did have on an Uber here, I wasn't going to give up a free ride. "I think you owe me this since you disappeared on me."

"I left you a note."

"Could have waited for me to come back and told me... communication is big with me, Alaia."

If I wasn't feeling guilty before, I was feeling ten times guiltier seeing how he looked at me. "You're right. I'm sorry... I could have waited and spoke to you. The good news is my lights are back on, so you don't need to spend a lot of money on a hotel suite."

"Was never about the money, mama." He winked, as we walked toward his truck that was parked a couple doors down from the studio.

When he called me mama, I nearly became a puddle of water. I can say with all of my heart that I had never been turned on in my life. Sex with Zayne was purely out of obligation and force. It wasn't something that I happily did, and I often enjoyed when he was gone for a week or more with his other wives.

The way my kitty felt was something that I had never experienced before. It only behaved that way when Cappadonna was around. I tried to play it cool like I wasn't about to melt right before his eyes.

"You so fucking beautiful," he caught me by surprise when those words left his mouth. I couldn't help but to blush at the compliment.

I didn't get the ick when he called me beautiful like I did

whenever I heard Zayne or Taz say it. They said it like I was a show pony, a possession, instead of a woman. Cappadonna said it like he meant it with every breath in his body.

Like I was a piece of art, a view, that had taken his breath away the more he stared at it. I liked the way he said it more, and I held it close to my heart because it made me feel worthy. Worthy of someone finding me beautiful, worthy of someone actually loving me the way I wanted to be loved.

"Thank you."

As we drove through Brooklyn back to my apartment, I looked over at him. He wore a Yankee fitted on his head and had his signature simple gold chain around his neck. He leaned back comfortably as he drove, stealing glances at me in the process.

"I really am sorry for just leaving the hotel room and not telling you." I felt the need to apologize again because it was fucked up of me.

"I'll forgive you only if you make me a promise."

"You are already up to two promises... how many more promises you need me to make to you?" I giggled.

He grinned, his gold teeth gleaming in the process. "I hate liars, Alaia. I'm easy going unless you lie to me, and that's something we can't ever come back from."

I gulped. "I haven't lied to you though."

"Which I appreciate. I'm not going to ask the questions that require you to choose between lying to me and keeping the truth to yourself. I promise, eventually, you're going to have to be honest with me."

"When that day comes, I have no problem being an open book with you. Just not right now, okay?"

His jaw tensed and I turned to see what he was looking at. Taz was walking down the block from the corner store, which meant he had been in the apartment and knew there was no food.

Capp shook off the grimace that came across his face when he turned to face me. "When that day comes, just know I ain't giving you back."

I smiled. "Thank you for the ride and today. I really appreciate you."

"You got my number, Alaia. Call me and I'm here," he reminded me, stepping out the car to open the door for me.

It didn't make sense to stop him because he was going to do it anyway. Taz had fire in his eyes when he saw me step out the car. There was no other way that I could explain myself to him. This was the second time he had caught me climbing out of his truck, after he told me not to.

"Aye baby boy... remember what I told you. Let me see her with a mark and that's yo ass," Cappadonna laughed while walking back to the driver's side.

Whenever he referred to Taz as baby boy, I wanted to piss my pants laughing because it infuriated him. Taz was so angry he didn't even have a rebuttal for Capp and rushed up the steps. "Bring yo ass, Alaia!" he growled, not bothering to hold the door for me.

Capp cruised slowly, looking at me. "You can come with me whenever you ready, mama."

I offered a weak smile and waved as I climbed the steps. My heart desperately wanted to get back in the car and go with him.

It was hard going with what your heart wanted and what trauma told you to do. My heart told me that Cappadonna was safety. Then my trauma got in my head and told me that Taz was the safe choice.

He was familiar.

My life hadn't been all that hard for me to go with someone

unfamiliar. I watched as his car sped off my block before climbing the stairs slowly to my apartment. Not even a second before I walked through the door, I felt the sting and pressure from the punch that Taz tossed my way.

I was off balance, but used the small table I kept by the front door to keep balance. My thought was on not falling on my stomach. He reached his fist back and sent another punch, causing me to fall this time.

Thankfully, I didn't fall on my stomach, but hit my back against the edge of the door. "You got to be fucking slow or something for you not to listen to what I said. I told you last time to leave that nigga alone and here yo' happy ass go climbing out of his truck. What the fuck is with you?" He kicked me.

Actually, kicked me like a fucking animal in the streets. Even animals didn't deserve to be kicked, and here he was kicking me like I was a stray that had eaten his sandwich off the table. "I'm...I'm sorry," I squealed in my pain.

The pain up my back was unbearable. I didn't even think I could get up from where I was sitting.

Taz got real close to my face, so close that I could smell the food he had probably eaten, when he was supposed to be fasting. "You always fucking sorry. I come here and you busy up in his car smiling up in his face. Alaia, I will fucking kill you before I allow you to get the fuck away."

"It won't happen again," I promised him.

He stood up straight and kicked the leg off the kitchen table. "Who the fuck does he think he is fucking with? Keep dealing with his ass and I can promise I'll sell your fucking daughter off the minute she's fucking born. Don't act like I haven't done the shit before. You got that good hair, too... could get more money for her."

His statement was so ignorant. Every baby had good hair,

and it was damn near impossible to see their texture right away anyway. My skin got goosebumps listening to how he would sell my baby. I was scared because Taz was the type to rip my baby away from me and sell her for whatever he wanted to.

In Delaware and Philly, he ran houses filled with women and teenagers. Some of the women he pimped were there willingly, they felt like they had no other place in this world but to have him trick them out to men. Then, he had some girls that were being trafficked. Some of them were missing girls from the area.

Raheem thought he was going to make it on Taz' level and it never gave that. He had no choice but to join forces with Taz and Zayne, which is how Raheem negotiated selling me off to Zayne.

From the way Zayne told it, you would have assumed it was a love story. He always speaks about how he fell in love when he first laid eyes on me. Meanwhile, I hated him the moment I met him.

I'd be stupid not to believe that Taz hadn't taken some of the babies born in those houses and sold them off. The only reason I had been safe all these years was because of Zayne. His mutual respect for his brother was the reason my ass wasn't turning tricks with the rest of them. What was stopping him now from putting my ass in one of those houses and selling my baby off to someone?

I finally found the strength to pick myself up from the floor while he was on the phone and watching the game. He looked at me disgusted as I limped to the bathroom and whimpered when I saw my face.

My eyes were completely swollen shut and the bruise on the side of my face was massive. I held back the sob that threatened to escape as I looked at myself. How many more times was I going to look in this mirror at the disfigurement of my face. This wasn't the first time I couldn't recognize myself in the mirror.

The only difference was Zayne would come after me and kiss me on the face, promising not to do it anymore. He would then pull our prayer rugs out and say this whole prayer about him changing and getting the anger out.

What made the entire charade sick was how I had to sit next to him, patting his back and saying how I forgave him. In those moments, I would rather have taken another punch to the face than do that. Taz didn't seem like he was going to apologize for nothing he did, and I thanked him for it.

I knew that I needed to get away from his ass before I had this baby. Even though he threatened it, I could see in his eyes that the idea didn't seem that bad to him.

11
CAPPADONNA

I STROLLED into the fancy ass country club that Capone said we were members of. Places like this always made me itch because of the way these people viewed me. They saw the tattoos and my black skin and immediately felt like I didn't belong in their funky ass country club. Meanwhile, I had more money than half they balding asses and they had the nerve to turn their nose up at me.

If Forty hadn't texted me to meet him here, I wouldn't have been up in this bitch. I don't even know why my brother signed us up for this bullshit. Aside from him saying that CJ had golf lessons here, I didn't see the need for me to have a damn membership.

When I walked out on the lanai that overlooked the golf course, I spotted Forty's ass sitting there. A big ass smile came across my face when I laid eyes on my best friend. It had been years since I had laid eyes on him, and his ass was a sight for even the sorest eyes.

His brown skin glistened under the sun, with specks of salt and pepper throughout his beard. It was his bald head that surprised me. Before I was locked up, his ass had a head full of hair. He finally looked up from his phone and stood up, waiting for me to come over to him.

"Long time no see, brother," he pulled me into a hug, kissing me on the cheek. "Missed you, nigga."

Forty was a couple inches shorter than me, but that didn't matter with the way I hugged him tightly. "Missed you more, pussy."

We remained hugging for a couple minutes before we both took our seats. It was difficult doing my time without being able to see my best friend. We spoke sparingly because the goal was for nobody to know we were even connected.

Forty was a DEA agent and his reputation wasn't anything to fuck around with. We both decided on two different paths, and that never changed the friendship. I could always expect for my guy to put something on my books, even though he knew I didn't need it.

Forty was the reason we stayed one step ahead of everything. That offshore account he had was stacked lovely. He looked out for my brother when I couldn't and I could never repay him for that shit.

"When the fuck did you go bald?" The server came over and handed me the small menu and sat a bottle of iced water on the table next to me.

"My fucking hairline was disappearing. It was either this or going to turkey to get a fucking hair transplant."

"I mean, you got the money."

"Fuck you."

"Ah, feels fucking surreal sitting across from you." I couldn't stop smiling seeing my best friend after all of these years.

Our energy picked up right where it left off. There wasn't an awkwardness about us at all. Forty took a sip of his whiskey and then looked over at me. "From what I hear... you been home for a minute. No hit up or nothing?"

"I needed to get my mind right and tap in with the family. Couldn't just pop out like nothing happened, feel me?"

"I'm fucking with you. I know Kendra's ass was all over you."

I snorted. "I didn't even tell her that I was home."

Forty choked on his drink. "Deadass?"

"Capo probably told you about the bullshit that she did."

He slowly nodded. "I've heard about the boy. Why the fuck would she keep that away from you? Ken already know how you feel about children."

"Forty, I feel guilty as fuck about not being in this boy's life. He's not even a fucking boy anymore. A whole grown man and I'm supposed to just tell him that I'm his father."

Forty chuckled. "How the fuck do you know that he doesn't already know? I mean, he has that Delgato DNA cruising through him."

I never considered that Chubs might know that I was his father. The thought never crossed my mind because the guilt had overtaken me. Even though it wasn't my fault, I felt guilty for not being there for him.

What was his childhood like? Did he ever miss having his parents around? Was the little nigga loved enough? Those were the things that sent me down a rabbit hole of my feelings at night.

"I brought her to Capo's crib for a little dinner for Josephine."

"Oh yeah? How did that go?" Forty laughed knowing how Capone felt about Kendra, and he was exactly right to laugh.

"Chubs was there. Kendra acted like she didn't even know her own damn son. It's one thing for me to play pretend, but she acted like she didn't even know his ass."

"She cold."

"He ain't say shit either, so that shit got me thinking what the fuck is going on. Are they in this together... like what the fuck is going on?"

When Kendra smiled and waved at Chubs like she hadn't pushed him out her own pussy, I knew that I needed to sit far away from her. How could a mother pretend that she didn't know her own son? Her cousin told me that she raised him for the first few months of his life before she was out.

She still connected and showed up for him throughout the years, so he wasn't a stranger. Kendra knew exactly who he was and she was acting like she didn't know his ass. The anger I felt for her was far beyond anything I had ever felt. Mostly because she was playing games with me instead of being honest.

"Just fucking tell him, Capp. Put all that guilty shit behind you and start fresh with him. You were in prison and you didn't know about him, he can't hold much against you."

"Yeah." I leaned back messing with my beard and taking in the view of the golf course. "Remember that chick I was telling you about that I met at the prison?"

"The Muslim chick, right?"

"Yeah."

"What about her?"

"Ran into her again, and she's big pregnant." Whenever I thought about Alaia, I always said a quick prayer for her.

"Damn... that's a wrap for you. She still with that fuck nigga?"

"Nah. He's dead... told me he passed away a few weeks before I ran into her," I explained. "He had more than one wife, and now his brother is stepping into his role or some weirdo ass shit like that."

Forty remained sitting back as he stared at me. "Capp, you not going back to prison, not even for her."

"What you mean?"

"I see that crazed ass look in your eyes when you talk about her. Stay out her shit and let her handle it."

"Nah."

Forty looked at me like I was crazy. "Nah?"

"You heard me... I want you to find me some information on this nigga." I told Forty all the information I had on this Taz character, and he knew that I wouldn't give this up.

Forty knew me enough to know that I wouldn't give up until I had what I wanted. What I wanted was Alaia next to me, but until then, I was going to find out all I could to see what the fuck I was dealing with when it came to him.

Alaia didn't seem like she was terrified of him, but there was this part of her that was scared to go against him. She could have come with me, and instead she chose to climb those six flights up to the apartment with him.

"Man, you and your twin always got me looking some shit up with your women. First him with Erin, and now you with this new chick... y'all don't know how to date regular women?"

"Where's the fun in all of that?"

Me and Forty kicked it for a minute before he had to leave. I sat on the lanai for a bit before I was about to call it a day.

Kincaid: she just hopped in a Mercedes... following behind.

Me: Copy.

I can't remember if I was born at night, but I knew damn well I wasn't born last night. That nigga in front of the building was there for her. Kendra's eyes nearly popped out her head when she noticed he was still standing downstairs.

She tried to quickly recover when she noticed me looking at

her. I wasn't a fool and had heard all the rumors about the shit Kendra was into while I was away. Capone was the main person telling me the shit he heard or had witnessed with his own eyes.

I told him off the rip to not tell me shit about Kendra. In order to do my time, I didn't need to be worried about what she was doing on the outside. Even though I had hoped that she would keep it tight for me and be loyal, who the fuck was I fooling?

Kendra had been for the streets when I met her, and I thought I could take the challenge and turn her into what I wanted her to be. Even though I knew she wasn't acting right out here, I still took care of her. There wasn't shit that she couldn't ask for that I wouldn't get for her. I made shit happen for her.

The one thing I realized was that the little act she had when she visited me wasn't the Kendra out here. She ain't lied when she said that she wasn't the same twenty-one-year-old anymore. I didn't even recognize this Kendra, and the shit made me mad every time she was near me. She rubbed me the wrong way. How could she act like she didn't know her own son?

If you didn't have loyalty toward your own son, then how the fuck could I expect the same from her as my woman? Chubs knew what her heartbeat sounded like on the inside, and she disregarded him like he was nothing.

I told Kincaid to keep an eye on her ass to see what the fuck she was up to. Like I knew, her ass was on the move and I was willing to bet it was that same Mercedes that was parked out front. I could tell the way she was acting all nervous that he wasn't her neighbor's son.

It took me a little while to make it from Jersey to Queens, where they were dining. Kincaid was parked on the block on his Ducati. When he saw me, he nodded as I double parked in front of the restaurant.

I've been locked up so long that I recognized a social media tourist trap when I saw it. The green grassed background in the restaurant told me that Hookah and lamb chops were on the menu. The music was playing while everyone was turning up with their people and enjoying the overpriced, watered down cocktails they were serving.

The hostess shoved up her breast when she saw me walk in. If you asked me what she looked like, I couldn't tell you from a can of paint. I maneuvered past her because I spotted the back of Kendra's head.

How did I know the back of my girl's head? Like I said, I knew my girl better than she knew herself. She was sipping her drink while twirling her hair around her fingers. Hair that I probably paid for, because it looked fresh from last week at Jo's birthday dinner.

The nigga that was supposed to be the neighbor's son, was too busy in his phone. I maneuvered around the table until I was beside him, pulling out the empty chair next to him. Kendra choked on her drink and was gasping for air when she saw me take a seat.

"You good, baby?" I laughed, taking the menu from her side of the table, and looking it over. Like I expected, lamb chops were right on the menu next to some remixed oxtail meal that nobody asked for.

Why the fuck would I want an oxtail beef patty? Who the fuck asked for shit like that? I had half the mind to go in the kitchen and slap the shit out the chef for creating some shit like that. Kendra was trying to control her breathing while homie was staring at me like I was lost or something.

"Cap…Capp." She cleared her throat, as her hands started to shake. "Cappadonna, what are you doing here?"

I ignored her and looked at the confused homie. "My fault,

Playa... we met the other day, and I didn't know you were piping my shorty. Call me Capp," I smirked.

"The fuck you mean *your* shorty... Kendra been wifey. She told me about you being in prison and like I said, I stepped up—"

He didn't finish his sentence because he didn't see my hand as I smashed his head into his plate of oxtail lasagna. He tried swinging and moving his head, and I slammed it back down into his plate, shattering the glass plate.

I yawned while looking across the table at Kendra. "You got five seconds to make your way to my truck before I snatch you fucking bald," I said through gritted teeth.

Everyone stared at us, some taking video of me slamming homie's head into the plate. I finally released his head and inspected the shards of glass that were now embedded in his face.

"You see that pussy hightailing it to the front of the restaurant? That shit belongs to me... feel me? Touch her again and I can promise it won't be glass embedded into your ass, but it will be fucking lead. My name may be Capp, but lil' nigga, I don't fucking cap. When I say some shit... I mean it." All that mouth he had was gone because he didn't say shit. I stood up, using the napkin beside him to wipe my hand. "Chill with all that wave grease, too."

Nobody knew what to do, and when I lifted my shirt showing my gun, the manager knew to mind his business. The restaurant wasn't in the best neighborhood, so he knew street code. Let that nigga rest before calling the ambulance or whatever the fuck he wanted to do.

Kendra was shaking at the passenger door when I exited the restaurant. I hit the locks and opened the door for her. "Get in my loose pussy hooker," I winked, and she hesitantly climbed in.

I slammed the door, checking my surroundings before getting into the car. Kincaid rode past, and then sped off the block with me following behind him. Kendra was terrified as she sat over in the passenger seat, not knowing what the fuck was next.

"You lied to me, *baby*," she started crying when she heard my manic tone, knowing that I wasn't playing with her ass. "I hate when people play in my face and then lie to me... asked you about homie, Ken."

"I...I didn't know how to tell you about him. It...It just happened, he wouldn't leave me alone and was persistent. I...I was lonely," she choked out while turning around, pleading with me.

"You was lonely?" I rhetorically asked.

"Yes. I swear it didn't mean anything to me. I swear to you Cappadonna he didn't mean anything to me. I was breaking it off with him tonight."

She held onto the arm rest as I zipped in and out of traffic on the expressway. Every time I came close to a car, I would zip over to the next lane. Kendra looked like she was about to be sick with the way I was driving, and I didn't give a fuck.

"You got me out here buying you whatever you want, upgrading your car whenever you complain and tricking money on you, and you out here giving *my* pussy away. I told you, Kendra... I told you not to give that pussy away."

"We didn't have sex!" she screamed, closing her eyes when I got up and close to a tractor trailer.

"Oh, no?"

"Capp, please... please can you slow down I'm going to be sick."

I made no attempt to slow down. "He fucked that pussy, Kendra?"

"No. We only kissed," she spoke with her eyes closed.

I knew she was lying. No nigga was going to go as hard as he was if he hadn't hit the pussy. I was the exception when it came to Alaia. The nigga I sat next to damn near had her juices dripping from his lips.

He didn't recognize that he was sitting next to a man that was a few screws shorter than the average person. Instead, he was willing to die for her pussy, and Kendra was still lying. I was going to allow her to continue to dig her hole.

"You lying to me, baby?"

She slowly reached over to touch my hand. "I'm not... I promise. I'm so sorry." Kendra broke out those fake ass tears thinking that she would gain some remorse from me.

"Strike one, Kendra. You only get two with me before I loose every piece of mind I have on you. Let me find out that you were lying and you gonna wish you didn't lie to me."

"Okay... okay, I love you."

I didn't reply as I took the exit to her condo. Kendra may have thought she won this round, but there was always a method to my madness, and she would soon learn why the fuck they called me the crazy twin.

~

It had been a few days since I heard from Alaia. She didn't reach out often anyway, but when I didn't hear from her, I became worried. I knew I couldn't fight her battles for her if she didn't want me to.

She was a grown ass woman and she had told me more than one time that she could handle herself. I was a man that took everything on, and I wanted to handle things for her. She deserved to have a man that handled shit and would air out the fucking block for her. There wasn't shit I could do if she was willingly going with that nigga and didn't want my help.

If I forced her, I wouldn't be no better than the nigga she was currently with. The only difference was that I would have given her a life she didn't need to daydream away from. I was willing to step up to the plate for her baby, too.

"How long have you've known?"

I looked up from the car magazine I was reading at Chubs standing in the doorway of the theater room. Closing the magazine, I nodded for him to sit in the chair across from me.

"For a little minute now... how long have you known?"

"Since I was seventeen."

I examined his face, the same one that we shared. It hurt staring at the man across from me because I had nothing to do with raising him. I didn't have the chance to be something I always wanted to be – a father.

"How did you figure out that I already knew?"

He laughed to himself as he took his seat across from me. "I saw the way you looked at Kendra when she was introduced to me. She missed it, but I peeped it right away."

"Shit is wild. How she act like she didn't even know who you were." That shit still bothered the fuck out of me.

"That ain't nothing new when it comes to Kendra. She has always come in and out of my life." He shrugged.

I tossed the magazine beside me. "I had no clue that you even existed, and I wished that I would have known. There wasn't much I could have done from prison, but I would have been there. A phone call or visit away."

Chubs looked down at his hands. "I found you because I believe we were both robbed of a relationship."

He didn't understand just how much I felt like I had been robbed. "Being real, the shit hurts. I would have been there. I don't know why Kendra did this, but I can promise you I'm going to find out."

"All she does is talk around the subject. A few years ago, I heard her and my aunt arguing because my aunt felt like I needed to know my father. Kendra refused. If it wasn't for Jasmine, I wouldn't have known shit. She told me because she felt like we both deserved to know."

"You grown as fuck now so it ain't like I can punish you or some shit... but I want to get to know you. I want to have a father and son relationship... I didn't get the chance to be there before, but I promise on my life that I'm here now...ight?"

He shook his head, and wiped away a tear that escaped his eyes. "I'm being soft as shit."

I stood up. "Fuck all that soft shit... when it comes to family, call me a teddy bear. I show emotions because that shit is real, and every real man shows his emotions... come 'ere." I waved for him to come to me.

Chubs stepped into my arms, and I held him, kissing him on the head. "Capella."

"What's that?"

"My name is Capella."

I smiled when I heard his name. Did I ever think I would be standing in my brother's movie room hugging my nineteen-year-old son? I never would have imagined some shit like that. Just like I wouldn't have imagined Kendra having my seed and keeping him away from me.

She didn't realize how much hurt and pain she had caused for her own son. Fuck my feelings and how I felt, it was more about how Capella felt.

"I like that. Where the fuck did you get the names Chubs from? You not even fat." I released him from my embrace.

He stood there; I could tell that embrace had meant a lot to him. "I needed a street name."

I pulled him back into my arms and hugged him tighter this time. "If I pull your ass into a hug randomly, it's because I'm making up for all the hugs that I missed."

"Ight."

I kissed his head once more before I spotted Capone standing in the doorway. He winked and left us alone to have our moment.

My brother didn't realize how lucky he had it to be there for every step of his son's life. He never missed anything because he had been right there all along. I never got to experience that, and I was bitter because of it.

I missed him taking his first steps, saying his first words, and playing sports like other little boys did. Kissing my son on the forehead once more, I released him from my grip, and looked him over.

"Can't believe that I have a fucking son… can't believe that shit."

He plopped back down on the couch. "I can't believe that I have a pops."

"My parents gonna be bugged out when they find out."

My parents didn't play when it came to their grandchildren, and knowing they had one all this time and didn't know would crush them. It was crushing me, but I needed to move forward. I needed to appreciate the fact that we were in this place where I had more time to build a bond with him.

"She kept staring at me and asking me who my people were." I started laughing because that sounded like some shit my mother would say.

"Sounds like your grandmother. Aye, I'm serious when I said I'm here, Capella. I'm here and I got you… where the fuck you living?"

"Got a little room that I rent for now… why?"

"Yeah, you moving out that shit… I'm gonna get us a fucking house. I don't care if you grown, either. I'm gonna make you fucking breakfast and all that shit."

We both started laughing because I know I sounded crazy;

I was serious though. I was getting the chance to be a father to my son, and I wasn't going to take that shit for granted, either.

12
CHUBS

Soon as I pulled into the narrow driveway at my aunt's house, I rubbed my stomach because I already knew she was cooking some good ass food. Sunday dinner was always a nonnegotiable when it came to eating at Francie on Sundays. She always got in her feelings when I couldn't make some Sundays, so I tried my hardest to always be there to grub and catch up on the drama she had going on.

Her drama was less intense than the shit that I was in. She was forever beefing with her neighbor because both their gardens backed up to each other's, so neither of them knew which plant belonged to who because they planted the same thing. The rundown of the drama was always entertaining while I ate.

These days I got a meal from wherever I could. The room I rented didn't have a kitchen, so I ate out mostly, and whenever I was over Capone's crib Josephine made sure that I always had a plate. Capone and Cappadonna paid their people well, and nobody could ever complain about not having money.

I used my money to pay my aunt's bills because I hated for

her to work. She had Lupus and was always in and out the hospital because of it. As far as she knew, I was heavily into gambling and always hit big. It was a stupid excuse, but a legal one to keep her off my back about what I was really out here doing.

When I opened the storm door and entered the house, the food hit my nostrils before I could fully step into the house. My aunt's house was home for me. I had memories all over this house.

"Capella is that you?" she called from the kitchen.

"Who else would it be walking in your house, Ma?" I called my aunt Ma because she was my mother in my eyes.

When I broke my arm in third grade, she was the one that sat in the emergency room for hours with me until they saw me. When I had the flu in sixth grade, she sat up all night with me to make sure that the fever broke. Everything that a mother does, she had surpassed that for me.

Soon as I turned the corner into the kitchen, her newly renovated kitchen that I had surprised her with for her birthday, Kendra's ass was sitting at the kitchen table looking like shit. Usually, Kendra came around dressed down and her face all made up. I was taken aback to see her ass looking like she had been dragged all through the Belt Parkway by her hair.

"What you doing here?" I remained by the wall, knowing she was coming to stir some bullshit up.

"I can't come and see my aunt and son. Auntie, you know he's been ignoring me when I call him."

My aunt turned to look at Kendra. "You've been calling him?"

Kendra looked offended that she even asked the question. "Yes. I want to start working on our relationship. He's older now, and I think we need to be closer."

"Now that all the work has already been done?" Francie put

her hand onto her hip, as she glared at her niece and the foolishness she was over here speaking about.

Kendra didn't give a shit about getting closer with me. She wanted to know what I knew when it came to Cappadonna being my father. That was the only reason she came here on a Sunday because she knew she would be able to catch me here.

"Let me holla at you outside, Kendra."

"Auntie, do you hear how he calls me Kendra?"

"Well, that's your name ain't it?"

Kendra looked at our aunt and excused herself from the table to follow me into the backyard. The backyard was another thing that I had paid to get done over, so my aunt could relax back here.

It would have been easier to just buy her a new house. She loved her house, and she would rather die before she moved off her block to anywhere else.

"The fuck you want, Kendra?" I asked when she closed the door behind her.

All that ulterior motive bullshit wasn't for me. I've always been a straight shooter, and she wasn't about to keep playing games with me. "Look at the way you speak to your mother. Do you really think that's right for you to do?"

"What. The. Fuck. Do. You. Want?" I spoke slower because I had always heard our family say her ass was slow.

"Why are you running around with Capone and Cappadonna? If Auntie knew, she would be upset… you need to step away."

"I'm a grown ass man. You haven't told me what to do all this time, we not going to start that shit now."

"Running with them isn't some shit to do for fun, Capella. Real shit happens and what Capone and Cappadonna do isn't for play. I don't want you caught in the middle of that."

I chuckled because she was a little too late for that. I've

been putting in work with Capone this long and had taken my fair share of lives. "I think I can handle myself, Kendra. I've been doing it before this conversation, and I will continue to do it."

It was a little too late for her to play mommy now. She wanted to live her life and pawn the responsibility of raising me off to everyone else. Why the fuck she thought I was about to sit here and listen to anything that she had to say.

"I forbid you."

I paused before I laughed in her face. "Don't be goofy now. I'm a grown ass man and I can do what the fuck I want. If you think snitching to Auntie is gonna do something, be my guest. At least I'm using my money to take care of her. She hasn't had to work a job in almost a year, and I'm fixing the house up. What the fuck are you doing, Kendra? Living in that nice ass condo, driving that G-Wagon, and carrying a fucking Birken bag, but don't give back to your own family."

She was shocked at the way I had come at her. The only reason I didn't mention anything about Cappadonna being my father was because he asked me to keep her ass in suspense a little bit longer.

It angered me that I didn't have my father around when I was growing up. Since Capp had been home, all I wanted to do was be with my pops and learn everything I could from him. Capone had no problem taking me under his wing. I suspected that he knew I was his nephew from the way he started to move.

He knew I was capable of handling shit on my own, but he stuck me with Kincaid or Big Mike when it came to putting in work. With my father home, I had been doing stupid ass errands and I didn't mind because that meant I could spend time with him. I started to suspect that Capp knew when Kendra acted like she didn't know me.

That nigga couldn't hide his facial expression even if he wanted to. He looked at Kendra like she was beneath him, and I didn't even blame him. For my own mother to act like she didn't know me for the sake of a relationship was crazy.

I still didn't know why the fuck she chose to lie to him instead of telling him that he had a son. Kendra was selfish and I had learned that pretty quickly growing up with her coming in and out. If it wasn't about her, she didn't give a damn about anyone else.

It was crazy because my aunt Kalisa was the complete opposite when it came to her sister. I remembered Kalisa coming to pick me up to spend the weekend in Delaware with her. She made time and made sure I knew who she was.

There was a time when I saw her more than my own damn mother. Even though she didn't agree with my mother's decisions, she never spoke bad or got involved with it. She just did her part as an aunt. When it came to Kendra's mother, my supposed grandmother, I saw her ass every once in a blue moon at a family function. She and Kendra were one and the same. It was no wonder Kendra was a selfish cold-hearted bitch.

"Capella, did I tell you that the water heater has been acting funny?" my aunt called out the back door.

"I'll buy you another one... it was time anyway," I called back.

She put her hand on her hip. "This boy has the biggest heart. Finish up this conversation so you can come in and eat."

"Be right there, Ma," I called back to her.

Kendra stood there with her arms folded. "I know I haven't always been there for you, but I do love and care about you. I'm just trying to look out for you, Capella."

Bae: Miss you.

I looked down at my phone before returning my look to

Kendra. "How about you do what you've always done... look out for yourself." I turned, leaving her ass in the middle of the yard stunned.

She wanted to be a mother now, and I needed one back then. I needed her to be my mom, not the older fly sister that swooped in to take me shopping when she felt like it. Kendra stole years that I could have had with my father.

Capp being in prison wasn't the problem. I know my aunt would have done whatever she could have to make sure I visited and had a relationship with him. Kendra stole that from me, so it was going to be forever fuck her.

13
KENDRA

I tossed my keys on the damn foyer table and kicked my sneakers off before rounding the corner to my living room.

"Sassy, you should hear the way that he spoke to me, and then my aunt had the nerve to co-sign with him... he acted like I wasn't his mo—Ahhh!" I hollered.

"Girl, what? What happened?" Sassy was on the other end of the phone waiting for me to explain why the hell I had screamed.

Cappadonna was sitting on the couch with his legs crossed at the ankle reading a car magazine in the damn dark. This nigga had on a pair of reading glasses sitting on the bridge of his nose, unbothered that I had even screamed.

He didn't seem phased that he had scared the living shit out of me. Ever since he slammed Ace's face into the table and he dropped me home, we hadn't spoken. I tried to send him text messages and he just read them, never replying back to me. Now he was just sitting here like we were on good terms.

"Sassy, let me call you back." I quickly ended the call before she could even say anything back or ask me anymore questions. Sassy was so damn chatty at the wrong times. "Babe, what you doing here?"

"I pay for this bitch... you telling me I can't come and chill in it whenever I want?" he nonchalantly replied, never taking his eyes off the magazine he was reading.

"When did you start wearing glasses?" I sat my purse down on the table and took a seat on the couch across from him. "You know you can whenever you want. You're the one that don't want to move in."

He finally looked up from the magazine and I could have sworn I saw a look of disgust in his eyes. "Your eyes eventually get weak when you have no choice but to read in the dark... I don't want to live with you, Kendra."

"How can I fix this? I know I messed up with Ace, and I'm sorry about it." I couldn't take him being upset with me.

I just wanted to fix things between us so we could get back to loving on each other, even though it had been more tension than love since he's been home. Was a girl wrong for wanting to be under her man and trying to fix things?

Cappadonna abandoned the couch and went into the kitchen. I took a deep breath and relaxed on the couch. "Why the fuck didn't you tell me about my son?" I felt his hand wrap around my extensions, and I yelped.

Capp had never put his hands on me, even when he threatened it when we were younger. This time, as he stared me in the eyes with those menacing eyes, I knew I had fucked up. How the fuck did he find out that he had a son?

"Capp.... Cappadonna, you're hurting me."

"Answer the fucking question then," he snarled, and I tried to focus on the question and less about the fact that I could hear my hair ripping in his hands.

"I...I was scared, Capp. I didn't know what you would

think," I sobbed. There was no need to fake tears this time because I was actually scared as hell.

His breathing was labored, his eyes were red, and he looked crazed. "The fuck do you mean you were scared?" My head snatched back once more before he finally released me.

I scrambled back on the couch, far away from him as he walked coolly over toward the pictures I had on the TV stand.

"A lot was going on between us and I was scared to tell you. I thought you would have thought that I was lying to you."

"You saying a bunch of nothing. A lot of shit ain't adding the fuck up. I promise you don't want me to start doing the math, Ken." He impatiently snapped his fingers, making the anxiety in my chest nearly paralyze me.

I kept Capella away because I didn't want to be a mother. If I would have come back to the city with a baby in tow, Capp would have done everything he could to make sure we were taken care of. He would have also expected me to sit down and raise his son. His ass was already on me whenever I went to the club. Capp never liked the club like that, and he hated whenever I went or hung out with my girls.

If I would have told him that we had a son, he would have sat my ass down. My life would have been over, and then I would have been stuck raising his son while he was locked up. That wasn't the life that I wanted for me.

When I moved back to New York from Jacksonville, me and Capp reconnected like nothing ever happened. Our relationship had always been fragile with us going at it like cats and dogs. We were in such a sweet spot when I came back that I didn't want to bring up something that could tear us apart.

I was young when I had Capella and didn't know any better. Leaving him with my granny felt like what was best for him. She loved the hell out of him, and she raised him good until she passed. It only made sense for Francie to take over and raise him. What the hell was I going to do with him?

Did I expect for Cappadonna to go to prison and for my grandmother to pass in the same year? Everybody was worried about why I pawned my son off and never asked me if I was alright after losing my grandmother and man within the same year.

I refused to step up to the plate and be a single mother. I've witnessed those mothers climbing off the bus with those screaming ass kids to visit their daddy. Capp liked to pretend that he always had money while he was serving time. Those first few years, I was getting my ass on those buses and going to visit him.

Capone didn't visit his brother for the first two years of his sentence because he was busting his ass and running it up to build the empire they had now. So, it wasn't like he was giving me free rides to come and see him. Imagine having to do that with a child who would end up screaming because they didn't want to be stuck on a bus for six hours with other screaming kids.

"Ouch." I jumped when he plucked me in the neck.

"You had nineteen years to come up with your explanation... chop fucking chop, Kendra." He walked around the couch and took his seat again.

"I was scared. You had just gotten locked up and I didn't know what our future looked like. It was best for my aunt to raise him."

He pretended to count on his fingers before looking over at me. "If my math is right... Capella would have been around four when I was locked up, correct?"

"Uh huh."

"You thought it was best for your aunt to raise him and not have his father involved? I get why you weren't involved; you were too busy being a conniving bitch... you know, that takes a lot out of a person so clearly you couldn't raise your son."

"You didn't always have all this fucking money, Cappadonna! I would have struggled trying to take care of him on my own."

"My fucking family would have helped!" he roared so loud that I nearly jumped out of my skin. "You had fucking options and you took that away from me. You took my son away from me."

"Bab—"

"I want you out this fucking condo by the end of the week." He stood up, taking the picture of us on the Brooklyn bridge.

He had taken me on a date and we decided to walk the bridge back to Brooklyn. It was my favorite picture because it was the one and only picture I had of him smiling. I cried while watching him launch it across the room.

"I'm sorry, baby... I'm so sorry!" I was stuck on that couch not wanting to move because I didn't know what he would do.

Cappadonna had this dark side of him that I had only seen a few times since we've been together. As much as Capone was a jerk and couldn't stand me, I would have rather got on his bad side than Cappadonna's bad side.

"Fuck all that 'baby' shit, Kendra. People told me you were out here tossing that pussy on whatever dick that was moving and I always kept it together. My own brother told me he saw you with his own eyes, and I went against him, not wanting to hear shit about my girl. I just knew you were out here holding me down and keeping it tight for me." He walked over toward me and grabbed my damn pussy. "Nah, you were out here giving that shit away to anybody with some money... filthy bitch." He looked me up and down before releasing me.

"Fifteen years, Capp. I was stupid and didn't understand... I was selfish," I pleaded with him.

It wasn't about the money and how Capp had always kept me comfortable. The minute he started making money, he was never worried about himself. He had his brother make sure I was taken care of.

I went from staying with Sassy on her couch to having an apartment of my own. He made sure I always had money and a mode of transportation. As the years went on, he continued to upgrade my life. There was nothing that he wouldn't give me. Money aside, I was in love with Cappadonna Delgato, and wanted to be with him. I couldn't picture my life without him, and being seconds away from losing him had me more scared than I had ever been in my life.

"That's the difference between me and you. Had you had to sit up for fifteen years, I wouldn't have been giving this dick up. I'd be fucking jacked because I would be beating this shit off every chance, I got thinking about you coming home. It's called fucking loyalty, Kendra!" Spit flew from his mouth.

"Please," I whimpered.

"You heard what the fuck I said... take the shit you fucked for, not any of the shit I bought. Leave the keys to that fucking whip on the counter, too. Any bitch that could turn their back on their own seed can't ever be with me."

"Capella was fine!" I screamed. "He was raised with love —" I quickly jumped over the couch when Capp tossed the coffee table and was coming for me next.

The front door opened and Quasim rushed in. "Yo, Capp... chill... come on." He pushed Capp away from me.

The man's eyes was fucking glowing red as he stared at me. What was even worse was the hurt I could see within his eyes from my actions. He was allowing Quasim to hold him back, because if he really wanted me, he would have gotten to me.

"I want you out my shit by the end of the fucking week. Let me come here and find you here, I'm going to pull you out this bitch kicking and screaming," he said low enough for me to catch chills at the tone of his voice.

He kicked the couch and headed out the door while I stood near the fridge. "You alright?"

Quasim was always nice whenever we ran into each other. He used to run with Capp back in the day, and it was nice to see that they had reconnected. Or maybe they never lost touch with each other. Either way, it was nice to see that they were still close.

"Y...yeah. Please try and talk to him, Sim," I pleaded with him. Leaving my home felt cruel, and maybe emotions were just high right now.

Capp didn't want me out of the condo. He needed to calm down and realize that I didn't mean to hurt him. I was always able to talk my way out of everything and for the first time I didn't think I would be able to change his mind.

"Not my beef, Kendra... just make sure you out of here 'cause I ain't gonna be able to stop his ass if he come drag you out."

When he closed the door behind him, I could still hear Capp yelling obscenities in the hallway. Sliding down the fridge, I buried my face into my hands and cried so hard I gave myself a headache. Where the hell would I go?

Ace: You either picking me or that nigga?

I looked at the text message on my phone and cried even more. This nigga got his face slammed into a table while Cappadonna looked at the menu and continued to slam his head with his free hand.

He wasn't going to fucking protect me.

Me: I choose you, babe.

14
ALAIA

Taz was back on his bullshit and there wasn't anything that I could do. I really didn't want to call Cappadonna, but I had been in this house for two days eating grilled cheese because I had no money for food. I was grateful that I had electricity, so I was managing with the grilled cheese sandwiches.

That was until I ran out of bread and all I had were two slices of cheese. The cheese wasn't all that good to begin with because it barely melted. I had called Taz for the past few days, and he refused to answer. The one time he answered, he laughed and said *you hungrier than a bitch, huh?* How could someone be so fucking cruel.

As if putting his hands on a pregnant woman wasn't enough, he continued to torture me some more because Capp had hurt his ego. I truly didn't want to call Capp, but I had no other choice because I didn't know who else to call. I hated that I had so much pride and would rather starve than call this man to ask him to help me.

It wasn't about me anymore; it was about the baby. I couldn't deprive her because I didn't want him to look at me like I was a charity case. Even though he never acted that way once.

The phone rang and he answered, sounding like he was asleep. "My phone must be fucking with me... can't be *the* Alaia calling me." Even with the sleepiness in his voice, he still found time to make a joke.

"Hey Capp."

"What's going on, baby girl?"

"Can you make me a promise?"

"Depends."

"Capp... I made you three promises already. I'm only asking for one... please," I begged him.

"Ight...what's the promise, Alaia?" I could hear him sitting up on the other end of the line and became nervous.

"That you won't think less of me for what I'm about to ask you."

"Come on now, I could never. I promise... tell Daddy what you need." I just knew he was grinning on the other end of the line.

I was in the middle of about to beg this man for money, and he had managed to make me blush. "Can I borrow some money to buy some food? Taz won't answer the phone anymore and I ran out of some things. I will pay you back soon as I get the money."

The line became quiet, and I was regretting even calling. I should have knocked next door and took my chances.

"Give me thirty minutes."

"You don't need to come over here. I have the number to the grocery store, you can pay over the phone, and they will deliver it."

"Get dressed, Alaia."

He ended the call and I looked at the phone knowing he was heading over here. I had time to think, and I needed to just tell Cappadonna what was going on in my life. After Taz mentioned selling my baby, it didn't sit right with me. It was all I thought about since the words had left his mouth.

Capp could help us, and I needed to stop being stubborn and ask him for help. It was clear that he wanted to help me, and I *needed* the help. This was the only way I would be able to escape this life I had been sold into. What's the worst that could happen compared to how I was already living?

Taz was worse than his brother and I was scared that if I didn't take this chance, my baby would end up paying for my mistakes. I quickly got dressed and packed as much stuff as I could without taking a break.

I had found out that Taz was in Mexico with Fatima this week, which pissed me off. She was over here living good, and I was surviving off cheese sandwiches while they were enjoying life. I packed the little bit of baby stuff that I had for the baby, and some of my clothes.

As I continued to scan the small apartment for anything worth bringing, I heard a knock at the door. I slowly walked over toward the door and Capp was standing there. Well, it was his chest because he was taller than the damn peephole.

I quickly opened the door and welcomed him in. From the look on his face, I had fucked up. I was hungry and concerned with leaving, I forgot about my eye that was currently healing. My face didn't look nearly as bad as it looked when it first happened.

He took hold of my chin and looked me in the face. I could see the anger forming in his eyes as he took in the bruises on my face. "He put his hands on you?"

"Yes." I refused to defend Taz to Cappadonna. He put his hands on me after Capp had warned him.

"Am I giving you money or a home, Alaia? I could peel off some money right now, but that won't solve your situation or hers," he touched my stomach, before walking around me and opening the fridge. The milk had spoiled and other than condiments, there was nothing inside of it. "What you gonna do when he decides to duck your calls when the baby needs milk?"

"Can you take me with you?" I pointed to the duffle bags on the floor. One with the baby's clothes and the other with mine.

He leaned on the fridge. "If you come with me... there's no coming back to this shit. I don't do the back and forth shit. The minute you walk out this door with me, you putting your life in my hands, and I don't take that lightly. I need to know everything, Alaia... don't bullshit me." He stared down into my eyes, as I stood near the door.

Freedom was right outside that door and my heart was beating in my chest harder with every second that passed. "I understand."

"Do you still wanna come with me?"

"Yes," I whimpered.

He abandoned the fridge and came over to hug me. I held onto him tightly, as we stood in the small kitchen that had so many bad memories for me. "Baby boy gotta see me." He held my hand and walked toward the door.

"My stuff."

"You got anything that is important to you?"

I didn't have anything that meant anything to me because the stuff that I packed that meant a lot to me had been destroyed to punish me. "The baby's clothes are in there."

He looked at the bags and then back at me. "Fuck all that shit...I'll buy everything that she needs."

I held tightly onto his hand as he helped me downstairs. We got into his truck, and he hesitated before he pulled away. "This wasn't about food, was it?"

I gave him a weak smile. "You told me to call you and you'll come... I knew you would come without any questions asked."

"Long as you know." He touched my thigh, and examined my face, his face ticking in the process because he was so upset.

He usually peeled off the block as quickly as he came. This time, he slowly pulled away while I looked at the building that had been my personal hell. I looked over at him and felt grateful to have crossed paths with this man again.

Before I even knew him, he had been saving me without wanting anything in return. I touched my stomach and promised my daughter that I would do whatever to protect her. Cappadonna looked over at me, putting his hand on my stomach.

She kicked soon as his hand touched my belly and he smiled. "Even she knows she is in good hands."

I smiled as he kept one hand on my stomach with the other on the wheel as we drove out the city. Relaxing, I closed my eyes and enjoyed the ride to freedom and my new life. I had been so scared to leave what was familiar that I almost stayed because I didn't know any better. Since meeting Cappadonna, I had never got a bad feeling.

He had been protective of me since he saw me walking to the laundromat. I've always questioned my faith, and how much Allah loved me. For the first time, I believed that he had sent Cappadonna into my life for a reason, and it was meant for our paths to align again.

"You naturally snore or is that the baby?"

I shoved him. "Be quiet. I haven't slept very much."

It was true.

I spent my nights staring at the wall thinking about my entire life and what my future looked like. I cried because I was scared for me and my daughter's future. It was one thing to deal with this when it was just me, but she didn't deserve that.

He touched my face so softly, zeroing in on the bruises. It looked like it actually hurt him that someone had hurt me. "We gonna grab stuff you need and then get some food into you so you can get some real sleep."

It was then that I noticed that we were in the parking lot of Target. He got out the car and opened the door for me. My back ached with every step that I took, so I held onto his arm until he got me a shopping cart.

Capp didn't care what I put in that cart. I couldn't pick anything up because he would ask me if I wanted it. I got some pajamas and a few pieces of clothing, along with food and toiletries. He tapped his credit card without looking at that total for everything we spent in there. I had never had that much money where I didn't care about the total of my purchase.

While I sat in the truck, he put everything in the trunk before getting in. "I'm gonna have my sis-in-law take you to do some real shopping once you're rested."

"This is good enough. I got some good stuff, and even got the baby some onesies."

He stopped to look at me. "Stop playing with me, Alaia."

He held onto the back of my seat while backing out the spot. Capp stopped at one more store before we drove for a little bit before we entered a gated community. The man with a gun strapped to him caused me to jump, and he held my hand.

"What up?"

The man nodded and opened the gates for us, as he pulled through. We drove down a bunch of streets of perfectly built homes. They were beautiful, and one could only dream of living here.

We pulled into the driveway of a two-story ranch style

home with a three car garage. The white ship lap and washed brick stood out against the black garage doors and front door. Capp hit the garage opener, and we pulled into one of the garages.

Pulling in, we pulled beside an old school mustang and a black-on-black Bronco that was so high that I don't think I could climb up unless I had some assistance. It didn't have a roof on it, and it was tricked out.

"Is this your house?"

"My lake house," he replied. "My brother and his wife are next door, my parents are on the opposite side of me, and my sister is across the street," he explained, killing the engine. "It's a lake house community, most of the people here don't live here full time."

The way he spoke was like it was so normal for his family to occupy an entire block with their own lake homes. "Wow."

When we entered through the garage door into the kitchen, which was fit for a celebrity. I imagined this was how some celebrities lived. I think I was too shocked to say anything because I stood by the door taking it all in. The white and pale blue cabinets, white marble countertops and three windows over the sink, looking out at a huge lake in the back.

The lake was literally in his backyard, with a pool overlooking it. I couldn't remove my eyes from the view, even if I wanted to. I was stuck in place taking in this beautiful kitchen.

"This is beautiful," I whispered.

Capp was busy with bringing the bags inside while I walked closer to the farmhouse sink and continued to look out the window. While he was getting the bags I ventured into the living room, filled with soft shades of beige and a huge cream sectional that covered most of the living area. The windows were massive, and I wondered who the hell were cleaning them. Instead of the couch facing the beautiful view, it faced the fireplace and the television.

Capp went to the front door and went outside, then came back in with a bag of food. "What is that?"

"I ordered food while we were in Target... come on so you can eat."

He unpacked the Chinese food and my stomach growled. I hadn't had anything to eat today, and it was clear baby girl was ready to dig in. He ordered shrimp fried rice, fried chicken, shrimp rolls, chicken and broccoli, and chicken sticks.

I sat at the counter and watched as he packed my plate full before sliding it over toward me. I've never felt taken care of ever, and in this moment, Capp made me feel like I was being taken care of.

"You live here alone?"

"This my first time coming here. I been staying with my brother at his crib... but I figured you would be more comfortable here."

"Thank you. Are you going to go back to your brother's house?" I questioned, not wanting him to leave me.

"Not if you don't want me to, Alaia."

I took a bite of the chicken. "I would like you to stay with me, please."

"Then I'll stay with you."

He went to do Wudu while I continued to stuff my face like a savage. I ate like the food was going to run away from me. By the time Capp had finished praying and broken his fast, I sat there stuffed.

"Damn, you couldn't even wait for me to come eat."

"You took too long... I think she could smell it too because she was damn near kicking me to eat."

"Don't go lying on her." He smiled, standing across from me at the counter. "Come with me real quick."

I allowed him to take my hand and help me up the stairs to a room upstairs. It was the way he held my hand, like I was a delicate flower that he didn't want to tear. We walked through the room and into the bathroom.

The lights were low, and candles were lit around the tub. The built in speakers played "Don't Change" by Musiq Soulchild quietly in the background. The water had bubbles in it, and my pajamas I had picked out in Target were folded on the sink with all of my toiletries. I had been so busy stuffing my face that I didn't realize that he had brought the bags past me and up the stairs.

"Cap..." I couldn't get the words out because I started choking on my tears that already started gushing down my cheeks.

He wiped my tears as they fell. "You don't got to thank me or say anything... I want you to relax and decompress. When you're done, we gonna sit downstairs and talk. I want to... I need to know about you, Alaia. I'm already in too deep when it comes to you."

I stared up at him and nodded my head while he swiped whatever tears fell down my face. "T...thank you."

"You never have to thank me, Joy." He kissed me on the cheek and slowly closed the door behind me.

I sat on the edge of the tub and broke down crying. All the years of abuse and trauma rained down my face like a rainstorm. My shoulders shook as I sobbed into my hands at the realization that I was safe.

A man I had only met in a prison visitation room made me feel safer than anybody I had ever encountered in my life. Slowly I disrobed my clothes and the past that I desperately wanted to forget and climbed into the bath.

When I came down the stairs, Cappadonna was sitting on the couch in the living room. He had taken him a shower and was wearing gray sweatpants without a shirt on. I swallowed hard as I took in his body.

All the muscles all worked together to make this man ten times more irresistible than he already was. He looked up and smiled when he noticed me standing there.

"I feel honored." He touched his chest.

When I was getting dressed, I debated on if I would cover my hair or come down with my natural hair. Every time Capp had seen me, I always had a hijab on. I decided to leave my hair out. It was wet from me washing it.

My hair was thick and curly. I had always complained about managing it when I was younger. It wasn't until I was forced to cover it that I truly fell in love with my curl pattern and everything that had to do with my hair.

It was my hair, and I should have had a say in if I wanted to cover it or wear it out. That decision was robbed from me for years. "You don't think less of me for showing you it?"

"I'm not that nigga. The decision to cover your hair or wear it out should be a decision that only you make, or if we ever got married, we make together. I think you're beautiful with or without one."

My heart thumped against my chest when he said if *we* ever got married. It probably didn't mean much to him, but those simple words did something to me and meant a lot.

"Thank you." He helped me sit on the couch, while trying to get comfortable.

We sat looking over our shoulder at the lake behind us. The different homes around the lake had lantern lights, and you could see some of the other owners on their back porches watching the lake.

"You ready to fill me in?"

I shook my head, and looked into his eyes, scared. Telling him my story meant that I was letting him into my world, and it had been so long since I've let anyone into my world. I've closed myself off the moment I got into that car with Zayne and left my yaya's house.

As I spoke, tears welled up in my eyes. I told Cappadonna everything, watching how his hands balled up and the anger flashed in his eyes. I paused to gather myself, and he pulled me closer to him, slowly rubbing his hand across my stomach in a circular motion.

After a dozen pauses and tears, I finally got the story out and the way he looked at me hadn't changed. "You don't have to worry about that shit anymore. I promise you'll never go through that again. I'm going to protect you."

"I don't want you to go back to prison, or to be hurt because of me."

He kissed the back of my hand. "You went your whole life never having someone to protect you. I'm not letting you go another fucking second never knowing what feeling protected feels like. I'm not letting you bring her into this world not knowing what being protected feels like... alright?"

"Okay," I whispered.

He touched my face and looked me in the eyes, softly kissing me on the lips. "I put that on my life that I got you, Alaia."

My heart raced as I stared into his eyes. "Thank you."

Cappadonna left me on the couch while he went outside to handle a phone call. I sat on the couch and watched as he spoke on the phone. He used his hands a lot and was so passionate about the way he spoke. I sat there rubbing my stomach and feeling safe for the first time in my entire life.

When he came back into the house his energy was different. I sat there watching as he grabbed some water from the fridge and then yawned. "You can go to bed if you want. I'm fine right here."

He chuckled. "Can I be honest with you?"

"I would hope, Mr. Honesty."

He laughed. "I've slept alone for fifteen years."

"So, I've heard."

He smirked. "Come on, Ma. I've slept alone for fifteen years... I'm not trying to sleep alone anymore."

Capp came over to me and pulled me up from the couch. We took the stairs one step at a time, and then went into the master bedroom. I climbed into the bed, pulling the covers over my body. I hadn't had a bed feel so good in my entire life.

He set the alarm and then stripped out of his sweats and was wearing his briefs. I turned on my side since that was the only way I could get comfortable these days. I felt when he slid into the bed, and I remained still, scared of what came next.

"Alaia."

"Huh?"

"Can I hold you?"

"Please."

He scooted over toward me and pulled me into his arms. His arms swallowed me up as I got comfortable in them. I felt him kiss the top of my head. "You can rest now."

Those four words meant so much to me as my eyes became heavy, and I drifted off to sleep with Cappadonna's arms wrapped around me and my belly.

Was this what safety truly felt like?

15
TAZ

"Nigga, I know exactly why my brother kept each wife. Those women are some fucking freaks. Fatima ain't let my dick breathe the entire time we were in Mexico. Soon as I pull into the driveway at her crib, she treats me like a fucking king," I bragged about my brother's first wife.

Me and Fatima went way back. When she and Zayne got together, I was the one telling him that she was for the streets, and she wasn't going to be a wife. I was the first to admit when a nigga was wrong because I now understood why I always had to come drag my brother from her crib.

"What about that young one? I just knew it wasn't going to last when he brought her around," Ralph, my cousin, asked.

Only reason his ass was asking was because he wanted Alaia for himself. His ass was pushing damn near fifty, and he still couldn't get over that Zayne scooped her for himself. I couldn't even be mad at him because I wanted her for my damn self, too.

Ever since I laid my eyes on her ass when he first brought her home, I had wanted her for me. I was pissed that her stupid ass brother Raheem offered her to my brother. Everybody knew that Zayne pretended to be hard but was as soft as fucking socks. He may have flexed his power a bit, but his wives did whatever the fuck they wanted.

Alaia was the only one he ever controlled or paid close attention to. Even then, he would be gone for weeks leaving her alone. She was too damn scared to run away, so I guess he did good when it came to instilling fear into her ass. Even though he said she was the easy wife, I wasn't seeing that.

Her fine ass was so fucking stubborn and hardheaded. If I told her not to be with that other nigga, then why the fuck was she with him? Imagine my surprise when I see her ass climbing out his truck like I hadn't just told her ass that I didn't want her near his ass.

Then his cocky ass had the nerve to be throwing empty threats like he was going to do some shit. I leaned back in the barber chair pissed about the situation all over again. Alaia was used to getting her way with Zayne and I needed to break her ass out of that shit. What other way than to withhold the things that she desperately needed. She needed electricity and I snatched that from her. Slick bitch found a way around that and wasn't even home to suffer in the heat.

Food was the next thing since she was pregnant and could eat. When she called me crying that she needed money for food, I laughed while I had my dick down Fatima's throat. It was funny how I had one wife on the phone begging me for money and the other one choking on my shit. Zayne didn't know how to get these bitches in control and now that they were mine, I planned to get them under control.

Starting with that fucking baby that she was carrying. All his other wives had his children and it pissed me off going over to their homes and having to deal with my nieces and nephews. You could say what you want about my brother, but he loved the shit out of all his damn kids.

Alaia was moving in with me and I didn't want no screaming fucking baby around. I was a person that didn't like kids, so I was going to sell that baby soon as she had it. It wasn't like this was something new to me. Soon as one of my bitches had a baby at one of the houses, I snatched that baby and sent it packing. Soon, a big lump of money was wired into my account.

I liked to think of it as me helping women become mothers. What the fuck was a hoe going to teach a child? How to lay on her back?

Tonight, I was popping out to the club to celebrate making the move to New York. We already had one house set up in Queens and it wouldn't be long before we had others around the city. Delaware was home, but the shit didn't pay as much as New York would. My clientele wasn't just the regular joe whose wife wouldn't give him pussy. I had fucking law enforcement, politicians, and men of important power.

Word traveled and it wasn't long before I had men from New York driving in or flying in to come get a piece of my girls. It was only right to make the move into New York and collect even more money.

"They out there with them damn bikes again," Ralph said, while I waited for the barber to start my haircut.

I was ten minutes from spazzing because I had been shooting the breeze for a few minutes and his ass still hadn't cleaned this after shave from my face. He was on the phone, and I was becoming irritated with waiting.

In Delaware, all I had to do was snap my fingers and shit was done. Here, I had to prove my muscle a little more in order to get some respect.

I felt hands on my shoulders and relaxed that he was

getting started. That was before my head was snatched back and I was eye to eye with Cappadonna Delgato. This nigga had been a thorn in my side since I discovered that he had a thing for Alaia.

His eyes were wild with anger, and I could have sworn they were fucking red. "Baby boy, I told you that you would have to see me if you put your hands on her."

I tried to talk, but his hand was around my throat squeezing so tight that I was seeing the light. "What's that? Nah... go ahead and put your hands on me like you did her...what's that bitch?"

He released me, stepping into view while I was trying to catch my breath. "Aye, get the fuck on wit—"

Ralph fell back onto the bench when Cappadonna slammed his fist into his mouth "You good?" he looked at the man sitting beside a now bleeding Ralph.

"I'm...I'm straight." He held his hands up and moved away from Ralph toward the front of the barbershop.

Ralph was over there spitting his teeth out while moaning and I was still trying to breathe from the pressure he applied around my neck. Cappadonna cracked his knuckles and looked at me. "I warned you twice that you would have to fucking see me... right?"

"That's my bitch... mind your fucking business." I spit at his feet, and he laughed in my face like a fucking maniac.

When I looked down, this nigga had a pair of fucking crocs on, and he was in here fucking choking me out like this was a normal errand on his list of errands to run. I remember Cappadonna because Zayne always complained about him.

Imagine your older brother calling you from prison to complain about another nigga, younger than him, herbing him. He would say that he would toss his food onto the floor, slam his head into the cell and snatch his commissary.

The nigga even told me that he snatched the phone from him and spent the next ten minutes talking to our mother using all his phone time. I called Zayne soft and told his ass that he needed to fucking tighten up.

As I sat in front of this big nigga, I realized that my brother wasn't bullshitting when he said that he was everything that he said and more. I was looking outside for my guys to bring they ass in here, and nobody entered the door.

Ralph's soft ass was still over there moaning in pain while Cappadonna didn't look bothered. "You and your brother are fucking weirdo pedophiles... the fuck you mean she's your bitch? She was sixteen when you bought her from her brother, and trust that nigga gotta see me, too."

"I tell you how to run your shi—"

He lunged at me, taking my head and pulling it way back until I became dizzy staring into his eyes. "It's up when it comes to Alaia, pussy. I'm doing you a fucking," he paused as he applied more pressure to my neck, "favor by not sliding that fucking straight razor across your neck... but I got respect for Brandon and his shop, so I'm gonna let you breathe. Whatever sick thoughts you had of Alaia being yours, end that shit. That's my baby, and when it comes to her, I'll paint the fucking city red... feel me?"

"Arghh," I gargled.

"I could just apply the right amount of pressure right here and make sure you and your brother are reunit—"

"Yo Capp... not yet." A man entered the shop and told him to ease up on me because I was on my way to fucking glory. I think I saw my fucking grandmother that passed a few years ago.

If I could, I would have thanked the other man, but I was so busy trying to breathe. Cappadonna swaggered toward the door. "Don't end up like your brother, Tweety."

This nigga not only punched my fucking cousin's teeth out his mouth, but he also choked me on multiple occasions while telling me that he took my bitch. If all of that wasn't enough, his ass called me fucking Tweety knowing that my name was Taz.

I was so fucking angry that when Brandon tried to cut my hair, I snatched away from him and ran outside with the damn smock still around my neck. Cappadonna had his back turned talking to another overly big nigga.

All these niggas were on bikes chilling and talking like this man didn't assault me and my cousin minutes before. Any sane nigga would have gotten off the scene quick, not this man. He sat there secretly praying that I would make a move so he could do what he really wanted to do. The murder in his eyes told me everything that I needed to know and how I needed to move.

The vest the other men wore told me that they weren't nothing to deal with either. I heard of some deadly things when it came to the Inferno Gods. They were a biker game notorious for causing horror wherever their wheels stopped.

I looked around for my peoples and they were nowhere to be found. "Oh, those pussies down the block. They gotta pay me to come on this block or I'm knocking the fucking wind out they chest." Capp smirked while looking down at me.

I've always been height challenged, and had been insecure about my height. It was something that I learned to deal with over the years and as I became older. I may have been short, but my money was long.

With the way Cappadonna towered over me, he was bringing me back to that little boy that used to be bullied on the playground. I turned and went back into the barbershop and sat down waiting for them to fucking leave.

When I made it to the crib, I was going to put Alaia's head

through the fucking wall. I told her to leave this crazy nigga alone and now he was over here trying to tell me what he was going to do with my bitch.

"Yo Taz, I think I fucking swallowed a tooth," Ralph choked out, probably wishing he had minded his business.

I watched as everyone outside parted a damn sea for Cappadonna to get to his truck. He got in, and sped off the block with a sea of motorcycles following behind his ass. If he thought he was going to take Alaia from me, he was dead wrong.

Bitches came a dime a dozen, but the fact that he wanted her meant that I needed her, and I wasn't willing to let go of her. That bitch had to be paid back for the way he embarrassed me. I wasn't letting this shit go.

16
CAPPADONNA

Saturdays were for me to run around and handle my shit and being that Tweety's ass was on the way to my actual destination, I made sure to stop and have a talk to his ass. When Alaia told me the shit she went through and how her own brother sold her to those pedos, I couldn't sleep that whole night. While she slept peacefully in my arms, I held onto her and her stomach tightly. I refused to let her go, and I would do everything I could to make sure she stayed protected.

How the fuck could a brother do that to his own sister? When I thought of my own sister, I would fucking kill for her and lay down and die for her. I got pissed even thinking of harm coming to her.

Alaia's brother sold her ass like she was a pair of fucking sneakers and didn't think twice on what her life would become. I sat there holding in my anger as she had to pause and take breaths because it was so traumatic for her to relive.

I've always felt a connection to her, and now the connection was that stronger. She was just a child; someone should have been there to protect her. Nobody protected her and left her there to fend for herself. It made a lot of sense why she never wanted to accept my help without me pushing it onto her.

I'd be damned if she ever had to struggle like that again. Every night since she'd been with me at the lake house, I had held her and promised myself that she would know what love felt like. For her, I would blow this fucking city up without a second thought.

I understood what my brother felt when he explained how he felt about Erin. How he would go to the ends of earth to prove a point when it came to her. Me and Alaia hadn't even known each other that long but I felt everything that my brother had said.

When I had Tweety's ass choked up, I wanted to end his ass right then and there. I hated when people played games. I warned his ass and told him that he would have to see me if he put his hands on her, and he tested me. He went ahead and put a bruise on my baby's face and there was no coming back from that.

I was on whatever he was on. I've sat up for the past few years living through the action through word of mouth. My hands were itching to show them why the fuck they called me Capp. I backed into the spot in front of the condo that Kendra's ass better had been out of.

When I hit the code on the door, I opened it and spotted her in the kitchen with her purse. I knew I told this bitch to be out this shit and here she was standing here like I didn't tell her ass she needed to be gone.

If Quasim hadn't come in, I probably would have choked her out. I became enraged whenever I thought of the selfish shit she did. The only people that paid the price of her selfishness was me and Capella. We lost out on time that both of us needed.

She stood there with dark circles and was clearly stressed because I was kicking her ass out. "Hey."

"I told yo' 'hey' ass to be out my shit when I slid through here."

She broke out into tears like I gave a fuck about her tears. Kendra didn't give a fuck about nobody but herself. "I want to fix this, Capp."

"Alright... where's the Time Machine then. If we gonna fix this, step in that bitch and give me back the last nineteen years that my son lost."

"I know I fucked up and I shouldn't have done that." She continued to cry while searching my eyes, praying she saw just a glimpse that I cared.

"You only give a fuck now because shit is being taken from you. I fucking gave you everything you could have asked for. Always held you down because I thought you were on the same time."

"Ella and Capone were able to fix their problems... I want the same for us—"

I held my hand up when my phone rang with Alaia's name. "What's up, baby girl?"

"Are you sure about me using your card? Some of this stuff is very expensive in this grocery store."

I laughed. "I told you to get whatever you want. You the one that swear you know how to throw down, don't back out now." My damn heart did backflips whenever I heard her voice.

She told me she was tired of takeout and that she wanted to cook, so Erin came over to take her food shopping for the house. I was getting used to sharing the house with her. It was our little piece of heaven away from the world.

I could tell the longer she was there she was becoming comfortable. A few times I had to stop her ass from trying to clean and force her to relax. Other than that, I couldn't wait until I was back in her presence.

"I do know how to cook so don't try and play me." She giggled. "I just wanted to check and see if you were alright. Oil is almost forty dollars in here," she whispered.

"You funny... I'll see you in a little bit."

"Okay."

I ended the call and turned my attention back to Kendra, whose mouth was damn near on the counter. "Where the fuck was I... oh yeah, because you're Capella's mother is the only reason you're walking up out of here and not in a fucking bag. Don't compare yourself to Ella because she didn't hide her son from his father, and she has more than proven herself to this family. Meanwhile, you couldn't be so bothered to come around with me being gone."

The shit bothered me how Kendra stayed far removed from my family while I was locked up. If we were building a future when I was released, wouldn't the person that I was with want to be closer to my family? Not Kendra's ass, she stayed away from them like they had the fucking cooties or something.

The difference between Ella and Kendra was that Ella knew her position. She knew her role as CJ's mother would mean she was family. With the way I heard she held down Erin when they were in a place where she could have greased her and been for herself, I admired her. Did I fuck with her for the shit she did with Capri?

Nah.

I gave respect when it was due. Kendra couldn't get respect because she was a fucking liar, and even standing in front of me she couldn't be honest with me.

"I want to fix this... please give me that."

"Get the fuck out my face and this crib before I do some shit I can't come back from," I snarled, looking down at her.

She slowly gathered the bag she had on the stool and walked toward the front door. "I love you, Cappadonna. I want to fix the relationship between me, you, and our son."

I didn't turn around or even acknowledge the shit she was saying. It was too late for her to want to fix anything between us. The chance to do that was when she found out that she was pregnant.

After she left, I looked around to make sure all my shit was still here. Kendra was selfish, not stupid. I knew when I looked in that closet that everything would be there. The maintenanceman had come on time to change the locks and code. I snatched the keys to her whip before locking up and heading to my brother's crib to grab some more clothes.

The lake house wasn't to live in permanently. I needed something closer to the city, and I had been putting it off for a minute because I had become used to being around my family. I enjoyed hearing my nephew running around the house, seeing my niece making spit bubbles when I poked my head over her bassinet.

It didn't hurt that Josephine was always cooking some good ass food. I could wake up from a nap and I had a plate waiting for me. Capone's ass thought he was slick with the way his house ran. He didn't have to do shit when it came to the women in the house. I respected it because he had created a village, and the house ran like one.

Whenever Erin was overwhelmed, she had my mother or Jo to tap in and take over. Capri and Ryai came over and took over from them if it was needed. If he needed to take his wife away, the house would still run and the kids would be taken care of.

Living with them for the first few months after being home, it forced me to look at my future. I wanted to have the life where I had a wife that fucking admired me. When Erin looked at her husband, it wasn't shit that woman wouldn't do for him. It was equal when it came to their marriage. Money wasn't a factor because their love outweighed it all. You couldn't tell my twin shit about his wife.

Soon as I stepped through the doors, I could already smell somebody cooking. I headed into the kitchen, and found my mother there. "Hey Ma," I kissed her on the forehead.

"Hey baby... I didn't know you were coming over today. Your brother said you been locked in the house at the lake."

I chuckled. "Oh yeah? Where is he?"

She gave me a tight squeeze. "He's in the office. Are you staying for dinner tonight?"

I headed out the kitchen, walking backward. "Not tonight... I have somebody making me dinner tonight."

"Kendra could cook?"

"Me and Kendra are not together anymore... we decided to go our separate ways," I smirked, seeing the happiness in my mother's face.

"Oh, I'm sorry."

"No you're not and that's alright... I need to talk to Capone real quick."

She wiped her hands on the dish towel. "I enjoy seeing both my boys in the same place. I've prayed for this."

"Reason why I stayed sane in there is because of your prayers." Anytime I thought I would lose my mind, hearing my father or mother pray for me kept me together. "Where's Pops?"

"Playing golf with his friends."

I knocked on the door twice before I twisted the handle and entered. Capone was on the phone and nodded at me. I allowed him to handle business while taking a seat in one of the chairs. Even though he stepped back, he had stepped up for our trucking business.

With how much shit he went through, he just wanted Erin to be able to sleep at night without worrying about him. He finished his call and then came around the desk to sit in the chair across from mine.

"You finally got some time to see the little people?"

"Fuck up." I laughed.

Capone messed with his beard. "What's your plan? Staying at the lake house with her forever. She's pregnant, Capp."

"She called me, and I came... I told her that I would come if she needed me, and she did."

When Alaia called me about needing money for food, I felt like it was more to it. I was coming because I was hoping I would be able to convince her to leave. To have better than what she currently had. Soon as I saw her face, I wanted to lose my mind and knew I had to be strong and calm for her.

"Fuck. How do we end up in shit like this?"

"This my shit, Capo."

He screwed his face up. "Nigga, fuck all that my shit... I'm banging my shit beside you if it comes to it." He held his hand out, and I dapped him.

"Erin gonna fuck me up," I laughed.

The knock interrupted us, and Jaiden came into the room. "Bro', how you knew I was coming to talk about you?"

"Explain, Kid."

He gave me his phone on that damn clock app and showed me a video of me slamming that nigga's head into his plate while reading over the menu. "It has over twelve million views," Jaiden was all excited about me causing harm to another person.

Capone took the phone and watched it before he looked over at me. "What the fuck happened to cool and chill?"

"That was. I had my gun and didn't shove it into his mouth." I shrugged.

He was complaining, meanwhile I thought I handled it pretty well. Ace was still able to talk about what happened to him. Not too many people got the chance to do it. Shit, I thought I was becoming soft with how easy I was on his ass.

"I've had my eye on him, and he been respectful. Careful not to put his traps near ours and not stepping on our toes. I allowed him to be, and then you go and do this."

My twin was peaceful and thought everyone could co-exist, and I was the opposite. There could only be one set of twin kings, and there was no room for nobody else.

"Nigga, this is why the fuck Trilla caused so much mayhem... why? Because you thought you could co-exist."

"He not even touching nothing near what the fuck we bring into the city. I ain't trying to make beef when there's no need for none."

I laughed. "It was beef when he started fucking Kendra."

I not only had beef with one bitch, but I had it with two of them and I couldn't care less. I craved this shit, and if that meant killing two birds with one stone, then I was game to handle that. I could see why my brother wanted to chill, he had been through a lot and he had to focus on his family.

"You've gotten soft on me."

"Fuck outta here... never soft, just not ready to bust my shit for everything."

Jaiden leaned on the wall. "You already know I'm do—"

"Get the fuck outta here... you going to college. Don't need you fucking getting involved. Matter fact, you need to be finishing that exit essay," Capone snapped, and Jaiden hung his head leaving the office. "I'm already trying to put another baby in my wife, and if she found out his ass was involved, she putting me on the couch."

"Pussy."

"Yeah, but only when it comes to my wife." He leaned back and sighed. "I got your follow up... always."

"I gotta tell you some shit."

"What up?"

I leaned up and told Capone everything that Alaia had told me, and I watched him go through the same emotions I went through when she told me. His fist balled up, and I could see the fire in his eyes. My fucking chest started to hurt when I listened to her telling me her story.

"Her fucking brother?" he asked disgusted.

"Word. I went to see the bitch that think he gonna have her, today. Choked his little ass out, and I feel like this isn't going to be the last time I see him. Capo, I had my hand around his neck and wanted to snap it so bad. Him and his fucking brother are fucking disgusting to have done that to her."

"She's safe now... we got her."

"You already know. I'm not letting her go." When I said that, I meant that shit with every fucking word.

I hadn't even slid inside of her, and she was already mine. Tweety was going to have to see me if he thought he would ever get the chance to fucking take her from me.

"The fuck is the move then?"

Capone knew he lived and breathed this shit. He tried to act like he was stepping back, but this shit cruised through his blood like it did mine. I couldn't imagine my twin not having my follow up.

"That's what I'm trying to figure out. I remember you mentioned something about that drive-by in Delaware. You said you would tell me over a drink... tell me."

"Since your ass don't drink... here," he tossed me a bottle of water, and then sat back down in his seat. "Kincaid took Capri out there to some lounge, and some niggas tried to rob him."

"Alright." I wasn't seeing the reason to shoot at them

niggas for Kincaid's dumb ass getting robbed. His ass should have been smarter and moved smarter.

"He ain't just want what Kincaid had... he wanted Capri, too. His cousin told us them niggas be trafficking women and shit. He was trying to get Capri and she let her shit go and got them out of there."

Nothing made me prouder than knowing that my sister could handle her own. She would always have her brothers, but the fact that she could let her shit bang and handle herself always made me proud. Capri was college educated and could still let her shit go when she needed to.

"My girl."

"Facts. I was proud of her and pissed at the same time. Kincaid wanted to get the get back, and we pulled up out there and cleared the fucking block... ain't thought about them until you brought it up to me that day in the visitation room."

The fact that those bitches tried to get my sister made me want to finish the job from earlier. Even though Capone handled it, I wanted to spin the block and let my shit go, too. "Turns out the bitch I choked earlier is connected to those people."

"However you want to handle the shit, let me know."

I chuckled. "I'm sitting until that pussy come and see me. After getting his ass choked out, I know he gonna come sooner than later."

"Heard you and Quasim linked up."

I smirked. "He may have stepped out of retirement when he heard I was home."

Quasim was the head of Inferno Gods, the biker gang that nobody fucked with. Inferno Gods had their hands in a little bit of everything. When it came to work, we always had a mutual respect, and supplied them.

He had stepped back after his baby mother was murdered.

Qua raised their daughter, and then his daughter had gotten cancer. Life was one thing after the other with him, and the streets wasn't a priority for him.

His daughter passed away a few years ago, and I remember crying in my cell. That shit hurt like nothing I had ever felt before. Not only did he lose her mother, the love of his life, he then lost his baby a few years after that. Even with stepping back, things still ran in his absence. He had come to visit me a few months before I was released and we had a conversation.

We've been playing big for a while now, and it was time to play bigger. I wanted to make sure that the shit that happened with Trilla never happened again. That anybody that went against us would know what to expect when it came to gunning for the Delgato twins.

"How is Qua? Haven't spoken to him in a while... nigga like a ghost." Capo poured himself a drink.

"He's straight. Grief takes time, but he's ready to return."

"Yeah." He nodded in agreement as we both sat in silence for a bit. I missed being able to soak up my brother's energy. It was different sitting across from him in a visitation room.

We made do with the time we were given, but nothing beats sitting this close to him and soaking everything in. Capone wasn't the same man that I left before I went in. He had to grow without me and I always worried it would cause a divide between us.

He had to fill both of our shoes while I sat back. When I looked at him, my chest filled with pride because he had done that shit without breaking a sweat. "How your health?"

"I'm straight. Erin been on me about my medicine and having me eat cleaner."

"You married the right one. She loves and worries about you. I don't want you fighting her about shit because she knows best," I warned him.

If it was one thing that Capone hated, it was people taking pity on him, and treating him like he was sick. He naturally took care of everyone, so he hated when the focus was on him.

"Look at the baby boys sitting together all nice," Capri poked her head in, and I stood up, grabbing her into my arms and kissing her on the forehead.

"Baby Doll, why don't I see you enough?"

She squeezed me, before going to kiss Capone. "I'm a busy woman these days. Actually, Kincaid has been teaching me to ride bikes."

"I told his ass not to teach you shit else!" Capone snapped.

"And I told him that I am a grown woman and I want to learn... remember the boundaries we set in place, Winnie," she teased him.

Hearing Erin run around this house calling this nigga Winnie always made me laugh. We hated our fucking middle names with a passion. I knew he loved her because he allowed the shit.

"Be careful out there, Baby Doll."

"I am... always. Kendra called me," she revealed and I looked away, not surprised that she would try and pull whoever she could onto her side.

Kendra never reached out to Capri before and because she got her ass put out, she wanted to try and talk to my family now. "I should have tossed her ass into the fridge when I had the chance."

"Hey. You need to calm your ass down," Capri's eyes widened. "You guys always break up so I told her to give you time."

"That ain't what this is, Baby Doll."

"Oh. Well, shit, I don't know what she gonna do," Capri laughed as she crossed her legs. "I think you're better off without her anyway."

I didn't need to tell her about Alaia right away. We were still getting to know each other, and I was allowing her time to breathe. There was no need for us to rush into something. All she needed to know is that even without a title, she was mine, and Daddy had her.

"You and everybody else seems to think so."

Capri smiled. "Sooo, with Mommy and Daddy's anniversary coming up, Erin thought it would be a great time for us to plan a family trip together to celebrate them. What do you think about getting away soon?"

"I'm all for celebrating them. They've held it down all these years, and we wouldn't be the men that we are without the example that they set."

"I agree. Even though I'm divorced." She rolled her eyes.

"You're not divorced because you wanted to be, Pri. Stop beating yourself up about that." Capone reached over and rubbed her back.

"Thanks, Capone."

"I see why Erin nearly slammed my fingers in her laptop when I was trying to see what she was doing."

"You know how close she is with Mommy and Daddy. I think we're bad children for not coming up with the damn idea our damn self. They're going to be married for thirty-four years, and we didn't think to plan something."

"Shit... thirty-four years," I whistled.

"The thought of being with somebody for that long of a time used to make me itch. Now, I can see why they have stood the test of time. Marriage ain't easy and takes a lot of work every day."

"Shut up, Capone. You just got married and trying to preach to us," Capri shoved him, and we all started laughing 'cause this nigga thought he was a fucking life coach or something.

I looked at the time and stood up. "I'm about to bounce... I'll hit you."

"Be safe." My brother stood up, hugging me. "Send my wife home too."

"Always... love you both," I called over my shoulder as I headed back to the lake house. I didn't want Alaia being by herself for too long. Not because I feared anything would happen, I just knew she didn't like being alone.

∽

As I pulled into the driveway, Erin was walking to her car. She stopped when she saw me and waited for me to park before walking over toward my car.

"Appreciate you helping me out today, sis'," I pulled her into my arms, dropping a kiss on her head.

"Anytime. You know I got your back. I had no idea she was going through all of that, Capp. I fucking cried when she was telling me everything."

I leaned back on my truck. "I wanted to fucking kill everything moving when she told me. You don't do no shit like that to fucking people, especially women. She didn't deserve none of that shit."

"At all. Then to be going through that while pregnant. She has my number programmed in her new phone, so if she needs anything I'm there. I also have a bunch of clothes that Cee-cee can't fit anymore, so I'll bring them over the next time that I come over."

"E, I can afford to buy the baby some clothes." I laughed, because she was so damn frugal, and always trying to save some money.

"Oh hell no. Those clothes are good clothes and designer. Like I told your brother, I don't care how many commas we got in the bank, the clothes are being handed down in this family." She paused. "She's right there, too, so you might want to get her a prenatal massage, and things ready for that baby."

I laughed and hugged her again because she was dead serious. Erin humbled my brother and reminded him of times when he didn't have it like now. I could appreciate her for that because we often lost sight of where we came from. It was so easy to just toss away money because we got it. Any other woman would have been in Capone's pocket spending it, while Erin was always trying to save her man money.

"Appreciate you, E. You need me to follow you back home?" I called behind her as she walked over to her car.

"You know, there used to be a time when I would have asked you to, but we're finally in a place where I am good." She patted her purse. "Plus, I'm secure... text you when I'm home."

"Be safe!" I yelled, as I watched her pull out the driveway.

I stood there, leaning on my car for a second longer before going in through the garage. Soon as my foot hit the door, I could smell the aroma of food. My stomach growled in anticipation of whatever Alaia cooked for dinner.

She was bragging about knowing how to cook, so I was excited to see if her cooking levels was up there. When you entered the house through the garage, you were right in the kitchen. Alaia was leaned on the counter and looked up when she saw me standing there.

"Hey. You had to have run into Erin on your way in, she just left to go home." She smiled at me, rubbing her back.

"Come 'ere," I motioned for her, and she waddled around the counter. Going behind her, I did the technique we had learned at her class. She rested her head on my chest like she did before, taking slow breaths. "How does that feel?"

"Not as good as before... I think she might come early, Cappadonna," I could hear the concern in her voice.

I instantly felt guilty for allowing her to go shopping and then cooking for me. "Don't even put that out there... she is staying in until she's supposed to come out. Tell me whenever you're ready," I whispered, kissing the top of her head.

We stayed in the kitchen while I held her stomach up. When she was ready, I put it back down gently, and walked her ass back over toward the couch. "I need to make your plate... I spent all this time cooking to show you."

"I'm a grown ass man, Alaia, I can make us both a plate of food so you can relax." She had this look on her face when I said her name. "What was that face?"

"I don't know... I kind of like when you call me everything except my name." She shrugged and I smiled, knowing I was wearing her ass down.

Taking a seat beside her. "Oh yeah? Tell me why you don't like your name?"

She looked out the window. "It's not that I don't like my name, I never had a nickname... it makes me feel, I don't know... I guess warm inside that someone thought I was nickname worthy."

I ran my hand across her face, where her bruises were healing. "I'll call you whatever you want me to call you, you hear me?"

"I know that I can't stay here forever, but I do appreciate everything that you've done for me."

It was my turn to make a face. "The fuck you mean you can't stay here forever?"

"You have a life of your own to live, and that doesn't include helping the battered girl with a baby."

I looked up at the ceiling putting my words together before they left my mouth. Usually, I said whatever came to mind, and I didn't want to do that with her. She deserved to know exactly what I meant when I said it. I didn't want to leave no room for her to overthink or overanalyze my words and intentions.

"When I asked you if I'm giving you money or a home, I meant that. I meant the home part, and it doesn't matter if we stay here, or when I find a place closer to the city, it's going to be home. What the fuck I look like leaving you out here alone, baby girl? I want you to know that I plan to be here. Fuck that, I *am* here. I told you; you call me and I'm running for you."

"You have a girlfriend, Cappadonna. I don't want to get in between that." She ran her hand through her hair, and I noticed that her hijab was layered around her neck. "You wore your hijab out today?"

"I did."

"Why?"

She smiled at me. "I don't know... I like how you look at me when I wear it, and I wanted to wear it for you, I guess." She shrugged, unsure on how I would feel about it.

I never needed to see her hair to know how beautiful she was. Even wearing her hijab, she was beautiful, and without it she was still beautiful. When I thought of marriage, I never thought about if my future wife would wear one or not. I would feel honored if she wanted to wear one because of me, but it wasn't something that I was going to force down her throat.

"You special, you know that?"

"No, I'm not."

I moved closer to her, placing one hand on her stomach and then holding her hand with the other one. "Don't say that shit. You're fucking special, and I saw that shit when I first met you. Wanna know how I know you special?"

"How?" I hated how the desperation entered her eyes, wanting to know what made her so special. Alaia should have known; even felt how special of a person she was.

I took her hand and placed it on my chest. "My heart don't do this shit for just anybody. When you're close to me, my heart starts acting crazy as shit for you. I'm on your time, Joy. Slow and steady will always win the race. We don't need to move fast... I've waited fifteen years; I can wait fifteen more if that's what it takes."

She smiled, allowing me to continue to rub her stomach and hold her hand. "The day I ran into you going to the laundromat, I had stopped to rest, and I remembered saying, I wanted something good to happen to me that day. It didn't need to be big, just something to show that I was worthy of something – anything good happening to me."

"And then my ass hit an illegal U-turn to get to you. No bullshit, I never forgot about you... I didn't know when we would meet again, but I knew I would be seeing you."

"I believe that."

"I'm gonna fix your food, then go do Wudu."

She looked at me with those eyes, and I swore every time she looked at me like that, I knew I could never let her down like life had done in the past. "Can I pray with you?"

"Word?"

When she told me that her faith was broken and how she didn't know if she believed anymore, even believed in the first place, I didn't force anything on her. I knew what being Muslim had done for me, so I couldn't push my beliefs onto someone who was struggling with their own.

She smiled. "I would like to... I would like for you to teach me your way. You seem so at peace... so respectful of our religion." The fact that she wanted to still wear her hijab and pray with me, after telling me that she didn't feel connected to our faith anymore spoke volumes on how safe she felt with me.

Kissing her hands, I said, "I got you."

17

KENDRA

I climbed off Ace's dick and rolled my eyes because his drunk ass couldn't keep his shit hard. Whenever he started drinking and got too drunk, he could never keep up with me. We were both rolling off ecstasy, and I wanted to fuck all the anger and frustration I had with Capp away, and this nigga couldn't even keep his dick hard for me.

"Come on, chill, come on its gonna get hard," he tried to convince me, and I knew that was the furthest from the truth.

The shit felt like a turtle hiding in its shell, and I was trying not to punch him in his shit because I was so horny, and he couldn't even please me. Then, when I looked down at this stupid ass ring, I became pissed all over again.

Why did I have to fuck up and mess with this nigga? He was so thirsty for Cappadonna to know that he was fucking with me. Like, what did that fucking do other than have your face all sliced and diced.

The nigga was over here looking like Edward Scissor hand had got a hold of him, and now I had to lay here and pretend I wanted to be here all along. I rolled over and avoided even saying anything because I was going to lose my shit on him if I said something else.

There was a reason that I never got too serious with his ass. The goal was always to be with Cappadonna when he came home. I entertained him because he made me feel good in the moment. What woman didn't like a man who worshipped the ground they walked on. I was stupid for even giving him money as much as I did.

Ace wasn't a slouch and was fine as ever. He reminded me of Nelly back in the day, and the bitches loved Nelly, me included. He was younger than me and easy to manipulate, too, which I thought would be a good thing.

I could use him for the moment and when my man came home, I could act like I didn't know his ass. Well, my plan failed when this nigga thought he could go against Cappadonna. It wasn't like we hadn't had a conversation about his ass, and how he got down. The reason Ace was able to move through the city and get money out here was because Capone didn't think he was a threat.

Ace pissed me off because I warned his ass that Capone was nicer than his brother. I mean, he wasn't all that nice, but compared to his damn twin, he was Mr. Rodger's. Do you know how embarrassing it is to get on the internet and see your so called man being slammed into a table? I had Sassy sending me the shit and then laughing because she thought I was done with him.

Her ass didn't realize that I had moved into his house with him and had no choice but to stick it out or else I would be homeless. I had money in the bank, but it wasn't enough to pay real bills. A bitch hadn't paid real bills in so long that I didn't know what that even felt like anymore. Cappadonna handled all of that, so I never had to worry, and I planned on continuing that when he came home.

Imagine my surprise when this nigga kicked my ass out and took my transportation from me. Then he held his fucking hand up to talk to whatever little bitch he was fucking with. I give this nigga my undivided attention all these years and his ass pays me back like this. Got me laying up with limp dick Magoo.

"Baby, can you make me something to eat?"

Had he fucked me so good that I was walking with a limp, I probably would have gone in there and cooked him a full course meal along with a baked cake. The fact that his ass couldn't even keep it hard, he couldn't get Lunchables from my ass. I pretended to be sleep while all I wanted to do was cry myself to sleep because I missed my condo.

I missed my own space.

Hell, I missed what used to be my man. Capp was probably teaching me a lesson, and I needed to act right so he could give me everything I needed back. Ella was riding around with brand new whips and a nice ass townhouse, and Capone was married to another woman. There were clearly perks to being a baby mama, and my stupid ass had fumbled it.

One thing about Kendra, I don't stay down long, and I will have my way. While Ace continued to talk to me, I pretended to be sleep because I was going to call my son early in the morning. The only way to fix things was to make it right with my son. If Capp saw me trying with him, then he would change his mind.

That nigga was acting like this wasn't the best pussy he ever had. He knew good and darn well that he wanted to climb up in this and had to just show me he wasn't playing with me. Well, understood, Daddy. I understood, and I was ready for him to come give me everything back so I could ditch the corn ball I was lying beside. Whoever said young niggas were the one, lied right through their teeth.

∼

Your girl was usually one that didn't roll out the bed until noon. Here I was up at nine in the morning on the couch with my phone waiting to call Capella. His ass was so mean like his father that it would take time to smooth things over and wiggle my way into his life.

"Kendra, why the fuck are you calling me this early in the morning?" he answered the phone, already with the mean shit.

I wanted to tell his ass this was the reason I dropped his ass off with family members, but I was trying to be a mama, so I took a quick breath. "Hey Capella, I wanted to see you today. Are you free for lunch?"

"For what?"

I hadn't been the mother that was involved at all, so I didn't even blame him for being skeptical for my call, and wanting to have lunch with him.

"We have to talk about something really important." It was time for me to tell him who his father was.

Hopefully, I was able to get to him before Cappadonna and I would be able to use him to talk to his father about me. Capp couldn't be that heartless to not care about the mother of his child, right?

"I got some shit to do today, so I'll let you know when I'm free."

"Please, Capella... give me a few minutes of your time. I promise not to hold you up," I pleaded with him.

I never thought I would be here begging my son to have lunch with me, but here we were. I was on this phone biting my nails that this little crumb snatcher that gave me stretch marks and tore me would give me a few minutes of his time.

"Text me where you want to meet," he replied, ending the

call in the process. I wasn't even hung up on the fact that he ended the call.

Long as he was willing to give me a chance and have a conversation with me, I was already in the game. Now all I needed to do was work my charm and hope that he wasn't so damn stubborn like his father.

Ace came out the room with his boxers on and his face greasy as hell. I could only assume he had just applied ointment to all the cuts on his face. If the cuts weren't enough, his ass had a black eye and busted lip, too.

"I get fucking pissed every time I look at my face in the mirror. That nigga sneaked me and think he gonna walk around like shit all good."

I wanted to object to the accusation that Capp sneaked him. Any smart man would have noticed the deranged look in his eyes, and the way he was almost too calm. Ace was too busy trying to prove himself that he missed all that, so of course he would think that Capp 'sneaked' him.

I sent Capella the address to my favorite Italian restaurant in Brooklyn. He sent me the thumbs up emoji and I rolled my eyes. Was it just me, or did you consider the thumbs up emoji rude. I even considered the thumbs up in real life fucking rude.

"Last night you tapped out on me." Ace came in my face to kiss me on the lips and I ducked him, climbing up from the couch.

I usually had to talk myself out of being delusional, but it was clear someone needed to do it for Ace, too. Where in the world was that considered me tapping out? "Yeah. I was tired."

"You excited to come meet my family. They been asking when I'm going to bring you around." Ace rubbed my ass, kissing me on the neck.

Couldn't he see I was mourning my relationship with Cappadonna? He was all over me, and I was over here fucked up without Cappadonna. The only reason I agreed to get drunk and pop ecstasy with him was because I needed to just let loose and forget.

When I started trying to pull him out his boxers, I was thinking of Cappadonna the entire time. He couldn't even let me imagine riding Capp because his ass couldn't keep it up for me.

"Oh damn. I forgot all about your sister's baby shower," I pretended like I really had forgotten and was sad about it. "I actually have to meet up with my nephew."

I wasn't about to tell this nigga that I had a son. "You can't meet him another time?"

I sighed, leaning on the counter. "His mom promised to give him money for college, and I told him that I would take him out to lunch, and then give him money." I pulled an excuse out of my ass because I didn't know what the hell I was saying.

Ace looked at me confused and then nodded like he understood. "Can you try to make it? My family want to meet my fiancée and they gonna start thinking a nigga lying," he joked, but I could tell he was serious.

I smiled. "I'll wrap it up quickly so I could swing by there. You made me leave everything that I know, so I'm going to need a car."

Ace didn't need to know that Capp tossed me out my condo and took everything away from me. All he needed to know is that I needed a new car, and he needed to come harder than he was in the past.

"You can take the BMW coupe... I'll look at getting you a new whip this week." He made his way over to me to touch me again.

Ace wasn't broke, and he had money coming in so he could afford to give me what I needed. He didn't have money like Capp, but he did pretty decent for himself. He made most of his money down in Delaware, Maryland and Virginia area. He was slowly trying to move his work here in New York.

I should have been smarter not to mess with his ass knowing that Capone and Cappadonna ruled New York. It would be hard for him to move into their territory and that would lead to beef. My stupid ass wasn't thinking of the day that Capp would actually be released. I was living in the now, and that was why I was staring at this nigga who thought I was in love with him.

"Thanks, babe." I kissed him and went to get ready for this lunch with Capella. I hope it went well and he didn't react like his father did.

For someone that was tossed out her home, I had to admit that I cleaned up pretty nice. My hair was blown out beautifully, and I had the top down on the BMW with my Prada sunglasses on. Capp was smoking crack if he thought I was leaving these behind.

Valet took the car and I strutted inside the restaurant, excited for their pesto pasta. I knew this was to tell Capella that his father was Capp, but I was excited for the meal, too. Maybe even a few glasses of wine to settle my nerves.

Capella texted me and told me that he was going to be a few minutes late. I was seated and ordered two glasses of their best white wine while I skimmed the menu. I needed to be a little loose when I told him the secret that I had been hiding from him.

As I sipped my wine, Capella swaggered right into the restaurant with his father's walk. It was something about the way those Delgato men walked. Capp had a slight bow leg that always turned me on whenever I saw his ass walking.

"What's up?" He sat down across from me, looking like he would rather be anywhere else but sitting across from me.

With the way he was seated, I knew I didn't have much

time with him before he was going to leave. "I ordered some starters for us to share... you want to order a drink?"

"I'm nineteen."

"As if you haven't had liquor, and you're about to be twenty soon. Relax and live a little," I waved the waiter over and ordered him a drink.

"Kendra, what the fuck is all of this about? You call me to come have lunch, for what? We don't never do shit like this."

I guzzled the rest of my wine down and stared at him. It was time to rip the bandage off and be honest with him. Hopefully, he understood what I was going through and respected the decisions I made for him.

"Cappadonna is your birth father," I revealed, taking a huge sigh of relief and leaning back in my chair.

Capella screwed his face up and looked at me like I was stupid. "You made me come all the way to fucking Brooklyn to tell me some shit that I already knew."

"What do you mean something that you already knew?"

"I already knew. Jasmine had more fucking balls and heart to tell me than my so called mother. What was this supposed to be? Some moment where we connected, cried and ate pasta to celebrate our new formed relationship as mother and son?"

Why were my feelings so hurt at the way he sarcastically replied, even laughing in the process. I did think we could come together and try to connect with each other since I was being honest with him. Instead, he made me feel all weak and low compared to my cousin Jasmine.

"Jasmine had no right to tell you."

"Shit, I'm glad that she did because you damn sure wasn't about to run your mouth to tell me. I get you not wanting to sit up and be a parent, you too selfish for all that... I get that part." He paused, staring me in the eyes. "What I don't understand is why you would rob me of the chance to get to know my father.

You stole that from me and didn't give me a chance to know my family. I have grandparents, an aunt, uncle, and cousins, and you took that away from me... What the fuck you thought this was going to be? That I was going to call you mom, and we would be good? You'll always be Kendra when it comes to me."

As much as Capella tried to play cool and nonchalant, the hurt in his eyes made my chest tight. He pushed out from the table, gave me a look like I was less than dirt, then walked away from the table. When I came up with this idea to have lunch, I didn't think I would end up feeling so low when it was all said and done.

∼

ACE WAS over the moon showing my hand with the ring he bought to his family. I smiled, while my conversation with Capella was in the back of my mind. I didn't expect to care as much as I did for the look on his face. Usually, I was able to brush things off and continue on with my life like nothing happened.

As I sat at the table listening to Ace shit talk with his cousins while playing Spades, I was miles away in my thoughts. I jumped when he slammed the card down onto the table, and everyone broke out into laughter.

"You handled that problem you were having with homie?" Zeke, his cousin, questioned, shuffling the cards to start a new game.

Ace was pissed with Cappadonna for doing what he did. It was all he ever spoke about, and I was tired of hearing it. Actually, I was turned off that he allowed this man to come slam his head into the damn table with such ease. I needed a nigga that could protect me and right now this nigga was on thin ice.

Cappadonna could come up in here and slam his ass into

the table again if he wanted. Ace looked at his cards with too much focus, and then looked over at me. "He mad because I took his bitch...I'm gonna get my get back though."

"Excuse you?" I snapped.

He was talking like I wasn't sitting right here and could hear his ass. "My bad, babe... he mad because I'm about to make her wifey."

Ace kissed me on the cheek and continued playing cards while I rolled my eyes. Instead of listening to them, I went to make me some food. I thought I would be able to have a big spread of food with Capella, but his ass didn't even stay ten minutes before he cussed me out and left.

"Hey, can you put some chicken on a plate for me?" I looked over at Aimee, Ace's sister. She was sitting in an extra ass throne chair looking miserable.

The empty chair next to her showed that her nigga was either in the party getting loose, or he didn't come. Nine times out of ten he was here, because why else would they torture the girl by putting the two chairs knowing he wouldn't come.

"Sure," I added some chicken onto the plate and handed it over to her.

The table was right near where she was seated, so it was no sweat off my back. "Thank you... are you enjoying the shower?"

I stepped back down and continued to fix my food. "It's beautiful... whoever planned it knew what they were doing," I lied.

This shit screamed gaudy royalty theme. "My mom did. She swore this was the theme since my son's name is King."

"I know that's right... royalty." I tried to quickly make my food to finish this conversation. I didn't even want to be here right now.

Ace was a fucking baby, so if I would have told him I wasn't coming then he would be all in his feelings. "Thank you for coming, though. Ace never brings anyone he's dealing with around, but I guess you're different because he's gonna marry you."

Little did she know, my ass wasn't walking down no damn aisle to his ass. I was playing my part until I could fix things with Cappadonna, and then I was as good as done with Ace. I couldn't shake the way he got his ass fucked up and then had the nerve to lie about someone sneakin' him.

"I wouldn't have missed it."

She was looking over at the corner of the room, and the Spades game had apparently turned into a game of fucking cee-lo. "Ugh, I told his ass not to even bring those dice." Aimee turned her nose up at her brother.

"Men don't listen to nobody unless they want some pussy."

She rolled her eyes. "Yeah, I know. I told my baby father that was a bad drop, and he went anyway, and now his ass sitting in Riker's Island waiting for a court date." I could tell he had her pissed all the way off.

"You got all the support you need with your brother. He's going to make sure that you're well taken care of."

Ace would do anything for his sister and his mother. That was one of the things I actually admired about him. After his father was sent to prison, he stepped up to make sure his mother and sister were taken care of. Aimee came to New York for school and then eventually decided to stay here. He always complained about how she wasted his damn money by not finishing school and then getting pregnant by a hood nigga.

She was raised around this life, so naturally that was what she was going to be attracted to. I watched my mother bring different men around and the vast majority of them were hustlers. When it came time for me to start looking, I was attracted to all the boys on my block that were selling drugs. It didn't matter how much he tried to keep her removed, she was going to find her way to a nigga that held a gun and sold work.

"Yeah, I guess." Her phone started ringing, so she quickly excused herself, and went to answer it.

I finished fixing my food and went over to the now empty table. Once I was done with my food, I was going to make an excuse to get the hell out of here.

18
ALAIA

Taz: **When I find you I'm going to break my foot off in your ass.**

Taz: **Bring yo' ass to the fucking apartment.**

Taz: **If I gotta come drag yo ass home it's gonna be ten times worse, lil' bitch!!!**

If the text messages weren't enough, he also called and left voicemails to go along with the text messages. It was hard trying to move forward when all he continued to do was send me text messages reminding me of what he would do to me if he got a hold of me. I was so uncomfortable that it was hard to sleep, and during the day I found myself lying in bed not knowing what to do with myself.

Cappadonna had made it where I didn't have to lift a finger or do anything. As he said, all I needed to do was relax and be pregnant. I couldn't relax because I had never relaxed in my entire life. I was always on go, doing something, or being someone for everyone else. It felt weird laying around and not doing anything.

"Baby girl, you sleep?" Capp softly asked from the door,

and I turned over and smiled at him. He was this rough and rugged man, but when he spoke to me, he was always so soft and gentle with me.

"Trying. My old phone keeps going off." I yawned, and sat up on the bed, a headache rushing to my head.

I felt like this baby was going to come early and I was scared. I've never been pregnant before, was I supposed to feel like this all the time? There were women who worked out and worked full jobs while being as pregnant as I was. Was something wrong with me because I felt this way?

Cappadonna abandoned the door and grabbed my old phone. He scrolled through the text messages and chuckled to himself. "Next time I'm gonna have to take my belt off and whip his little ass."

"Next time?"

"Don't worry about it," he kissed me on the cheek, and rubbed my stomach. "My son is coming over here today for dinner."

"You have kids?"

"A son." All of our interactions had always been about me and my fucked up ass life. I never asked if he had children. "I didn't find out about him until a few months ago. My ex-girlfriend lied to me about him, and it got back to me."

"That's horrible. Why did she hide it from you?"

He shrugged. "Who the fuck knows why Kendra's simple ass does anything. I know that her ass lucky she alive to speak about fucking me over."

"You have to co-parent with her, no matter how you feel about her," I tried to convince him, and he laughed.

"My son is nineteen, 'bout to be twenty. I don't have to speak to that bitch ever in life. She lucky she has the ability to talk, and I didn't cut her fucking tongue out."

"If he's coming over for dinner then I can make us something." I tried to stand up, and he parked my ass right back down.

"Look at me, and let this be the last time I have to repeat myself... ight?" he sternly replied, and I stared up into his eyes. "You are pregnant and in pain. I'm not that nigga that needs you to run around cooking and cleaning for me. Do I prefer my woman barefoot and pregnant? Hell yeah... I think it's the sexiest shit ever. I'm also the type that will keep her spoiled to the point where she *wants* to do those things. Being that you got the barefoot and pregnant down, you don't need to be cooking and cleaning."

"You want more kids?"

"Hell yeah. I want like six of them... I love kids."

I gulped, because six was a big number. "Oh."

He looked into my eyes. "I got something for you, though."

"What's that?"

He pulled me up and walked me out the room and down the hall to the master bathroom. When I walked in, there was a massage table and a black lady standing there. "I booked you a prenatal massage. Erin told me that it would help with a lot of the pain you're feeling."

"Thank you, Capp." I hugged him, and looked at the lady.

"While you relaxing and getting your massage, I got to head out for a couple hours. You good here alone?"

"Yes."

"The chef I hired should be coming, too. I gave her the code to the door, so don't be all scared when you hear her downstairs. Don't nobody get in this bitch or out of it without me knowing, alright?"

"Okay."

He hugged me and kissed me on the nose before leaving me to get my massage. I disrobed and got on the table, and allowed her to do her job. Just the touch of her hands on my swollen body felt amazing.

The smell of lavender made me feel so much better. I felt congested and couldn't catch my breath to save my life. As I lay here and had this woman perform a miracle, I smiled at Capp thinking about me and getting me a massage.

My pregnancy had been lonely. Being around him had made me not feel so lonely in this. I felt like I had the support I used to pray for. He made me feel like I mattered, a priority and not a burden. As she massaged my hips, and lower back, my eyes continued to flutter, until I had fallen asleep.

My hands trembled with blood on the finger tips as I sat on the edge of the tub. I used my hand free from blood to cover my mouth as I tried to withhold the sob that I wanted to release. I dry heaved as I looked at my bloodied hand.

The knocking on the other end of the door startled me, and I quickly washed my hands and continued to hide in the bathroom. How could my life have ended up like this? Why did Raheem have to send me away to hell? I lay awake at night listening to Fatima and Zayne having sex, crying because I never wanted to be in this situation. I should have been having fun with my friends, going to the mall and getting good grades. Instead, every other night I felt Zayne slide into the full sized bed and climbed between my legs. When I cried, he would slap me in the head and tell me to act like I enjoyed it.

"Open this damn door, lil' girl...your ass done pissed me the fuck off!" Ralph hollered through the door, scratching at the door like a blood hound.

My heart was beating out of my chest as I looked around the small bathroom with no window. I looked for a way out of this hell. Zayne and Fatima went away for her grandmother's funeral, and Ralph volunteered to watch me. Zayne didn't trust me to stay in the house alone, so Ralph was the next best thing. Anytime that Ralph came over, a sick feeling washed over me because I knew he was no good.

None of these men were any good. They were all sick and hid behind the Quran for their sick actions. I hated when bad people hid behind religion to make themselves seem good. There was nothing good about any of the people I had been around in the year I've been living in Fatima's house. I knew Ralph was a creep, but I never expected him to do what he had just done to me.

As I slept in his daughter's room, he climbed into bed and put his gun in my mouth. As he aggressively raped me, I cried and tried to fight but my body refused to move. I was watching myself from above and couldn't move a muscle. I felt liquid coming down my legs, as he continued while calling me the prettiest thing he's ever saw. I listened to him grunt and tell me how I was almost his. As if I was a pair of sneakers, or an object that you could just buy in the store. When he finally rolled over to catch his breath, I elbowed him and ran down the hall to the bathroom while he hollered. How could someone do something like that on their daughter's character sheets?

Ralph kicked the door open and grabbed me by my hair, he snatched his basketball shorts down...

"Alaia, baby... baby girl, it's me," Cappadonna said as he pulled me up and wrapped his arms around me.

My face was wet with tears and my arms were sore from swinging them around. The masseuse stood over near the shower scared as I cried into his arms. He held me tightly while kissing me on the shoulder, and rubbing my back.

"I'm sorry...I...I can't," I choked out, still in the moment. I couldn't shake off what he did to me.

I tried to bury it in the back of my head, and laying here relaxing triggered it to come back to me. It was easy not to relax because I didn't have time to think of everything that I had been through.

Capp still held onto me and turned toward the masseuse.

"Here... take this and I'll send more for the table and shit... just go ahead and dip," he told her, and she took the knot of money he placed in her hand, grabbed her bag and left the oils and massage table behind.

I held onto him, around his neck tightly while taking in his scent. He smelled like fresh laundry and the smell alone calmed me down as I tried to breathe. He held me tighter and kissed me a few times on my temple.

"I'm sorr...I'm sorry," I dry heaved as I looked at him. "I didn't mean to ruin this... or waste your money."

"I don't give a fuck about the money... I was about to leave and heard you up here screaming and dropped everything... shit scared me. Money is always going to come... you more important than that."

I nodded my head and held onto my chest because the flashback was so vivid that I could see his face when he was on top of me. How crazy he looked in the eyes as he assaulted me without a care in the world. Even after he finished with me in the bathroom, he had the nerve to kick past me and leave me on the floor.

"Do you mind if I come out with you to go wherever you going? I don't want to sit in the house alone."

He smiled. "I was going to figure out what a baby needs, so yeah, we can figure it out together." He helped me stand up. "Go put something on, and we can head out, probably stop at that diner you love so much."

"The food was gross, why are you playing?"

He laughed. "I'll take you to a better place."

"Okay."

"Aye. When you're ready to tell me, I'm all ears, baby." I could tell in his face that he wanted to know so he could make whoever pay.

Cappadonna didn't give a damn if I told him Thanos was

responsible, he was going to find him and make him pay for whatever he did. "Thank you."

We took the Bronco out, which seemed to be a bad idea because I had a hard time climbing up in it. All Capp had to do was lift me and put me in the seat and we were all good. I wasn't skinny before I got pregnant, so the fact that he lifted me up with ease just proved how strong he was.

The warm breeze kissed my face as we sped through the streets with the top down. Capp turned up the music and started singing to me. Conveniently "Joy" by Blackstreet was playing, and he sang as he looked over at me.

"That girl brings me joy," he sang, and rubbed my stomach while I laughed at how horrible he sounded.

I didn't even know this song, but he was singing it like he had listened to it a bunch of times. This was a welcomed change from how I felt in the bathroom. I needed something to take my mind away and this was the perfect distraction to it. It didn't hurt that the man beside me was so beautiful to look at.

We pulled into the parking lot of the store, and he killed the engine, not bothering to put his top back on to his truck. "You not going to put it back on?"

"Only somebody stupid would try and touch my whip. You ready to grab the baby something other than onesies?" he clowned me.

Every time he brought up something that babies needed, I always brought up the onesies that I bought in Target. "Ha, really funny."

Capp held the small of my back as I pushed the shopping cart in the store. We headed straight for the children's section and I fell in love with all the pinks and purples for little girls. I loved my baby, and over the past nine months, I had grown a bond with her that I never thought I would.

This was the first time that I had gotten excited about

shopping for her. All the clothes I left at that apartment was stuff I picked up because I had a little extra money after grocery shopping or saw it for a cheaper price. As I picked up the pink linen baby doll dress, I imagined her in it. Kicking her feet and sucking on her fingers while looking up at me, her mommy.

"Damn, Joy. We just started and you already crying," Capp wiped my eyes as he looked at the dress.

"It's so little... look at it," I held it up to him, and he smiled as he held it.

In my hands it looked like a regular baby's dress, in his hands, it looked like it could fit a doll. "This shit is cute... get it in every size so she can always have one."

"We only need one." I grabbed a zero to three months size and put it in the cart, as I continued to look at the different things that I would need.

I've never done this before, so I didn't know what I needed. What did a baby need when they were born? Capp tossed things in the cart that I wasn't sure we would even need. We were both clueless about what we needed. When we got to the strollers, I looked at each one, pushing it to see which one I liked.

"That little shit fire... let me see how I look pushing it." Capp took over, and even with the handle extended, he was still too damn tall for it.

I grew excited when he was interested in seeing how the stroller fit his needs, and it also made me nervous. What if this was all too much for him. A baby was easy when it was inside, but when it was born, what happened then?

"You don't have to do that," I blurted out, before I could stop myself from saying it out loud.

He turned and looked at me. "Not this shit again, Joy."

"I can't help it, Cappadonna. I'm sorry, this is who I am.

I'm somebody that has a hard time trusting someone's word. I want to believe yours, so bad. My body is telling me to, but my mind keeps reminding me that I could trust no one. I know that I will be there for her... I can't depend on you to be there."

He pushed the stroller to the side and walked over toward me. "I can sit here and try to convince you until I'm blue in the face. I'm not doing that because I know where I'm going to be... I'm going to be here helping you. The fuck you think I came and got you for? To add onto the long list of fucking disappointments you experienced. I'm here, ba—"

Both of our heads snapped in the direction of the floor where water flooded from between my legs onto his sneakers, and my sandals. I held my stomach and looked at Cappadonna who was still in shock.

"Baby, please don't tell me that was your water breaking."

I looked down and then back up at him. "My water just broke."

I always imagined when your water broke that you would start screaming in pain because the baby was coming. Even though I was nervous and my shaking hand was evident of that, I calmly walked through the puddle. All day I felt this incredible amount of pressure down there and couldn't figure out what it was, or if I should have been worried.

"That mean the baby coming, right?"

"I'm pretty sure that's what it means," I laughed, as he grabbed hold of my hand and pulled me next to him.

"Shit...alright," a million thoughts were going through his mind at the same time and I touched his arm. "Fuck, you alright?"

"We need to go to the hospital. I can walk, and I am fine," I let him know.

A lady walking by noticed what was going on. "Do you need me to call the ambulance?"

I hated to be put on the spot and I was fine enough to make the drive to the nearest hospital. "I am alright... thank you. He's going to drive me there."

Cappadonna looped his hand into mine and we headed toward the exit while he was on the phone. "Calm down, Dad... everything will be alright," she called behind us, and Capp turned and smiled at her.

When I heard her refer to him as Dad, it made my heart swell. Although he wasn't her father, it was nice to not be alone like I had feared. He was on the phone with his mother, and that was when I got worried.

"Yeah... Lennox Memorial is the closest one to us right now." He pulled the phone away from his ear. "Baby, you ain't in pain?"

"Not yet," I replied, as he lifted me up into the car while still holding a conversation. "Is that your mom?"

"Yeah... she gonna meet us there with Erin."

"Oh, no... she doesn't have to do tha—"

"Alright, Ma... see you in a little bit. Drive safe... love you," he said and ended the call, backing out the parking spot.

"Your mom doesn't have to come up there, Capp."

It was funny seeing him nervous. "In this family, we show up for everybody. I don't want you to feel like you have to have me in the room."

I touched his arm. "No, I want you in the room with me. I don't mind."

He took my hand and kissed it. "You about to become a mother, Joy."

I smiled, starting to feel those same nerves he was experiencing moments before. As he held my hand and I tried to do my breathing exercises, I was preparing to step in one of the biggest roles I would ever have.

By the time we pulled up to the hospital's valet, I was nearly screaming because I felt like somebody was trying to rip out of my body. Cappadonna abandoned all the nerves and stepped into protective mode. The whole ride to the hospital, he was trying to talk me through it, and not in the good way.

They rushed me to labor and delivery while he followed behind us. I was put in a room where they checked me, and I was five centimeters dilated. After an hour, they allowed me to get an epidural and I felt good as a bitch. The pain didn't matter anymore as I watched Capp pacing in the room.

I should have known that nothing ever goes as planned when it comes to me. We had been at the hospital for over eight hours now and I hadn't moved from five centimeters. The nurses and doctor kept talking to each other, then called Capp out the room to talk to him. When he came back into the room, I could tell he didn't want to tell me what he had to tell me.

They told him that I needed a C-section because I wasn't dilating fast enough, and they needed to get the baby out. I begged them to wait another hour to see if I moved, and they agreed. When she checked me again, I was still in the same place, and it was time for me to do it their way. I watched them move around the room, preparing my bed to be transported to surgery.

"I don't want to go alone... please. I can't have this baby all alone," I held onto the nurse's arm while she took the brake off the bed.

She started to push me out the room and I wanted to scream. "Aye, wait a fucking minute. You see she fucking scared and you pushing her out the room." Capp was on the phone, and walked over toward me. "I promise I'm going to be in the room with you, Alaia... I wouldn't let you go through this alone, alright."

"Al...alright." I shivered.

It was funny because I wasn't even cold, but I couldn't stop shivering. "Give me kiss."

I kissed his lips and held his hands as they pushed me out of the room. Everything was a blur as they got me down to the operating room and transferred me onto the operating table. It was so bright and cold.

When everything was prepared, this huge sheet was put in front of me, and I couldn't see anything. How was I supposed to see my baby being born? My arms were on single tables of their own, I felt like I was Jesus on the cross or something.

"We're bringing your husband in now," another nurse told me, and smiled, as she went to the door.

Capp entered the room and sat on the stool next to me. He kept kissing my forehead. "You're going to be alright... you strong. We gonna have this baby and then I'm gonna bring you food from your favorite diner."

"That... isn't ... my favorite," I smiled through the shivers, and he kissed my forehead again.

When I got undressed, he was right there to help me, asking for a surgical bonnet so I could take my hijab off. How did I get so lucky to have met such a man like him. The doctor spoke and I felt a shit ton of pressure.

It felt like someone was pulling my stomach down and standing on it. The pressure felt unbearable almost, but Capp kept his lips on my forehead as we listened to the doctor talk about what he was doing.

"You... gonna... think... I'm gross with a big cut." Why my mind was on what Capp would think with a huge C-section was beyond me.

He laughed and kissed my forehead, before getting closer

to my ear. "I'm trying to swap spit with you for the long haul, Joy. I ain't worried about a scar."

I smiled as I closed my eyes. When I heard crying, my eyes popped open and the doctor held my daughter over the sheet for us both to see. "She's here," I whispered, too tired.

"She's beautiful... look at that hair." I expected him to go over toward the baby, but he stayed with me and continued to kiss my forehead.

"We're going to bring baby up to the NICU...Dad, would you like to come with us?"

Capp remained seated. "Go with her... I'm going to be alright."

"Once we close her up, she will be in recovery."

He kissed me on the lips before going with the other nurse who pushed the baby out the room in an incubator. She was early, but not nearly enough where it was considered dangerous. I closed my eyes counting down the minutes until I was able to see her fully and hold her.

I felt lightheaded, and my head turned slowly when I heard the machine I was hooked up to beeping. "She's hemorrhaging!" was all I heard before my eyes flickered and it went dark.

19

CAPPADONNA

Her little hand was wrapped around my finger as I looked at her through the incubator. She was beautiful, with the same kind brown eyes that her mother had. Her chubby cheeks, pink lips and curly black hair showed me that Alaia had given birth to her twin.

It was crazy because she wasn't my daughter, but I felt like a proud father in this NICU. All the nurses continued to call me Dad, and I never corrected them. When I made that promise to her mother, it trickled down to her and I would forever protect her like she was my own.

Fuck that.

She was my own, and I would do whatever that was needed to always make sure she and her mother were protected and loved. The nurse from the operating room came upstairs and from the look on her face I could tell something was wrong.

"Mom is hemorrhaging, the doctor is doing everything to stop the bleeding. I wanted to come up here to tell—"

I ain't heard shit she said since she said, "Mom is hemorrhaging." I rushed out of the NICU back down to the operating room to my baby. She ran behind me. "Wait... you can't go in... one second." She was trying hard to catch her breath.

Her ass was lucky that I had to wait for the elevator. "I need to be in there with her. She doesn't want to be alone."

"We cannot allow you back in there right now. I promise I will keep you updated. You can wait up here, or if you have family in the waiting room you can wait there." She reached up and placed her hand on my shoulder. "I will let you know what happens, I promise."

My fucking heart was beating out of my chest thinking of her being all alone in that room. Yeah, the doctors and shit were in there, but she was alone. She didn't have me with her and that shit worried me.

I was too damn nervous to go back into the NICU, so I went downstairs to the waiting room. My mom texted that they had gotten there, but I didn't have my phone with me until I left the operating room.

When the elevator doors opened, I saw my mother, Erin and Capone sitting in the waiting area. My mom got up from her chair and stopped when she saw my face.

"Is everything alright?" Erin beat my mother over toward me and waited for me to respond. My fucking chest hurt thinking of all the things that could be wrong.

"Yo, come 'ere," Capone came over and pulled me into him, and I hugged my brother. I was strong about a lot of things, but if they came out here and told me that Alaia didn't make it, I was going to lose my shit. "Nigga, she strong as shit... you think she going out like this? Come the fuck on... you smarter than that," he continued to talk to me while we hugged.

My mother and Erin stood to the side and allowed Capone to console me. Tears welled in my eyes when I remembered how Alaia looked at me and wanted me in the room with her. I felt like I was letting her down by being down here.

"They said she fucking hemorrhaging... she could die, Capo."

"She's not, though. Don't even speak that... how's the baby? Beautiful, right?"

He let me go and I sniffled, wiping my eyes. "Mad beautiful. Looks like her mother."

My mom came over and hugged me, while Erin held onto her husband. "I know it is hard to do because you're worried. Pray, Cappadonna. Go on and pray for her and the baby."

My mother was Christian, but prayer was universal. We were all praying up to a higher power. "I hear you, Ma."

Other than Capone and Erin, I hadn't told anybody about Alaia. All I had to do was call my mother and she dropped everything to be there for me. "Parking is ridiculous."

We turned and saw my father walking toward us. He stopped when he saw my face and tapped right into pops mode. He pulled me into a hug and rubbed my back, not knowing what was going on.

"Breathe... I can see in your eyes you haven't taken a breath. Remember all that good shit we spoke about that would happen when you got out?"

"Yeah," I replied, not understanding where he was going to go with this. None of this was even remotely fucking good.

"Even the good things have a struggle at first... that's how you really know it's good." He kissed me on the cheek. "Alright?"

Kincaid: They hit the trap in Astoria.

Me and Capone locked eyes with each other, and he nodded his head. "Worry about Alaia... I got it."

Erin grabbed her husband's arms and looked up into his

eyes. "You come home to us, Capone." She closed her eyes before she finished speaking. "Please be careful."

He kissed her lips a few times. "I got you."

I watched as he headed toward the exit and felt guilty for being here. "I'm about to go with hi—"

"You stay here. Cappadonna, you care about this girl?"

"Yeah, Ma."

"She has a baby, so that means being with her is accepting her child and that makes them your family." My moms was saying a bunch of shit when all I wanted to do was fuck some shit up.

"Jean get to the point." My father felt the same way as I did.

"She's saying that this is the part of the game that your brother has experienced, and you haven't. If she and the baby are your family, there is going to be a time when you have to choose. Your brother has had to choose, and now it's your turn to choose them… you could handle that when you know they are good," Erin explained.

I hugged her and agreed with her. Alaia and the baby needed me, so I needed to be here. Soon as I knew they were good; I was going to rip a nigga's head off his shoulders.

The doctor politely tried to tap me to wake me up, but I was already awake. "I'm up."

"Oh, shit," she cursed, as I leaned up.

I had my hat over my eyes, but I was watching everything and waiting for them. Erin was asleep beside me while my parents went home to be with CJ and Cee-cee. Nudging Erin, she stirred out of her sleep and sat up once she noticed the doctor in front of us.

"Is she alright?" She held her chest, waiting for the doctor to let us know what was going on with my baby.

The doctor took a seat across from us. "She is being moved to recovery, and from there she will go to the intensive care unit. For the good news, she is alive and came out of surgery fine... we're just waiting for her to wake up."

"There's bad news?" Erin beat me to the punch.

She looked away and took a deep breath. "We had to perform an emergency hysterectomy."

Erin gasped so loud I thought her damn teeth was about to fly out her mouth. "Oh God... no."

"What...what the fuck does that mean?"

"We had to remove her uterus. She won't be able to naturally have any children in the future. It was our last option, and the one that saved her life. I've been through this a few times with patients and I always advise to wait to tell them. Let them recover, and then let them know."

"Lie to her?" Erin shrieked, tears pouring down her face. "She's too young, there was nothing else that you could have done?"

I leaned back, fucked up by the news that I had been told. If that shit had me fucked up, could you imagine how Alaia would feel when she found out. "Fuck."

"I take no pleasure in taking a woman's ability to carry life. Especially being that she's only twenty-six years old. I hate to give you this news, but she's here and alive because of us removing it."

"I'm not blaming you. I just... I feel for her."

"How is the baby?"

"The baby is doing well. She was only thirty-eight weeks, so she isn't too premature. We will keep her in the NICU overnight and go from there."

"When can I see her?"

The doctor stood up. "I can bring you to her recovery room. You both can come," she waved for us to follow her.

When I walked into the room, she was still asleep. The IV machine and everything was hooked up to her. I walked around the bed and softly kissed her lips, taking in every part of her. Erin stood at the foot of the bed looking at me and her.

"You really care about her. From the moment you first met her," she whispered, while trying to avoid crying. "Cappadonna, you love this girl."

I didn't reply, I continued to kiss her forehead and smell the fruity shampoo she used through the surgical cap. My heart ached when I thought about having to tell her that she could never have any more kids – my kids.

Kissing her once more, I walked out the room because I needed to breathe. Erin followed behind me, and we went to sit in the small waiting area near the nurse station.

"How much is enough? Why the fuck does she have to go through all of this? Damn... she ain't been through fucking enough?"

"I know. I hate the whole God gives his toughest soldiers speech." She rubbed my back, as I leaned forward with my head in my hands. "Is that something that you can accept, Capp? I know you want children. I remember when me and you had that conversation about you wanting your wife barefoot and pregnant. That's not a possibility anymore for her, is that something that you can deal with?"

Erin wasn't just a sister-in-law for me, she was my sister for real. I remember when I called her, and she was on bed rest by Capone. We talked about my future and when I came home. She told me how she needed to find me a wife, and I joked that as long as she was cool with having a lot of my babies, we were cool.

"My chance to be a father was robbed from me once. I feel like that shit is being stolen right in my fucking face."

"Not necessarily. There is a baby girl that is down the hall that needs a father. It doesn't matter if you're her biological father or not. Alaia didn't have the best start at life, don't let the same happen to that little girl."

I listened to her while looking down at my sneakers.

My son: Heading to Astoria now... Nah got hit.
Me: Be careful.
My son: I got you.

My hands were shaking while I put my phone away and walked down the hall to the NICU. Erin didn't ask any questions, she walked into Alaia's room.

20
ACE

THAT NIGGA THOUGHT I was going to sit back after he fucking embarrassed me the way he did. He fucking had me trending on social media, and I was supposed to let that slide. If I let that slide, then everybody was going to think I was fucking soft.

Cappadonna thought his ass was untouchable until I touched something that was his. He thought he would just put hands on me and I would run my ass back to Delaware with my tail tucked between my legs. I wasn't built like that, and I needed to let him know he wasn't fucking with some soft nigga that just allowed shit to happen to him.

It was hard finding shit out about him because his team kept shit under a lock and key. Niggas usually ran they mouths, so it was always easy to find some shit out. Not the niggas that ran with Cappadonna and Capone. They kept they mouth shut, and nobody knew shit unless you were within the inner circle.

It took me a little minute, but I found one of his little niggas and thought he would run his mouth. That little bitch looked at me like I was crazy and kept it pushing. Instead of pushing him to the side, I continued to follow him, and I admit he moved smarter. He never went the same route, and made sure he checked his surroundings. A few times I had to abandon the damn mission because he got suspicious and was driving like he was being tailed.

All it took was a few drinks at the bar, and this nigga wasn't so hypervigilant. I followed him to a house in Astoria where he switched shifts with another nigga. He was so busy on the phone with some chick that he didn't notice me parked across the street. I staked that shit out for a few days before I learned the ins and out of how they switched and maneuvered.

Me and gang waited for the right moment before we ran up in that bitch. They were so caught off guard that they wasn't expecting that shit. I'm not going to front, for them to be caught off guard, they came with their A game, but ours was quicker. I shot one nigga, and he fell over the couch holding his arm, but still letting his shit go.

Gang was in and out with work in under ten minutes, and none of us were hit. I jumped in the whip and sped all the way back to Brooklyn, never stopping. It was less about taking their work, but more on letting him know that I can be on his type of time, too.

"Chinese food again?" I complained when I came in the house, and Kendra was on the couch with her best friend.

"What you complaining about? This food not even for you," she rolled her eyes and turned up whatever show they were watching.

I've always said I wanted to date an older bitch because I knew the pussy was fire and they could throw down in the kitchen. A older chick made time to throw down in the kitchen, dress they ass off, and keep the crib clean.

Not Kendra's ass.

She wasn't dirty, her ass just didn't like to clean. Every

week she was asking when the housekeeper was coming. Bitch, you the damn housekeeper, I wasn't about to hire one. Why the fuck did she think I put a ring on her damn finger.

Cappadonna had her ass kept to the point she didn't have to lift a finger. The Delgato twins name rang big fucking bells. Everybody heard of them, even Capp and he was locked up at the time. Did I get a thrill knowing I was fucking this nigga's bitch while he was sharing a cell with another man?

Fuck yeah.

After the way that nigga slammed my fucking face into my plate, I had a fucking concussion. Even after all of that, Kendra still chose me over him and that took away the sting. He thought coming into that restaurant and forcing her to leave was going to keep her with him. My baby chose me, and what we built over the bullshit that they had.

Kendra wasn't that bad, and the reason I wanted to marry her was because of her sacrifice. When money was tight for me, she stepped in and was breaking me off with money. She always had money, and when I needed it she never had a problem handing it over to me.

"Sassy feels like you don't like her," Kendra complained as she did her skincare routine. I would never understand why the fuck she needed to put all that stuff on her face before bed. She always complained that she needed to stay young looking.

Kendra was thirty-six and could still compete with the bitches around my age. When she told me her age, I was fucking shocked that she was even interested in me. From the way she carried herself, you could tell someone was keeping her kept, so I was intimidated.

I dried off from my shower and looked at her as she put some drops in her hand and massaged it into her face. "I don't even be paying Sassy's ass any mind."

"You could say hey and act like you like her or something," she sucked her teeth, looking at me through the mirror.

Sassy didn't like me, and Kendra knew that shit. I don't know how many under breath comments the bitch had to make for her to see that she didn't fuck with me. I was cool with that because I didn't fuck with her ass either. I believed she held onto their friendship because she wanted to be Kendra and live vicariously through her.

"The bitch sitting in my living room and I gotta be the one to talk to her?"

Kendra sighed, washing her hands before tying the silk robe around her body. I followed her into the bedroom, and she pulled the blankets back. "If you can't get along with my friend, then I don't know if I could get married to you."

I was flabbergasted by the bullshit she was trying to start tonight. After a long day, I wanted to shower and get some pussy, and here she was starting some shit because of Sassy's ass. What the fuck did Sassy have to do with us in the first place?

"You fucking with me, right?"

She folded her arms as she stared me down. "Dead serious. Sassy is family, and if you can't fix things with her, then I don't know if I can be your wife." With that, she turned over in the bed and pulled the covers over her.

Here I thought I would get some pussy and instead all I got was a fucking attitude. I went back into the bathroom to take care of myself before climbing into the bed next to her. At times, I felt like Kendra made shit up to avoid marrying me. I asked her hella times to go away and lets just get married.

We didn't need a big ass wedding, anyway. From what she claimed, she wasn't all that close with her family anyway. Why the hell we needed to have some big drawn-out wedding that neither of us cared to have?

As I dozed off, my phone buzzed with a text message.

Zeke: We might have fucked up. Both them crazy muthafuckas gonna be tearing shit up now.

Me: I ain't scared. Fuck them.

Zeke: yeah. One was enough but both? Bugged. Get up with u tomorrow.

Me: bet.

Zeke scary ass was acting like we couldn't handle them. I yawned, rolling over and trying to put my arm around Kendra. She shoved me away from her and mumbled something before I ended up rolling over and going to sleep.

21
ALAIA

When I opened my eyes, I winced from the bright sun and the pain that I felt. Last thing I remembered was having a C-section and my daughter being shown over a sheet. I could still feel Cappadonna's lips on my forehead as he talked softly to me, encouraging me that I was strong. I moved my arms and saw the IV still attached with other things connected to it.

I had never had a C-section before, so I didn't know you were supposed to be knocked out after. Leaning up, I cleared my throat and looked around the room. Cappadonna was balled up on the small pull out couch in the corner.

Where was the bassinet and where was my baby at? He didn't look comfortable, but he seemed to be resting peacefully. He didn't understand how much I appreciated everything he had done for me. I don't think I would have been able to get through this without him. Reaching up, I touched my head and felt a silk bonnet instead of the surgical one I had worn going into surgery.

I made sure not to tangle my IV's as I slowly tried to get out the bed. The pain was unbearable, but I wanted to see my baby. "Shit," I muttered when I finally got to the edge of the bed.

When Zayne's other wife had a baby, she had a C-section. Fatima was talking big shit about how she took the easy way out, and she had all her kids natural. I didn't have an opinion on the matter, nor cared. Now, as I sat on the edge of the bed, birth in general was hard. However, being sliced up and a baby ripped out of you wasn't the easy way.

"Joy?" I heard Capp's raspy voice as he stirred from his uncomfortable position. After his eyes adjusted, he quickly got up and came over to where my feet were now dangling on the edge of the bed. "You up... why the fuck... fuck it... you up," he took my face in his hands and kissed me on the lips.

The kiss was so passionate that if I wasn't already sitting my knees would have been weak. "Where is the baby?" I held onto his forearm, desperate to see my baby.

I wanted to meet the little goblin that I had to be cut open for. "She's in the nursery. They moved her from the NICU yesterday."

"Yesterday? How long have I been out from surgery?"

The look on his face told me that everything wasn't all good. I hadn't known him long, and I could already read his facial expressions to know how he was feeling. "You've been out for three days."

I held my chest. "Is that normal for C-sections?"

He sat down beside me and took my hand into his. "You had some complications during the C-section, and you were hemorrhaging. They tried their best to stop it, and they couldn't."

"Capp, what are you saying? The baby didn't make it"

He kissed my hands. "She made it, and she's beautiful, Joy."

"Then what are you *not* telling me?" My chest felt like

someone was in there beating a drum, and I couldn't take it anymore.

"They had to give you a hysterectomy, baby." He stared into my eyes, pain evident within his eyes.

You would have thought it happened to him with how he looked. I knew what a hysterectomy was, and I felt lightheaded knowing that they had given me one. I wouldn't be able to have any more children.

"Can...Can I see the baby?"

The doctor softly knocked on the door just as I asked to see the baby. She came in and had this gentle smile on, unsure on how she should proceed. "She knows," Capp told her.

"I thought we agre—"

"We didn't agree on shit. I told you to let me handle my girl, and I told her the truth. I don't lie to her, and I damn sure wasn't about to start now. She needed to know."

The doctor remained quiet and agreed silently. She went on to check my vital signs, my incisions, and asked me a bunch of questions. "Can I see the baby?" I stressed again.

"I will have the nurse bring her in. While you're waiting, I want you to walk to the other end of the hallway. We need to get you up and walking to avoid blood clots."

Cappadonna stood up and lowered the bed until my feet were on the floor. He held my hands as I stood up, wincing in pain. I wanted to run out this room and down the hall so I could see my baby. The way this pain was, I could barely make it out of the damn room because I was in pain with every step that I took.

I held onto Capp as we walked slowly out the room and down the hall. He slowed his pace and took his time while I clung onto him. "Talk to me, baby."

My heart always did a leap hearing him call me *baby*. It was a feeling that I couldn't explain, but one that made me happy. I tried to increase my speed and he held onto me, slowing me down. "I need to make it down the hall and don't have all week."

He wanted to talk about how I felt, and I was feeling a lot of things right now. Although I didn't want my baby at first, I had grown to love her. Not that I had any plans to have any more kids, but it was different when the choice was taken away from me.

"Tell me what you feeling and then we can pick up the pace."

I looked at him with a half-smile. "Is that a promise you're making me?"

He chuckled. "Yeah."

I took a deep breath as I stopped in the middle of the hall. Capp continued to hold me as I looked up at him. "Can I have time to really think on how I feel? Like, I know how I feel, but there's so much I'm feeling at the same time. I guess I just need time to truly digest it."

He kissed me on the nose. "Take all the time you need. I want you to promise me one thing though."

"How you gonna exchange a promise with a promise?" He continued to look down into my eyes. "What is it?"

"That when you're ready to talk about it that you're gonna come to me."

"Okay."

Capp walked me down the hall where the nursery was. I was so excited that I was nearly running down the hall to the huge window filled with babies. When we finally made it, he stood behind me holding me while I scanned the row of babies looking for my last name.

When my eyes landed on the bassinet, I stood there looking at her name tag. In the nursery, everyone knew her as Baby Delgato. I felt Capp's cool breath in my ear, as the hair on my neck stood at the same time.

"You fucked up by allowing me to witness her being born, Joy. When they asked me to fill out her papers, I went back and forth on what felt right to me." He wrapped his arms around me and kissed my neck. "When they told me you were having complications, I ain't never been that scared in my life. My only thought was to pray for you and make sure that little girl would always be taken care of. The only way I can assure her of that is for her to have my last name."

"A...are you sure? That means you would be respon—"

"I would be her father," he cut me off. "Alaia, when I ran into you walking to the laundromat, I don't take that shit as some coincidence. We were supposed to fucking meet that day. I've thought about you ever since the first time I saw you. Knowing that I could have almost lost you had me fucked up. I want you forever, and I'm taking responsibility for healing the heart that I had nothing to do with breaking." He continued to hold me as we looked out at the row of newborns.

"Why would you want to take on the responsibility of us? I can't ever have children again... that's not fair to you," tears slid down my face as I looked at my daughter.

He gently pulled me away from the window so we could have some privacy. I could see in his eyes that he was serious and meant every word that he had said to me. I wanted to reach up and touch his face.

God, this man made me feel things that I had never felt in my entire life. I've never felt so strongly about someone, and so safe. Cappadonna made me feel safe whenever he was near me, and even when he was away. I knew I could call, and he would rip up the road to make it to me. It was a feeling that I never thought I would ever experience.

"What's not fair to me is not having you, Alaia."

He kissed my lips, tasting my tears in the process. "You told me that you wanted at least six kids," I said, with our lips still connected and he pecked mine softly.

"Having six kids is cool, but having you is more important. Why do you think some fictional kids are more important than you and the baby?"

I reached up, careful not to choke him with the IV cords, and hugged him tightly. "Why does everything always happen to me?" I sobbed.

He softly kissed my ear. "I promise that I'm going to make up for all the bullshit you've went through."

I continued to hold onto him, smelling his signature scent. It made me feel comfortable whenever I smelled him. Even the bed smelled like him, and it helped me to sleep some nights since staying at the lake house with him.

"She's been nameless for three days."

He laughed. "Let me make you a promise."

I finally pulled away and looked at him before rolling my eyes. "You and these promises... what is it now?"

"I want to give you a real one that you can hold."

"What?"

"I want to name her Promise." He looked at me to see how I felt about it. "Because I promise to love that little girl with everything inside of me. I promise to never let her or her mother down, and I promise that nobody will ever hurt either of you even after the breath has left my body."

Why he decided to tell me this now knowing that I was still hormonal was beyond me. I broke down loudly sobbing as he pulled me into his arms. "I love that name."

He kissed my ear. "Don't ever fucking scare me like that again, Joy."

I giggled through the tears. "I promise I won't."

Capp kissed me on the lips and took my hand, walking me

back to the nursery window. He gently tapped on the window letting them know to bring her to the room.

"Promise Delgato," I whispered.

"Alaia Delgato has a ring to it, too." He kissed my hand as we slowly walked back to the room hand in hand.

∼

Jean was like the mother I never had. This was my first time meeting her, and she had gone out of her way to do any and everything to accommodate me and make me feel comfortable. Even things that I never asked for, but she did it because it was who she was.

Cappadonna told me that she had been here since I had delivered Promise. As she sat on the couch with her legs crossed feeding Promise, I could tell she was in her element. Since I had been out for the past three days, they started Promise on formula. Even when I tried to pump, there wasn't enough to feed her.

"She's so beautiful," Jean smiled, as she placed soft kisses on her head. "Finish that soup... I'll have to bring up another batch tomorrow."

I slowly sipped my soup. Jean made green papaya fish soup because she said it was good for postpartum and would help increase my breast supply. The soup was delicious, just too fishy for me.

"Is tomorrow's soup fishy, too?"

She pursed her lips and smiled. "I made Erin the same soup after she gave birth and kept her in the house for a whole month, aside from doctor appointments... soon as you are discharged, I plan to do the same. I'm going to come stay at the Lakehouse with you to help with the baby."

"Thank you, Mrs. Jean. I don't have any clue what to do when it comes to a baby."

I was smart enough to know that while I recovered, I would need all the help that I could get. "We take care of our own in this family, so you have nothing to worry about."

I smiled as she burped the baby, and I finished the soup. As I was about to lay back, Capp came through the door with flowers. The sight of him always made me excited and I couldn't help how fast my heart sped up for him.

He was dressed down in a pair of sweatpants, white T-shirt and sneakers. "Hey Ma."

I watched as he walked over to drop a kiss on his mother's head, and then kissed Promise. "Hey baby... everything alright?"

"Yeah. Erin should be on her way up here so we can go and get stuff for the baby." It was hard not to feel like a burden.

I had appeared in this man's life pregnant without even a shirt on my back. He turned his attention to me, and sat the roses on my lap, and then reached over and kissed me on the lips. Each time I tried to focus on the flowers, he wasn't done and gave me another kiss.

"Your breath fishy as hell, Joy."

I giggled. "It's the soup that your mother has me eating."

He gently grabbed my chin and kissed me a few more times. "How you feeling today?"

By the time I had woke up this morning Capp was already gone. I knew he would be coming back up, so I never stressed myself out. Whenever he left me, I found myself worried about him. I knew how Taz was, and even though he was quiet right now, I knew that would only last for so long.

"Tired and sore... I walked down the hall by myself this morning." I smiled up at him, as he continued to stare into my eyes.

I desperately wanted to see what Capp saw whenever he saw me. Whatever he saw, was the complete opposite of how I felt about myself.

"Bet you only walked down so you could tell them to bring Promise."

I smirked. "I can't help that I wanted to be with her."

He kissed my forehead and then went to wash his hands. Every time Capp went to hold Promise, it was funny because someone had to show us how to hold her. We both were like a fish out of water while trying to figure out how to hold her the correct way.

Jean put her into his arms, and he cradled her bouncing in place slowly. "What is this movement, Cappadonna?" She laughed.

"Don't they like motion and shit?"

"I guess." His mother shook her head, then came over to my side of the bed. She reached over and kissed my head. "I will see you tomorrow... get some sleep and let the nurses help you, okay?"

Since I've been awake, I wanted to do all her feedings and have her in the room with me all the time. Capp was the one to convince me to let them take her at night so that I could get some rest.

"Call me when you make it to the house."

She touched her son's face and looked at Promise. "Okay. I need to get the house together for you both to come home."

It was the way she said *home* that made me feel so warm on the inside. Was this truly happening to me, or was I dreaming? Jean was staying at the lake house with us for a month to help me get adjusted. Cappadonna didn't realize how lucky he was to have parents that loved him that much. His mother didn't ask questions or even question his decision about me. She jumped into mom mode and made sure that I felt taken care of.

He softly kissed Promise's forehead as he did his weird bounce move around the room. I relaxed a bit and watched them in their zone. He continued to kiss her as he swayed around the room. I could already see that she would have him wrapped around her little finger. As he looked into her eyes, I could see there was nothing he wouldn't do for her.

"I think I love you, Cappadonna," I whispered.

Love wasn't something that I was familiar with. If you asked me if I hated someone, I could tell you without hesitation. Love was one of those feelings that was foreign to me and had been for a long time.

He raised his eyebrow and looked at me. "How you know?"

I wasn't expecting his response. Hell, I thought we would have one of those moments where we both said it and then fell into a deep kiss. He was still holding the baby as he watched me, waiting for my response.

"Never mind," I faked a yawn so I could pretend to go to sleep, and act like this embarrassing moment never happened.

"Nah. Don't try and pretend to be sleepy."

"I am sleepy," I argued.

"You opened this door, Alaia... we gonna talk about it." He sat on the edge of the bed, and continued to stare at me.

His stare was so damn intense that it naturally made you nervous. "The only example of love I have ever experienced was with my yaya. Whenever I'm with you, I feel that way about you, too. Like how I felt about my yaya, but it's different when it comes to you. I want you around all the time. Whenever you're not around me, I become anxious and think about you. You make me feel safe, whole, Capp. You make me feel seen, like a woman and I hadn't felt like that ever. My body does things for you that it has never done before."

He licked his lips as he took all of me in, while tears fell down my face. "I don't think. I know I love you. I loved you before I even knew you, Joy. I shook it off because the shit sounded crazy. The thought that I could have lost you solidified my feelings for you. All I kept thinking about was the chances I could have told you."

I touched his arm. "Your actions have shown me that. I don't think words were needed because I could feel how you felt about me. You saved me, Cappadonna." I rubbed my baby's soft curls. "Saved us."

He switched where he was sitting so he was next to me. I closed my eyes as he placed those same soft kisses that he did on Promise onto me. I inhaled his scent, and never wanted this moment to end. I always wanted to be beside him, and never wanted to be without him – ever.

22
CHUBS

"You don't know how to call and let me know that you were fucking shot?" Capri stormed into the kitchen, and slapped Naheim in the back of his head. "Where the hell is the baby? The nanny hasn't picked her phone up once to tell me anything... are you alright?"

Capri was hella late with finding everything out because she was away for her college friend's wedding. I guess she must have found out as soon as she landed because she still had her luggage with her.

"Chill out, Muf...Capri... the shit grazed me," Naheim quickly corrected himself. "I'm always going to be good."

Capri was examining him like she would have been able to remove a bullet if he had one. I found it funny because this was my aunt, and she had no idea that I was even her nephew. Capri wasn't that much older than me herself.

"Naheim, you can't..." she choked. "I can't go through that again. You nearly lost your life before... this isn't something to joke about."

Cappadonna came from Capone's office and looked at his

sister and Naheim going back and forth. "You would think you would argue less now that you're not married. The fuck we arguing about today?"

"Why didn't anyone tell me that he was shot? I had to hear it from Erin when she let it slip... don't you go call her a big mouth either." She waved her finger up in her brother's face.

Capp came over to me, squeezed my shoulders. "You straight?"

"No doubt."

"He's a grown ass man, Baby Doll. If he didn't want to tell you, the fuck you wanted us to do?" Capp shrugged, as he finished his water.

"Where's my baby at?" she snapped. "Since his father wanna play bang bang shoot 'em up." She stalked out the kitchen.

"Stop fronting like you don't be playing bang bang shoot 'em up... he upstairs with Jo!" Naheim called behind her, tickled that his ex-wife was so bothered he didn't tell her that he was shot.

"Why don't y'all kiss and make the fuck up already," Capone swaggered into the kitchen. He was dressed down in a pair of sweat shorts.

"This one told me that I'm being delusional...my baby know she misses me." Naheim snorted.

Capp looked at his brother. "You good? Erin told me you were in pain last night...don't fucking lie either."

"Nigga, let me get the fucking words out before you accuse me of lying... damn. I'm straight." He looked at his brother, then leaned on the counter. "When you gonna tell Mom and Pops about Chubs here being a Delgato."

"Shit, Capri don't even know," Naheim added.

I looked at Capone. "You knew?"

"That's my twin... I know everything he know." Capone chuckled.

"I don't know yet. I need to sit them down and have that one on one... they gonna be fucking hurt. Kendra hid this shit." Capp's phone interrupted him and he answered it. "What's going on, baby girl? Yeah... me and Erin going to handle that today... yeah... I got you... alright."

When he ended the call, Capone and Naheim laughed. "Shorty got you down bad. I asked you to bring me formula and you hung up on me."

"Cause I'm not your fucking baby daddy... the fuck. You asked me like I was five minutes from the crib. I was all the way in fucking Jersey... let the shit go."

"You got a lot to tell Mom and Pops. Two grandchildren at one time... one damn near grown."

"Not damn near... I'm grown," I laughed.

"You and Jaiden keep thinking that." Capone laughed as Erin came downstairs and slammed her purse down on the counter. "Damn, Gorgeous, you 'bout to make me...."

She shoved her finger to his lips. "Don't you start. You the reason I've had Capp waiting... ready whenever you are, Capp."

Capone pulled his wife over toward him. "Let me talk to you real quick."

"Two grandkids... why the fuck are we bypassing that?" Naheim stared at all of us confused as hell.

"Capp put his name on the baby's birth certificate." Erin filled him in, while trying not to be pulled into the hallway by Capone.

"The hell?"

"Don't gotta understand it but respect it. I held her and couldn't see myself ever letting her down. I already let down one kid."

"Yo Capp, stop saying that. You didn't let me down," I

stepped in, because I refused for him to feel like he let me down. "It's not your fault or burden to carry."

No matter how much I said it, I knew he would always feel like that. Capp was used to being there for his family, even with him being locked up. He was hours away and in prison, and still managed to be a vital part of the family.

"Honestly, you need to go kick that bitch neck in for doing some shit like that," Naheim added.

"Her reason was very selfish. It's not even a good reason to forgive her." Erin shrugged, still holding onto the wall so Capone didn't bring her down the hall.

"Oh shit... I need my medicine," Capone faked, and Erin looked him up and down. "Come with me, Gorgeous."

"Winston, don't piss me off. We need to get everything that we need for Promise."

Capri came back downstairs with NJ, as she shot daggers at Naheim from across the kitchen. "You kind of ate with that name... I can't wait to come see my new niece and meet Alaia."

"She's so sweet, Capri. You're going to really like her," Erin told her.

"Why the hell do you keep looking at me like that?" Naheim blurted.

I peeped Capri giving him this look while holding the baby. "Because you got him out here with nonmatching socks and what is this outfit, Naheim? I color coordinated all of his clothes so you shouldn't have a problem," she continued to get on his case.

Naheim stood up and waved for her to follow him, and she followed behind going off about the outfit choice he put on the baby.

"For someone that swore she didn't want anything to do with the baby, her ass sure making a fuss about him." Capone chuckled.

"They miss each other," Erin shrugged.

"I'm about to head out… you going to handle that?" Capp looked to Capone.

"You already know… 'bout to get dressed and head out… Chubs you riding?"

I was so in my own zone that I wasn't even paying attention to the fact that he was talking to me. "Nah. I gotta go handle something… you need me?"

"I'm straight… Kincaid gonna pull up."

Capp looked over at me, as if he was observing me. "You sure you straight?"

"I promise… just got a lot of shit going on in my head."

"Come to me when you ready to sort it?"

"I got you."

∽

Capone was just talking about Kincaid, and I pulled up to my aunt's house and here he was on his motorcycle talking to Jasmine. I pulled into the driveway and hopped out, walking past them.

"Boy, I know you see me standing here," Jasmine slapped me on the back of the head and laughed.

Jasmine was the only person that knew I ran with Capone and Cappadonna. She knew how my aunt was, so she would never snitch on me. That was probably the reason she decided to come out with the truth. She figured if Capone or Cappadonna knew they would take me under their wing and make sure I was good.

"You both seemed into your conversation… what you doing over this way?" I hugged my cousin, and then dapped Kincaid.

"I came to visit Mom and see if she needed anything."

"You were checking to make sure my aunt is good, too?" I fucked with Kincaid, and he smirked.

"Fuck up. Why didn't you tell me that Jas moved back to New York?" Kincaid asked, as he sat comfortably on his motorcycle.

"Didn't think it was important." I grinned, knowing that it was very important. There was no reason that Kincaid needed to know that Jasmine had moved back to the city.

"We're damn near neighbors. He lives the next block from me... that's so funny." Jasmine giggled, unaware of how Kincaid was taking her in.

Jasmine just bought a townhouse in Bushwick, and I never mentioned that Kincaid owned a house over there. I feel like there was some unresolved history between the two of them. Jasmine took off and never looked back, even after she moved back. The first-person Kincaid dated seriously had been Capri. Before her, he had bitches, but none of them were on a serious level.

I went into the house to find my aunt on the couch watching her court shows. When she saw me, her eyes lit up, excited to see me. After being raised by her, that look on her face never got old to me. I was her entire world, her pride and joy.

"Hey Capella. What are you doing here? I expected to see you on Sunday." She leaned up on the couch and I kissed her on the cheek.

"I figured I would come and see you." I plopped down in the recliner and leaned my head back, my head swarming with everything going on. "I met with Kendra the other day."

"Hmm. How did that go?"

"She finally admitted that Cappadonna is my father." My aunt shook her head, pausing the show that she was watching before I came in.

"How do you feel about that?"

"Why was she so selfish? Taking that away from me... it's hard knowing how hard Cappadonna is on himself."

"Kendra has been selfish her entire life. She gets it from your grandmother, and I don't understand it. If she wants to mend the relationship and right the wrongs, why not allow her to do it?"

"Because it's not something that I want to do right now. Why should I make things easier for her? Just accept her apology and then have her play mother."

"Not forgiving her for herself, but for you. You don't need to make anything easy on her. Forgive her whenever you are ready to do so. Just don't let that anger and hate eat you alive on the inside, Capella."

I heard my aunt, but I was conflicted on what to do when it came to my mom. Shit, even when it came to my pops. I wanted to give him space, so I didn't come around much. He was the one that invited me over for dinner before Alaia went into labor. It was this part of me that didn't want him to feel like I was invading his space. He just got out of prison and had a lot of shit on his plate.

"I love you, Bean... know that it has been my greatest honor to raise you, and I am so proud of you as a man."

"Thanks, Ma." I smiled, as she turned the TV back on, and we both tuned into her court shows like we used to do when I was younger.

23
CAPPADONNA

My mother was putting Promise in the bassinet right as I came into the room. Alaia was asleep, and the lights were low as she pointed for me to meet her outside the room. I sat down the food and bag of clothes that I had brought for Alaia. She wanted to take a shower tonight, so I went and got her a bunch of stuff to make her as comfortable as I could.

"Thanks for coming up, Ma," I kissed my mother on the cheek and leaned on the wall as she fixed something in her purse.

Nine times out of ten, I knew it was her gun. She hated carrying it whenever she was alone. It wasn't a negotiable when it came to me, my father, and Capone. Whenever she was with someone, she didn't have to carry it because I was going to let my shit bang behind my mama.

"You never have to thank me for being your mom," she smiled, and put her purse onto her arm. "She was in some pain today. I tried to get some soup into her, but she was sleeping most of the time. Get some food in her and put the baby in the nursery so she can take a shower and get refreshed."

"Yeah. That was the plan."

My mom looked up at me. "Are you alright? I know I haven't checked in with you often. You, Capone, and Capri are still my babies."

I chuckled. "I'm good. Just trying to make her as comfortable as possible. Neither of us expected for any of this to happen."

"What's next? Are you sure you are ready to be a father?"

I wanted to laugh because little did she know, I had already been a father for nearly twenty years. "Were you and pops ready to be parents? Especially to two kids at one time?"

"Lord no. I remember your father passed out when we found out it was two of you. I also know that your father would have done anything for me and you boys."

"So, know that I would do anything for Alaia and Promise... those are my girls."

My mom leaned and hugged me. "When you and your brother fall, you both fall harder than a tree in a rain forest." She looked up at me and winked. "Like your father. I love you and will call you when I make it back to the house. Your father is at our lake house, so I will stay there tonight with him, then go back over and get everything prepared at your house."

"Appreciate you, Ma." I hugged her tightly, taking full of advantage of hugging my mother. I never realized how important the small shit was until it was taken from you.

"Love you, baby." She cupped my face and then headed toward the elevators, blowing me a kiss when she stepped on one.

I entered the room and took out the food, and unpacked the clothes that I bought for her. Erin was supposed to be going to get shit with me, and Capone's ass dragged her back upstairs. I wasn't about to go upstairs and knock on their door, so I left and texted her ass that she was weak. Whenever it came to Capone, she could never stand on business.

Capri sat on FaceTime while I tried to find clothes that might be comfortable for her. I picked up some nightgowns a few sizes big, so it was loose on her incision. Quickly washing my hands, I scooped my girl up and kissed her on the cheeks. Promise was so fucking perfect that it killed me to even think of any harm coming her way.

I couldn't even sit and think of the shit her mother went through for too long before it had me seeing red. Knowing I had a responsibility to protect her and make sure she never knew what hurt felt like wasn't something I took for granted. When I signed her birth certificate, I meant that shit.

"Look at you peeking at yo' daddy." She was swaddled, but was squirming around like she was trying to get comfortable. "My most important Promise," I kissed her.

When I came back from pushing Promise back to the nursery, Alaia was sitting up in the bed worried. The minute she saw me, her expression softened, and she was relieved. "What's the matter, baby?"

"I had a dream and jumped out my sleep to the room dark, your mother and the baby gone. I'm alright."

"Moms went home."

"I told her to leave hours ago... I feel bad that she comes up here for me. She comes so early; I know she has to be tired."

"Jean Delgato is gonna do what she wants."

She winced as she leaned up in the bed. "She doesn't think it's weird. The whole situation has to be weird to her."

"She trust her sons, Alaia. I'm a grown man and have always made my own decisions. Moms know that if I make a decision than she's rocking with it because I'm never wrong."

She smiled. "You're not wrong about me?"

"Fuck no. I could never be wrong about you," I kissed her

on the lips, and pulled her bonnet off her head, running my hand through her hair. "You still want to shower tonight?"

"Yeah. I'm just mentally trying to figure out how I'm going to do this."

I pulled the blankets from her body. "I'm going to help you... come on."

Alaia looked up into my eyes. "You gonna see my body."

"Joy, I'm going to see it sometime... with the things I want to do to you, I'm def gonna see it."

"Not like this. I'm all injured and it's not sexy," she continued to complain while I walked her to the bathroom.

They unhooked her IV pole, so she didn't need to pull it around with her like a granny. The room we were in had an attached bathroom with a shower. I sat the little bag filled with all her toiletries that she would need down.

While she stood in the mirror combing out her hair that was pushed to the front of her head, I ran the shower and made sure the temperature was warm. I noticed she was hesitating on taking off her hospital gown.

"Baby, if you want me to step out the room... I can."

She looked at her feet. "I just don't want you to look at me differently. We've already met when I was pregnant, so I know you didn't find me sexy. But this..."

"Who the fuck said I didn't find you sexy? I found you sexy then, and I find you even sexier now." I pulled her close to me, staring down at her. "Look at me, Alaia."

"You're just saying that because you don't want me to feel bad."

I took her face in my hands. "I need you to know a few things about me. I don't say shit that I don't mean. Baby, I can promise there's gonna be times you're pissed because I didn't say what you wanted me to say. I'm not fucking shallow where I would ever think you weren't sexy because of this. You just gave fucking life... I find that shit to be so sexy."

"Promise?"

I kissed her lips softly. "I put that on Promise."

She smiled. "Real smooth."

I helped Alaia get undressed and she showered slowly because she was in pain. While she was washing up, I laid out everything she needed. Soon as she stepped out the shower, I had the towel open and wrapped it around her.

"Moms said that you were in pain today."

"Yeah...I couldn't get comfortable because the pain was unbearable... the pain medicine worked though."

I opened the diaper and held it open so she could step inside of it. "I'm getting the guest room downstairs prepared for you. I don't want you walking up the stairs."

"Thank you." She allowed me to pull the diaper up on her. "This is embarrassing. I don't care what you say about this being sexy."

"I said you sexy not the diapers, diaper booty."

She pinched me and giggled while holding her stomach because she couldn't laugh too hard. That's when she looked up at me. "You're tired... I see it all in your eyes."

"I'm straight." I helped put her nightgown on.

Me being tired was the least of my worries. After all she had been through with this delivery, I was more concerned with taking care of her and nursing her back to health. I'll sleep when I knew she was good.

"Did you eat?"

"What's with the twenty questions, Joy?" I kissed her forehead.

"I'm not attached to anything, so you can sleep in the bed beside me." I looked at her and broke out into laughter.

"We can cuddle up next to each other."

"Alright."

She held my hand, pulling me into the room. I helped her get into the bed, and she moved all the way to the side making room for me. I grabbed the food, and put it on the table so she could eat. Once I had her all set up, I got in the bed and Alaia put the covers over me.

"Here... have some fries," she shoved fries into my mouth as she turned on the TV and settled in beside me.

"Just gonna choke the fuck outta me, huh?"

"Oh be quiet." She kissed me on the cheek. "Thank you for helping me in the shower." I heard her talking, but my eyes were getting lower and lower.

It may have not been that much room, but the shit was more comfortable than that chair in the corner. "Anything for you, baby," I muttered.

"I love you, Cappadonna." I heard her say, as I drifted off to sleep. I felt a kiss on my cheek as she pulled the covers up over me. "Hey Erin, he made it up here... he's sleep." I could hear her having a conversation as my ass knocked out.

∽

Erin had done me a solid by coming with me to get everything Promise needed. I didn't know the first thing a baby needed. Me and Alaia were trying to figure that out when her water broke. Between Erin and my mother, I didn't know who had been up there more with Alaia. They didn't know how much I appreciated them for being there for the both of us. If I could depend on someone, it was my family. She took time away from her own baby to make the drive to Lennox Hills to visit her every day.

I knew Alaia felt less alone having her come up there. I mean, I was there and only left when someone was up there with her. I also knew she couldn't really talk to me about what she was going through. Whenever Erin came up, I went to the crib and showered, and brought something up for her to eat. As nice as this hospital was, the food was nasty as shit.

"You know it won't be like this forever. It's a lot for her to process right now. Knowing that this is her one and only child is tough." Erin brought me back from my thoughts.

"Feel like it's my fault."

"How? Capp, you couldn't have known this would happen. I love you and your brother, but you two can't take on everything within this family, you know? What you should be grateful for is that you ran into her before all of this. Imagine her having to go through this with that creep?" Erin shuttered out of disgust.

As much as I knew she was right, I still carried the guilt and her pain. I wanted to make everything better for her. She fucking suffered enough, and now she had more shit to heal from. I promised myself that once we were past all of this, she would always have a smile on her face. The only pain she would feel is her cheeks hurting from smiling every day. I would always make her smile.

"Tired of shit fucking hurting her."

"You're in love with her, Capp," Erin smiled while she accused me of being in love with Alaia.

She didn't need to accuse because I *was* in love with Alaia. When she told me she thinks she loves me, I needed to hear her elaborate. I had to know if she felt the same way that I felt about her. She had been through so much shit that I never wanted to put more on her plate, or have her feel like she *has* to love me back because I helped her.

I would have done whatever for her, even if she told me she wasn't interested in me. If a woman was in need, it was in my

DNA to help her out and not expect anything in return. Only weak men wanted something in return for their help.

"Why you so nosey?"

"I can tell she feels the same way about you." Erin shifted her body so she was facing me as I drove. "Man, I thought I had it bad when it came to your brother... you both are something."

I laughed. "That's my baby before she was even my baby."

"You would glare at her across the room whenever she happened to be on a visit at the same time... it was meant for you two to be together. Are you positive about taking all of this on? You know, I worry about you. With Chubs, and then Kendra. A new baby and then Alaia."

"Let me worry about how much I can take on... I'm good," I assured her. Once Erin got it into her brain to worry, she was going to fucking stress herself out.

Capone wasn't going to come to me complaining because his wife had ulcers about my life. "So, Kendra took the break up and eviction well?"

"She ain't have no choice after I tried to beat the shit out of her." I wasn't proud that I was about to put my hands on her, or I pulled her damn hair.

In my defense, I paid for that expensive shit, so it was mine to pull out of her fucking head. Whenever I got like that, I saw red and nothing ever mattered. When I went to prison, I had no choice but to work on that shit.

An old head named Mink introduced me to Islam and taught me the way. I spent the first few years whipping ass and always being tossed into the hole because I was causing hell in the prison. He showed me how to be calm and not fly off the handle.

Being Muslim saved my life, because I probably would have still been in prison on a different charge. Kendra had a way that pulled that part of me, and I wasn't proud of it.

"No Capp... if she makes you feel like that then you know it wasn't good."

"She hid my fucking seed away from me. I feel torn between wanting to be in his space all the time and giving him space. Kendra fucked me over when she took matters into her own hand. If she didn't want to raise him, my parents would have stepped in."

"Yeah. She had so many other options than to hide him." Erin sighed. "Look how the universe works, though. You have the chance to build a relationship with your son, and now you have another blessing... a chance to experience all the firsts you missed. I know it doesn't make up for missing out on the first time, but you have a second chance to do it."

Erin leaned back, enjoying the warm breeze that having the roof off the Bronco provided. I didn't think to switch cars since since Alaia went into labor. My choice of car was the least of my problems. I've been driving around in this shit since we headed to the hospital.

"Do you think the stroller and car seat is good for my baby?"

"Yes, and you lowkey threatened the damn salesman to make sure of it... I get it, though... it's scary. Do you know how scared I was bringing Cee-Cee home? Capone had to drive fifteen miles per hour to the house because I was so scared." She paused. "I'm still scared. Especially since Capone wants to try again."

I raised my eyebrow. "You didn't seem all that scared the way you ditched my ass to go upstairs with him the other day... you don't want another?"

She laughed. "I was helping him to find his medicine. Capp, I love my baby. You know I do, right?".

"Hell yeah. You're the best mother I know." Erin wasn't only a mother to her baby, she was also one to CJ, and she was one of the best mothers that I knew. Jo always gave her praises for how Jaiden came out because it was all Erin's doing.

"I'm afraid if we try for another baby again that something will be wrong. Cee-Cee has Down Syndrome and I'm still coming to terms with that. What if I'm broken and can't have a child without a disability?"

"Aye, knock that shit off. You can't blame yourself for Cee-Cee coming out the way she did. Sometimes we don't have any control over what God gives us. I do know that you and Capo both have a strong support system. My niece and nephew are my fucking heart and I would do anything for them."

"Thanks." She smiled, looking over at me. "This isn't the way to the hospital."

I happened to be looking at my rearview mirror when she asked the question. "That car been following us for a minute… slight detour."

She turned to look out the window while I drove. "Make a right and see if they follow."

I made like I was making a right, then quickly hit a left turn and the car did the same thing. Pussy wasn't even discreet with the way they were following me. "They are following us."

Erin went into her purse, while I hit the code for the safe in my whip. Capone had every one of my whips fitted with one. "Chill. Let me see what they doing."

Capone had Erin still taking lessons, even more now since they had a baby and she wanted to be independent without Big Mike. She watched the rearview mirror the same as I did. We were on a long strip of road that split into two lanes on both sides.

I looked at my sister-in-law, and she didn't appear like she was scared. She seemed more ready for whatever the more I looked at her. My only priority was getting her out of this. I'd be damned if I had to tell my brother something happened to his wife, and I couldn't hold it down.

While driving with my knees, I cocked my gun back and looked over at Erin. "You good?"

"Yeah... I need to make it home to my babies, Capp."

I hit the touchscreen in my whip and called my brother. "Yo."

Capone been handling shit in Queens, and making sure everything was held down while I been at the hospital. I felt guilty as fuck because he was supposed to have been stepping back.

"Baby, somebody is following us back to the hospital," Erin spoke while I continued to watch the nigga in my mirror.

"Fuck!" he roared. "I'm about two hours away... fuck. Where Capp?"

"Don't know why you worried. I'mma hold it down and get her back to the hospital... ight?" I explained calmly how I was going to fuck shit up and make it back to my babies in the hospital.

"Take care of my wife, Capp."

"Always."

"Gorgeous, hold it down... you got it, baby."

"At this point, I'm more pissed than scared."

Capone laughed. "That's my baby... I'm on the way to you."

"Head straight to the hospital." By the time his ass arrived we would have already been at the hospital.

Erin finished the call, and I stomped on my brakes and the car behind me had to swerve into the other lane to avoid hitting me. He swerved over toward Erin's side, and I hit the recline button on her seat. She fell flat back, as I held my hand out the window, not even waiting a second before I let bullets fly.

The muthafucka had the same idea because his gun was

already out and ready, but his ass was too slow. I sped the fuck up, jumping in front of him, so he could get on my side. I bit down on my bottom lip.

Bullets hit the car, and I ducked down because the roof was off. I was way too exposed, and I didn't like that shit. Erin took her seatbelt off, cocked her gun back and stood up in the front. I watched as she tried to get her balance and then she started shooting at the car. His front window shattered with how many times she hit that shit.

She missed maybe two shots while trying to get balance, but all the shots after that one she hit perfectly. "E, get down... he on my side."

She jumped back down in her seat, and I looked out my window, and waited until he was right beside me before turning the wheel and pushing him onto the opposite side of the street. Traffic on our side was light, but the traffic on the other side was a little more than ours.

My truck was lifted and had bigger tires than that little ass Infiniti he was trying to push. He hit his brakes and got on the opposite side, Erin's side, and I didn't have to say shit. She was already waiting and that's when she let her gun out the window.

I pushed his whip off the road, where there was dirt and trees. My Bronco had mud tires, but his wheels kept skidding and he was turning that wheel like it owed his ass some money. Our wheels were locked so Erin had the perfect chance while he was trying to struggle to get away.

Erin looked to me to give her the word. I smiled, as this nigga looked at me horrified that I was smiling when his ass was about to die. "Get 'em, E."

She sent two shots into the window while he was trying to get his wheel from being stuck with mine. Soon as the bullets hit him, he let go of the wheel and the car veered off into the tree. Erin pulled her chair up and looked over at me.

"Good shit, sis'."

She didn't look pleased to be in this shit, and I didn't blame her. I quickly hit a U-turn, pulling in front of the now totaled car. "What are you doing?"

"I'm fucking offended whoever sent a fucking amateur for me. He came at me with my family... E, I'll fucking kill for you... feel me?"

When I got over to the car, his ass was alive. His legs were stuck because the entire front of the car was now damn near part of the tree. Erin had got him in his arm and chest. I snatched the door open and shoved my hand around his neck, staring him in his eyes.

"Who the fuck sent you?"

He gargled, staring at me with fear in his eyes. I applied more pressure to his neck, and paused when I heard his phone ringing in the passenger seat. Reaching over him, I grabbed the phone and slipped it into my pocket.

I didn't even need homie anymore. I held him around his neck until I felt something snap, and his eyes slowly closed. I spit in his face, and then kicked the door to his whip closed, going back to my car.

I whipped the truck around and sped away, with the phone ringing in my pocket. We weren't too far from the lake house, so I drove there so I could park this up and switch cars. After I backed into the garage, Erin hopped out to call Capone, and I remained seated in the truck, clutching the phone in my hand.

"The phone is ringing again," Erin snapped me out the daze I had fell into.

I slid my finger across the broken screen and put the phone to my ear. "You better have good news for me... a week and you wasted my damn time with excuses." I immediately recognized Taz's voice.

When I was on the inside, I swore when I got out that I was going to live a peaceful life. I would handle business, but all that extra shit I wouldn't involve myself in. Now that I was out, my ass had made two enemies within the same time frame.

"Tweety, I thought we were good? Thought we had that heart to heart in the barbershop?" I manically laughed into the phone.

I wished I was a fly on the wall because I could tell this nigga was shook. "Where the fuck my cousin?"

I laughed. "Damn, that was your cousin... I'm a little pissed that you sent somebody for me and didn't come yourself."

"Then bring me my fucking wife back, and I'll call whoever I send next off. Capp, can I call you that? Anyway, this shit won't end well. I want my wife, and you need to bring her."

This little bitch had grown some balls since I choked his ass up in the barbershop. He thought I was going to just hand Alaia over like she was his property. I was being nice by sparing him, taking a note out my twin's book, but I knew I couldn't be peaceful. Niggas didn't listen when you were peaceful. They only reacted to you when you went full blown manic on they asses.

"Nigga, I don't negotiate with little people." I was done being nice because I could feel the heat rising to my face. Leaning forward, I held the phone in my hand as I spoke. "You sure you want to die over someone that was never yours, bitch? You fucked up coming at me when I had my family in the car, but you good... I'm gonna teach yo' ass." I tossed the phone out the roof, sending the phone crashing onto the floor.

24
KENDRA

I was trying hard to enjoy tonight out with Ace. It was a block party out in Staten Island, and everybody was out. Both the Vanducci-Cromwell family and Inferno Gods came together and threw a block party and car show. There was almost always a race at one of these parties, and it was never planned.

Me and Ace drove out here in his Jeep Wrangler. He took all the doors and roof off, so while he was shit talking with Zeke, I was sitting in the passenger seat watching the guys ride their dirt bikes.

I spotted Kincaid a few minutes ago doing a wheelie on the dirt bike. His ass needed a helmet or something because one wrong turn and his ass would be a vegetable. Everyone was hype with the way he and the guys with him were turning up on their bikes. That was what this event was about. The Vanducci-Cromwell family were neutral to all the beef in the streets. If you attended one of their events, you already knew you were coming to Switzerland.

"Who pulling up in that?" Ace whistled when a destroyer gray challenger with the darkest tints pulled onto the strip slowly. Like they were in sync, the dirt bikes rode on the side of the car as it slowly cruised until it parked in front of the car in front of us.

Kincaid stopped the bike, and sat on it waiting for whoever to hop out the car. When the door opened, Capri came stepping out. How was it possible this girl looked perfect in this hot ass weather. The sun was setting so it was becoming cooler, but damn, she got out without a hair out of place.

She wore a pair of jean shorts, sneakers and a crop top. "She fine as fuck." Zeke bit his knuckles taking her in.

Kincaid walked over to her, pulling her into him and kissing her on the neck. They spoke for a minute before he got on the dirt bike, and she got on the back and they pulled off with her holding onto him.

Me and Capri had never been close, even with me being with Capp for so long. We didn't have that sister-in-law bond that she seemed to have had with Capone's wife.

"She fucking with that nigga?" Zeke sounded mad that she was messing with someone else, as if she even knew he existed.

"You don't have no luck when it comes to messing with her. That's Capri Delgato... be for real," I rolled my eyes, tired of the conversation between the two.

It took me back to when I was their age and didn't give a fuck about shit. Now that I was older, I couldn't pretend I was even remotely interested in their conversation. Things between me and Ace had been tense since I got into an argument with him about Sassy.

I didn't give a fuck about him and sassy not getting along. The longer I stayed in this shit, the harder it would be to get out of it. I knew one thing; I wasn't going to marry this damn man. Sassy didn't mind me using her as an excuse because she knew how I felt about Ace. He was cool to fuck with, but not for the long haul.

The black-on-black Durango pulled onto the strip with another challenger following behind. Both cars were the same color, down to the wheels. They hit a U-turn and parked on the opposite side of where we were parked.

I just knew the minute I saw the construction Timbs step out the Durango, and the body followed that it was Cappadonna. My heart skipped in my chest while my mouth became moist when he fully stepped out the truck.

He wore a leather Inferno Gods motorcycle vest with no shirt on, and the body was fucking bodying. I knew it before, but prison had done a body fucking good. I was now doing what Zeke was doing not too long ago and was biting the back of my knuckle.

His single gold chain hung on his chest as he made his moves and dapped everyone up. Capo hopped out the challenger behind him, and went over to the passenger side, helping his wife out the car.

He kissed her before grabbing her on the ass, and then they walked where Cappadonna was. Capella hopped out the passenger side of Capp's truck while on the phone. I'd be damned if I denied that he was a Delgato.

Capella had the walk and the swag of his uncle and father without ever being raised around him. I watched as he dapped everyone up, and did the step back, same as his father. Cappadonna was laughing and then grabbed his son by the shoulder, as if to introduce him.

I wanted so desperately to run over there and partake in how proud he was of his son. My eyes didn't leave Cappadonna, and I wanted him bad. I regretted ever fucking up the way that I had. I'd do anything for him to run over here and grab my ass up.

"Why the fuck you staring so damn hard?" Ace nudged me, and I realized that I was nearly drooling out the mouth.

"Huh? I'm not even paying them attention," I lied, wiping the drool that accumulated in the corners of my mouth.

Ace looked at me. "Don't get me tight, Kendra. You want that nigga? I can call him over here... you want him?"

He continued to taunt me, which annoyed me. This was the immature side that I hated about him. Any other man, a real man, wouldn't have ever let another nigga see him jealous.

"If that nigga ride by us one more time and grill me, I know something," Zeke grabbed his gun and Ace stopped him.

"Chill out, we not on that tonight," Ace warned him.

Ace was new to New York, so he already knew niggas were already watching. Everyone knew the rules and if you attended one of these parties, you left the beef at home. Kincaid had been riding by since we got here, and kept grilling Zeke and Ace.

Me: Girl, Capp just pulled up and he look fucking good...

Sassy: get that old thang back. Get rid of the student and get with the teacher.

Me: ugh. I wish. I miss him.

When I looked up from my phone, Cappadonna was walking over here. I was so damn nervous I flipped the mirror down and started fixing my fucking hair. Ace was leaned on the front of the truck, and I continued to fix myself.

"The fuck up, pussy," Capp laughed, as he cupped Ace's face, then slapped it a few times. When he laughed, I saw he had his gold teeth in his mouth, and I was nearly a puddle in this damn Jeep.

Capone stepped toward Zeke. "Pull that shit only if you doing something with it... ight?"

Zeke was pretending to be down, but his ass was scared as

hell. He didn't have not one, but two of the Delgato twins in his face.

"Get the fuck off me," Ace pumped his chest out, slapped Capp's hands away from him, and moved back. "You look happy for a nigga that's missing out on some paper."

Cappadonna and Capone looked at each other and then laughed in Ace's face. If I was him, I would have gotten in my car and drove away.

"Bitch, that's what you think you did? There's more where that came from, but since you felt it was worth your life... let me tell you something," he cleared his throat, and stepped closer. "I put this on my daughter, you gonna pay for that shit. Not tonight because we chilling, but you mine, lil' nigga."

What the fuck did he mean by his daughter? As far as I fucking knew Capone only had a damn son, so when the fuck did he get a daughter? It was like he knew I was thinking about him because our eyes locked.

I used to be able to tell how much Capp loved me by the way he looked at me. This time, I saw nothing in his eyes. "What up, Kendra? Still wanna fuck me?" He had that sexy ass smirk on while he looked at me, and I wanted to fuck him desperately.

"Um. Hey...Hey Capp." I tried to play it cool, and completely fucking failed because I started stammering and shit.

"Don't say shit to my bitch. You mad 'cause she chose up, and you salty about this shit." I wanted to be anywhere but right here because Ace was about to look stupid.

"*You mad cause she chose up* ass nigga," Cappadonna mocked him. "Kendra ain't chose shit... I got rid of her, not the other way around. If I told her ass to come with me now, she would be hopping out this shit to come chase behind my dick like a puppy with a treat."

I hated how he was so cocky about it because he was right. If he told me to come on, I would break a heel trying to chase behind his ass. Even if he wanted me to suck his dick, I would do it because I wanted to get back in Capp's good graces. I was tired of being out here with Ace. He had us looking stupid.

"Fix that aim... my fucking sister got better aim," Capone flinched at Zeke, and he nearly toppled over the fender.

They walked away, not even scared enough to watch their back. It was like they knew these bozos wouldn't have done anything. I sat here looking away because now Ace was about to get on my case because his ass got bullied.

What the fuck did he want me to do? Kiss him and make everything all better for him. Ace wanted to poke the bear and now the bear was awake. I was smart enough to know that this was less about me and more about the fact that Ace touched what was his.

"What the fuck was he talking about?" Ace got on my case the minute they were a good distance away.

"Look, you not about to have me in your bullshit with Cappadonna. You knew he was my nigga, so don't get mad when he reminds you of it."

Zeke walked over on my side as he watched Capri across the street.

"And you. Why the fuck you nearly jumped out of your skin when that nigga flinched at you."

"You the one that wanted to go to fucking war with them. I came out here to get money, fuck some fine bitches and get more rich. I ain't come down here to get into no fucking beef with that crazy nigga."

"He all bark... nigga ain't gonna do nothing."

"Um, didn't he slam your head into your plate at the restaurant?" I slapped my hand over my mouth because that was supposed to be a thought.

"And just cupped your face like you his seed or something. That nigga think less of you, Ace," Zeke added on.

Ace was looking at the both of us like we were fucking traitors. It was the truth, so he needed to stop acting like Capp wasn't about that. With the way he looked at him, I knew this wasn't the last that Ace was going to hear from him.

"She ride bikes, too," Zeke continued to watch Capri as she got on the bike. Kincaid was on one behind her.

You could tell she was still new to riding, but she had the basics down. I looked over at Cappadonna, and he was laughing with a bottled water in his hand. It was as if he hadn't come over here and told this nigga that his days were numbered.

I watched as Ace pulled off the strip, and I closed my eyes wishing I could rewind the time. Instead of leaving with Ace, I wanted to be over there laughing and kicking it with Cappadonna. Ace was on the phone venting to somebody and I zoned out, looking out at the water as we crossed the bridge back into Brooklyn.

I was not going to marry that nigga, and I put that on my son!

25
ALAIA

I HAD NEVER BEEN SO happy to be out of the hospital and back at the lake house. We were discharged last week, and I was slowly trying to get into a routine with Promise. Everyone rotated through the house to help us out and I appreciated them. Jean and Erin had set up a nursery for Promise and I couldn't see it because climbing the stairs felt like torture.

The downstairs guest room had been where I was staying at. Capp slept down here with me because I didn't want to sleep alone. Not that he would have slept upstairs without me anyway. I sat on the couch with Promise beside me in the bouncer, as I tried to pump with the breast pump. Hardly anything had come out and I was so discouraged. I've eaten everything, and had even used the manual pump, and my breast supply still hadn't increased.

"Why you looking like that?" I lifted my head to see Capp making his way over toward me. He kissed me on the lips, then went to peek at Promise.

"I'm a failure... I can't even produce milk to feed her... look at this." I showed him the pumps still attached to my breast.

It was hard to focus on my failed breast-feeding journey when he was standing in front of me without a shirt on. I knew he had just come back from his run around the neighborhood. Sweat dripped down every inch of his exposed body.

"I told you about that shit, Alaia." He pulled me up from the couch and walked me over toward the kitchen. "You been eating these nasty ass cookies, eating everything suggested, and trying to pump every hour on the hour. You're doing your part, stop saying you're a failure."

"You're right. I guess I feel like I should be doing more. Everyone is helping me out and I'm just sitting here doing nothing. The least I could do is pump some milk."

He guzzled his water and headed to the guest suite on the main level. I followed behind him, while he went into the bathroom. "Why do you feel like you need to always be doing something?"

I knew it wasn't the end of the world that I couldn't breastfeed Promise. She was healthy and formula had been doing its job, so I needed to stop being so hard on myself for not producing enough milk. Erin had already told me she had a hard time producing milk and that I needed to stop stressing and allow my body to do its job.

"Why you got quiet on me?" I walked into the bathroom, and stood by the sink that I used, while he showered.

"I want you to stop being hard on yourself. How are you feeling today?"

"Not as good as you... you get up and go for a run damn near every morning." I had my days when I felt like I could run right along with Capp, then days where I didn't want to move from the bed or the couch.

"I want to take you out on the lake tonight. Capone just got him a boat, and that nigga ain't using it tonight." He turned the shower off and stepped out.

My eyes immediately fell down between his legs. Everything about Capp told me that he was working with more than the average, and it was all true.

"Yeah," I agreed, not knowing what the hell he was talking about. My eyes were too focused on his dick, just hanging freely.

I mean, I got a glimpse when he wore those grays sweatpants, but it was nothing like what I was experiencing right now. When I realized I was staring, I looked up, and our eyes locked. Capp stood there with a smirk on his face, as he slowly wrapped the towel around him.

Walking over to me, he stood in front of me. I looked up at him, as he put his hands on the sink, closing me in the middle. "Yeah... what, Joy?"

When he spoke, he was so close to my ear that it sent chills down my spine. "To whatever you said," I whispered, never removing eye contact with him.

"You not ready for this just yet, Joy... I told you I can wait." He took my hand and placed it on him, and I nearly fainted from feeling how thick it felt in my hands.

He was saying that he could wait, but I wasn't sure that I could do the same. I was ready to say fuck surgery and have him touch my body. I craved to feel his hands on my body, to feel him inside of me. I've never craved for anybody to touch me the way that I did for Cappadonna.

"I know," I admitted.

As much as I craved for Capp's touch, I knew it wasn't the time. I was still healing, and sex was the last thing that should have been on my mind right now. He held my chin and kissed me on the lips, shoving his tongue into my mouth.

I accepted his tongue into my mouth, as I held onto him, wanting to go further than this. It should have been illegal to be in the same house as this man and not have had him in that way. He pulled away from our kiss, sealing it with a single kiss on my nose.

"Allow your body to heal. Once it's healed... I'm gonna wear you out." He kissed my nose once more, before going into the bedroom.

I held onto the sink because I wasn't sure that I could even walk behind him. My heart was beating out of control, and I had to cross my legs because the insane amount of pressure I was feeling down there should have been illegal.

I wanted Cappadonna.

Bad.

I stood in the doorway and watched as he got dressed. This was around the time he got ready to leave for the day, and I missed him when he was gone. Sometimes I called him just to remind him to eat, and then we would have a conversation. Those small conversations always made me feel so good.

Our situation was unique, and not everyone would understand it. Sometimes I pretended like we had been together for years and this little family of ours was planned. That I had never gone through the horrible things I did, and he never sat in prison for as long as he did.

"Do you want me to make you some breakfast?" I slowly detached the breast pumps from my breast and sat them on the nightstand.

"Nah. I'll grab something while I'm out."

"You don't like eating fast food and you don't trust everybody's food." I folded my arms and continued to watch him.

He pulled the shirt over his head. "Nah. I'm straight."

"This works both ways. You wanted me to let down my guard and allow you to help me... us. I did that, and now you're not allowing me to help you."

Capp walked over to where I was standing, and I stood my

ground. His ass wasn't about to make me fold. "You standing on business behind your man, huh?"

I stared up at him. "I want to cook for you and take care of you."

"I feel guilty, baby... I don't want you feeling like you some fucking slave or some shit. I do what I do not because I want something in return."

"And that is why I want to do things for you. I'm still recovering so it's not much I can do, but I would like to make your breakfast and even wash your clothes. I want to do those things for you."

Cappadonna made me want to do those things for him. I wanted to wash this man's dirty draws while feeding him grapes. He took on a responsibility that not many men would, and he never complained about it. Every morning, he was up praying, working out, and then was out in the streets. He had given me and my daughter a safe place where we could sleep without any worries. Every time he came in, he had flowers for me because he knew they made me smile.

He held my face and kissed me on the lips. "I don't like runny eggs."

I got excited and did a little jump before I realized that I needed to not ever do that again. "I'll go make it now."

He shook his head as I took off out the room to make him some eggs. I wanted to feel like I was useful, and lately, I had felt like I wasn't good for anything. I knew that I had my own shit that I needed to sort out, but for right now, I was gonna make this man eggs and even do his laundry.

26
CAPPADONNA

When Alaia gave me that look, I was ready for her right then and there. She didn't even know how much I wanted her ass. I've waited years to get in some pussy, so I was a patient man. I knew the minute she allowed me in, I wasn't going to let up off her. The sexual tension between us was strong as shit. The way she scooted her butt back onto me to get comfortable before bed was about to kill me.

Holding her in my arms had always been enough, but damn, a nigga wanted to be inside of her. I wanted her to hold my face as she looked into my eyes as I drilled her shit. She was so fucking beautiful to me that she was all I ever thought about. When I left the house, Alaia and Promise were always on my mind.

Which is why Tweety's ass was on my mind. His ass had been laying low since we had our little fender bender with his cousin. I don't know why he thought he would be able to take care of me easily. His ass was probably ducked off in Delaware. His ass was on my list of shit to handle, and because his ass was scared, he wasn't going to come out to play.

When I got my hands on his little ass, I was gonna shove my foot so far up his ass he was gonna taste the rubber on my sole. It was the fact that he had the nerve to tell me to bring *my* woman to him.

Until I made my way to Tweety's ass, I was going to handle the pain in my ass right now. Ace was like the little engine that fucking could. How you bigging your chest up like you did some damage. The house in Astoria didn't hardly have any work in it, and his ass only grazed Naheim.

When I pulled up on his ass at the Vanducci-Cromwell block party, I knew I couldn't do what I really wanted to do. Everyone knew anything tied to the Vanducci-Cromwell's was Switzerland. I had too much respect for them to disrespect their event, and cause problems for them. Ace's ass knew that which is why he showed up and thought he was big shit. Had I been able to do what I wanted to do; his ass would have been under his own Jeep while I ran over his fucking head.

When I kicked Kendra's ass out, I already knew that she would go running to that nigga. She could never stand on her own, so she needed someone to take care of her ass. Ace thought he won the prize when in reality, Kendra would come running back if I wanted her ass.

I headed into the hospital and headed up to the gift shop to grab some flowers and balloons. As I headed upstairs, I checked my messages to make sure my baby hadn't called me, and I missed it. I switched to my text messages and found the room that I was looking for. As I rounded the corner, the nurse walking opposite of me slowed down and took me in with her eyes. Her ass was supposed to be saving lives and she was out here drooling over me.

"Can I help you, Sir?"

"Nah. I'm good." I continued walking past her and went into the room that I was looking for, pushing the curtain back.

Ms. Aimee was fast asleep while the baby was in the bassinet next to her. I sat the flowers and balloons down and went to wash my hands. I was unhinged, not irresponsible. I had my own new baby at home and knew I needed to wash my hands before picking up a baby. I expected her to wake up when she heard the soft baby gurgles as I picked the little nigga up.

He was cute.

Ace was an uncle out here and had the nerve to keep poking me until his nephew was visiting him in the grave. I did my little bounce walk as I stood near the window and looked at Aimee. I wondered what the fuck they gave her to be so knocked out like she was.

"I'm gonna kill your uncle, lil' homie."

Capone allowed this nigga to exist and now his ass thought he had balls the size of Texas coming for me. You don't touch my shit, and his ass touched two things that happened to belong to me. Then he had the nerve to puff his chest up like shit was going to be sweet. I wondered how Ken would look when her ass was wearing all black.

"Who...who are you?" Aimee's sleepy ass finally woke up and sat up in the bed. Not for nothing, this little nigga looked like he put her through it when it came to birth.

Capone had his own rules on how he didn't get women and children involved. That was why we were two different people, because while he didn't get them involved, I brought the whole family tree into shit.

You fucked with me? Oh bet. Now, I'm going to bring your old ass granny in this. I didn't have any plans on touching Aimee or her baby. I got the drop that Ace had a sister that he was fond of, and I wanted to make sure she was taken care of.

"Friend of your brother... Ace."

She relaxed. "Did he send you up here?"

I smirked. "You can say that. How you feeling?" I sat near the window, still holding her baby in my arms.

Ace was lucky I was a different man because had I been the Capp from fifteen years ago, and I didn't have my own bundle of joy at home, I would have tossed this baby at her ass. Since I was different these days, and I had to be an example for my daughter, I was carefully holding this baby.

"I'm alright. Just tired and ready to finally go home. Is Ace going to come up here? He said that he would."

This is why everybody wasn't meant to live this life. Had this been Capri in the room, she probably would have pulled her shit from under the blankets. She wouldn't have trusted that me or Capone would have sent anybody other than family to come up here with her.

Ace was so preoccupied with fucking with me, and pretending he was that nigga that he left his sister vulnerable. Had her exhaustion and naive demeanor not tugged on my heart strings, I probably would have choked her ass with the IV cord.

"He'll be up here real soon... I can promise you that." I laughed, as I switched arms with the baby.

"Do you have any children? You're so good with him."

"I have two."

"Oh."

Alaia: I can't remember what you said earlier.

I chuckled as I put the baby back down in the bassinet. Aimee rested her head back, and I replied to Alaia.

Me: Taking you out on the boat tonight.

Alaia: Boat? Where did you get a boat?

Me: Too busy looking at dick to pay attention. I'm bringing Promise over to moms.

Alaia: lol. Okay.

I could tell that she was tired, so I dipped out because my point had been proven. "Thanks for coming."

"Don't mention it... congrats."

"Thanks."

It took me no time to leave the hospital and run the few errands I needed before tonight. When I made it back to the hood, I pulled up in front of the corner store, and Capone was already there. Quasim, Chubs, and Naheim were all standing in front of the store shooting the breeze.

"Look at the new father... you got that new father glow," Quasim joked, dapping me up in the process.

"The fuck you doing over this way?"

"Came to get a hero and ran into these niggas." He laughed.

Quasim was a nigga that wasn't on the scene at all. Even with him being the leader of Inferno Gods, that nigga was hardly ever out. Before his daughter passed, he was always with her. After she passed, he had become somewhat of a recluse, always tucked in the cut. I don't remember the last time he mentioned he was in a relationship.

"I'm surprised you not hiding in yo fucking bat cave or some shit."

"Chill out. The fuck you doing out? I thought you would be up in the house since having a little one... she beautiful, right?"

I touched my chest. "She got my heart, nigga... can't even picture life before her little ass."

"Little girls are different, bro'... they have a special part in your heart." I could see the pain in his eyes as he spoke about having a little girl.

I was already knowing because Promise had my heart, and she hadn't even been in the world all that long. When I peeked in her bassinet at night, I couldn't picture my life before she and her mom came waddling into it.

"Why the fuck you need my boat. I ain't even take my own

wife out on it yet." Capone sat on the ice cooler outside the store.

"Nigga, just give me the keys. Alaia been stuck in the crib with moms and her birth ritual she swears by. I want to do something for her to get out the house for a little bit."

"On the real, how she been?" Naheim questioned.

"She been taking it day by day. It helps that moms and Erin have been around. I think they help her realize that none of this is her fault. I can say the shit until I'm blue in the face, but I guess it feels different hearing it from a woman."

Capone whistled. "Erin was emotional as shit after we had Cee-Cee. She would sit and stare at her for hours with tears pouring down her face. I think she still feels guilty because she has Down Syndrome. Now, her new thing is to talk about when she goes to school and kids make fun of her. My baby ain't even a fucking year yet."

"I fight kids, so if they know what's good for them, they better leave niece alone." Chubs and Naheim both started laughing.

"Why this nigga seem like he dead serious?" Naheim pointed at me.

"Cause his crazy ass is," Capone added onto the laughter.

I ignored they asses because I was ten toes down behind my niece and nephew. Let one of them come to me with a problem, and I'm running behind them. "You still renting that room?"

"Yeah. I'm looking for something bigger, though."

"Move into the lake house with me. I got more than enough room, and you don't need to be renting a room like you on the verge of homelessness."

"When the fuck are you gonna find you a crib closer to the city?" Capone interrupted our conversation.

"I don't think I need one. It's peaceful out there, and it's tucked away from everything." I enjoyed being at the lake house because it was quiet.

"Yeah, well, nobody got time to keep coming all the way out there for yo' ass. I thought we were done with the six-hour drives."

I chuckled. "Fuck up."

"The realtor told me there's a crib in my neighborhood on the market. Check it out before deciding to stay all the way out there."

As of right now, the lake house was where I was at. I knew I needed to be closer to the city to be able to handle shit when I needed to. I also didn't like the idea of Alaia and Promise being all the way out there when I was in the city. I wanted to be able to get to them quickly.

"I'll look at the house... damn."

"Just looking out for you, son." Capone shrugged.

"I hope the shit smaller... I don't want all that fucking house that you got."

He shrugged. "I got my whole village under my roof; I need the space."

Capone and Erin did have a whole damn village staying with them, and he liked it that way. "Not for long with Jaiden going away to college."

"I'm gonna miss his stupid ass," Chubs sighed.

"Word. I ain't looking forward to him being miles away," Capone added.

Naheim cleared his throat. "Shit, I'm gonna miss NJ when he goes away to college, too... that boy is my whole world."

We all turned to look at him, and I slapped him in the back of the head. "Nigga, your son isn't even a year old and you over here getting emotional."

Even with Naheim having help when it came to his son, he was a hands on father. The shit made me proud to see him step into his role. I wasn't a fan on how he became a father, but I could respect a man that showed up for his own.

"Capri the one got me thinking about the shit. She texted me about fucking preschools. He can barely hold his head up."

As much as Capri wanted to say she couldn't see herself helping him with his son, she had been there every step of the way. I wouldn't be surprised if NJ started calling her ass mama because she was always with him. When Naheim had to handle shit, he was either with the nanny or Capri.

"I'm about to head home... you know... since I got a long ass drive," I sarcastically replied, dapping them all up.

"Why the fuck you acting like you don't." Capone continued to fuck with me, and I flipped his ass the bird before hopping in.

"I'm out."

∽

CAPONE TALKED ALL that shit and had them keys to the boat over at my parents' crib when I got home. While Alaia was in the shower, I went and brought Promise over so my mother could watch her. Alaia had packed a whole diaper bag like she was staying over there for the next six months. I had the diaper bag on my arm while I pushed the stroller across the street.

"Don't your back hurt pushing that stroller?" my pops called from the front porch. "The handle doesn't come up any further?"

I pushed the stroller over toward him and he peered inside before taking Promise out. My parents trusted me and Capone and knew if we felt strongly on something to trust our instincts. It was very rare that I was wrong.

Maybe about Kendra's ass.

He held Promise in his arms as I took a seat in the empty chair beside him. "I've been meaning to talk to you."

"Oh yeah... what's on your mind old head?" I laughed.

He patted Promise's back as he rocked in his chair. "Something got back to me about Kendra."

If he was about to tell me about Kendra and Ace, his ass needed to keep his ear from the streets because he was late. "What you heard?" I entertained him by asking.

"That she was giving your money to help put that nigga on."

"How credible is your source, Pops?"

He gave me that look, and I understood enough. My father was like me, he didn't speak on shit unless he already knew and verified it himself. Even though my father was never a hustler, he knew things and people.

If it wasn't for him, we wouldn't have this empire that kept our family comfortable and paid. I bit the inside of my cheeks as he explained what he knew, and was gripping the arm of the chair like it had done something to me personally.

Whenever Kendra would ask Capone for money, he always checked in with me. There was a time when she was asking for large amounts of money. She claimed she was helping her aunt out, and I trusted that was the reason. Capone told me he didn't trust it, but he respected what I wanted. I gave him the approval to give her the money. I trusted you until you gave me a reason not to, and Kendra at the time hadn't given me a reason not to.

I made a promise to always take care of her and I held up my side of the deal. She promised she would hold me down, even when I told her that she didn't have to. There was a few months when I cut her off because it wasn't fair to her. Kendra fought tooth and nail to see me, and I thought she wanted to hold me down until I came home.

All those conversations about what we would do when I came home meant nothing. While I was sitting across from her, planning on giving her the world for her loyalty, she was fucking other niggas. I wasn't stupid, and shit got back to me about Kendra. I chose to ignore the shit because if I didn't then every nigga on my cell block would have been beat the fuck up.

It was easier to pretend than to pay any attention to it. I couldn't pretend I didn't hear that this bitch not only hid my son from me, but she was giving my money to help put another nigga on. At this point, I was starting to think Kendra was fucking slow or wanted to be put in a pine box, too.

"I'm already knowing you going to handle it."

I looked over at my pops. "Chubs is my son."

He raised his eyebrow, the same look I gave whenever someone revealed some crazy shit to me. "Who the fuck is his mother?"

"Kendra."

My father damn near tossed Promise with the way he turned toward me. "Don't tell me what you about to tell me."

"She hid that shit from me."

"From us."

I could always step out my shoes and place myself in someone else's shoes, but I couldn't do that with Kendra because she had so many options. She could have had all the help that she needed with my family, and she decided to hide my son from me.

"Yeah."

"Your mother had mentioned that he looks like you in the eyes and I waved her off. You know how her imagination takes over."

"Yeah, well, she wasn't wrong this time."

He kissed Promise's head as he continued to rock her. "I raised you and your brother to step up to the plate. You both have made me proud with the men that you have become. Stepping up and raising a child that's not biologically yours isn't something many men would do. You did it, and without hesitation because that's what a real man would do. You missed years of his life, but that doesn't mean you can't make up for those now."

"I feel so guilty, and I know I shouldn't because it ain't my fault, but damn."

He looked at me. "Cappadonna, you are a good man. This isn't your fault, and I refuse for you to act like it is. Put that guilt behind you, and focus on your son. There's nothing like a son and father relationship." My father smiled as he looked down at Promise. "Then there's the relationship between a father and his daughter...you'll see exactly why Capri gets away with murder with me."

I spoke with my father for a little bit more before I went to the house to get Alaia. When I entered the house, she was in the kitchen washing her hands. She had her hair wrapped in a cream scarf that matched the dress she had on.

"You like?" She looked up from washing her hands at me drooling over her.

She had on a cream floor length maxi dress with frills at the ends of her sleeve and bottom of her dress. It was modest where it covered her, but it also did little to hide her shape that she had been blessed with.

"I love it, baby." I stayed near the door, and continued to admire her from afar.

"My stomach is still... you know," she shrugged.

She was worried about her stomach when that was the least of my worries. "Stop doing that, Joy."

"Doing what?"

"Finding something wrong with everything about you. Your stomach is fine... you just had a damn baby. I think you look fucking stunning, and I want you to see yourself that way."

"You don't think I want to see myself that way?"

This conversation could either make or break our night, and from the way she was looking I wasn't going to give it the chance to even ruin our night tonight. Holding her by the hips, I kissed her neck.

"I appreciate you. I respect you. I think you're worthy of all good things. You belong to me in the best way. I need you to know and believe all of that."

"Okay." She reached up and rubbed my beard, her favorite thing to do.

"I like the way you tied your hair up... it's different." Her hair was tied up, with the scarf having a bun to the back. You could see small pieces of her baby hairs in the front, but the majority of her hair was covered.

"Really? I wanted to try something new." Her eyes lit up when I told her how much I liked how she wrapped her hair.

"I like this look... it looks good on you, Joy," I kissed her ear, and she wrapped her arms around my neck. "Can we start our night?"

"Is Promise alright? She doesn't need anything, right?"

I laughed. "And you were worried about how you would be as a mother. You sent me over there with six month's worth of shit... she's gonna be alright."

The sun was setting when I finally figured out how to unhook the boat from the dock. Once we were out on the water, Alaia laughed as I sped around the lake with ease. She sat on my lap as water splashed us some, and the air blew in our faces. She held her scarf down as I held her on my lap with one hand and controlled the boat with the other.

It was summer, so everybody was out on their boats or swimming in the lake. I found a sweet spot where we had enough privacy, and got a good view of the sun setting behind us. My mother did me a solid and packed us some food and had it waiting in the boat when we got on.

"She packed so much food for us." Alaia giggled while she unpacked the food.

My mom made me fish cakes, something I had been wanting since I got out. I just knew she would have more waiting for me when she brought Promise back over to the crib. The boat had a small table on the back, so we sat there while eating, enjoying the view.

"This view has to be my favorite."

"Thought New York was your favorite view?" I kissed her temple as she continued to eat her food.

"It's a toss-up."

"Wanna know mine?"

"What?"

"When you fall asleep with Promise in your arms drooling out the side of your mouth." I started to choke on my food.

"That's what you get for being shady." She patted my back.

"Nah, for real... that's my favorite view."

"I would tell you mine, but you know..." she blushed as she looked away. I knew she was referring to my dick.

"This is yours, Alaia. It doesn't belong to nobody but you."

She gave me a skeptical look. "So, it doesn't belong to your ex-girlfriend? She's not going to be a problem."

"She may have had it, but you got something else."

"What?"

"My heart." I reached into my pocket and pulled out the small jewelry box I picked up earlier.

"You mean that?"

"Baby, I don't say shit that I don't mean. I got you this."

She took the box from me and opened it. Inside was a necklace with a small diamond C on it. "This is beautiful, Capp... can you put it on me."

Alaia turned around as I roped the chain around her neck. "I never want you to take this off. I would never refer to you as property, but Joy, you're mine... you belong to me." I kissed her neck, and she turned around to face me.

"Wait, so I can't date anybody else?"

"Joy, you are free to embark on a suicide mission if you want."

She touched my face. "Calm down... I'm joking with you."

I puckered my lips and she kissed them. "Yeah... ight."

Alaia was my heart and I would do any and everything when it came to her and Promise. It didn't even sit right with me that Taz was walking these streets. I had detailed plans on handling his sick ass.

"I cried in the shower earlier."

"Tell me why." I kissed her hands, as she looked out at the sun slowly setting in front of us. The air had a slight cool breeze to it.

"It hit me that I could never have kids again. I don't know... it was easy to pretend it never happened while in the hospital, but every time I feed Promise, or I change a diaper I think about the fact that it will be the last time I'm able to do those things. I never had a baby shower, or took maternity pictures. You know, the things that women get to do and enjoy with their pregnancy. I feel so guilty because at the beginning of my pregnancy I wished I wasn't. I would wish I miscarried."

Instead of interrupting her, I continued to hold her and allowed her to get what she needed to get out. "I look at her and I can't imagine a life without her. I'm so grateful that Allah spared both of our lives, but I can't help but to feel sad because I'm broken. I can't give you babies... that's not fair to you, no matter what you say." I stared at her. "Stop looking at me with those eyes, Cappadonna." She turned around away from me.

"What you mean?"

"The way you stare at me... your eyes. I don't know how to describe it."

I looked out at the view getting my words together. "The best gift and blessing you have given me is allowing me to be Promise's father. I don't need six kids, as long as I got you, Promise and my son. I'm straight, and I mean that. If there comes a time when we want to give her a sibling, we will do what needs to be done to make it happen. I'll spend whatever to keep a smile on your face."

She laid her head on my chest. "I love you."

"Oh shit, you don't think?"

"Can you let it go already," she giggled.

"I love you, too... you gonna be my wife one day, Alaia. When I was sitting up all those years, the only thing I wanted was a wife and a family. Did I expect to come home and find that in months? Nah. But I know he makes no mistakes. You were mistreated in the past, taken advantage of, and I put this on my daughter and son's life that you won't ever feel like that again. I'm gonna always respect you and love the fuck out of you."

"Promise?"

"I put that on Promise." I kissed her on the head, as we enjoyed the view in front of us.

I wanted my baby to live a life where she woke up happy every damn day. I'd bust fucking heads to make sure she always felt protected and loved with me. She didn't need to know the Capp that should have been committed. She just needed to know Cappadonna, her man, her daughter's father that would do whatever for his family.

She was my family.

27
TAZ

"Why are you so concerned with her anyway? If she moved on with her life, then let her go. The infatuation that both you and Zayne had with her was a little crazy." Fatima sat the plate of food in front of me.

I wanted to slide this plate across the table, sending it onto the floor. Zayne allowed her to have all that mouth and I was tired of hearing that shit. She was jealous because when Alaia came into the family she became Zayne's favorite. He would never tell her, but he loved the fuck out of Alaia's ass.

"Because she fucking belongs to me, and I want what's mine. He gave her ass too much fucking freedom... had she been my wife, her ass would have been under lock and key."

Fatima sat across from me with her food. "Well, he had three other wives he needed to be worried about. Plus, you can't keep someone under lock and key when you are the one under lock and key."

We both started laughing because that shit was funny. This was why me and Fatima always got along. Whenever my brother was on her nerves, she would call me and we had this connection. Like best friends that could get on each other's nerves.

"You right. You right. Raheem's ass been calling talking about he got another one like Alaia. There is no other one like her."

"Raheem is broke and will do anything to make some money."

I smirked. "He sure would do anything."

After his ass got shot, he had a bunch of medical debt because he thought he was paralyzed. His ass was in a wheelchair for a few months before I saw him walking again. Money was what moved Raheem, and I knew all I had to do was wave the right amount in his face and he would do anything.

"Did you go to Cam's funeral?" Fatima asked about my cousin that I had sent to handle Cappadonna.

Cam was the man you called when you needed him to handle somebody. I never expected his ass would end up being the one handled. They said someone snapped his fucking neck. I knew exactly who was responsible and while I wasn't stupid to come at him without a plan, I knew how to get to him.

Alaia was important to him. A man like Cappadonna didn't give a fuck about much, but I was certain he cared about Alaia. If I wanted to bring him to his knees, then I needed to take the one thing that he cared about – Alaia.

28
CHUBS

"Nigga, act like you wanna play... how the fuck did I beat you for the third time." I mushed the nigga sitting beside me.

He sucked his teeth when I beat his ass for the third time. "Ain't easy to fucking play the game when you sitting here with a gun pointed at me."

The minute that Capp found out that Kendra's slow ass was giving money to Ace to help him, we ran up in one of his traps that was around the corner from ours. We walked in this bitch, slapped the main nigga, and then snatched the controllers for the PlayStation out of their hands. Ace and Zeke were gone, so we were posted up in here.

"Even more of a reason that you fucking suck. How you letting me beat you with one hand... Aye Ma, keep fucking massaging," I ordered his girl, who was massaging my shoulders.

Nigga should have known that it was a hell no to try and get some buns in the trap. Soon as we came up in this bitch, he came running from the back with pants down. She was butt ass naked still in that twin size ass bed with no sheets.

"S...sorry," she cried.

"No, you should be sorry for fucking on a twin mattress with no damn sheets. Who raised you?" I scolded her, even though she was probably the same age as me, or younger.

Just when I thought shit couldn't get worse when it came to Kendra, she managed to double the shit. How the fuck, or why the fuck would you give Ace money from Cappadonna? I should have been feeling sorry for her ass, and I didn't.

"What the fuck is this?"

Bingo.

When I heard Zeke's voice, I kicked my sneakers up on the cheap ass coffee table. "What up Zeke the freak?"

He walked around the couch and stood in front the TV. "Give me a reason I shouldn't fucking pop your top right now."

"Cause then I would have to pop your top, your grandma who is in a nursing home in North Jersey, and her fucking dog that she loves so much." Capp came from the back spraying air freshener. "I fucked that bathroom up, so give it a few before you go up in there."

"What the fuck are you doing here?" It was clear that Zeke wasn't about this life from the way he acted.

Any nigga that walked into his trap and some other niggas was in it, was gonna come in here busting they shit. This nigga ain't pulled his shit once. "Can you move? I'm trying to beat this nigga."

His stupid ass stepped to the side. "I heard Kendra gave Ace a little loan... he ain't never paid me back."

"What the fuck that got to do with why you in here? You should be looking for Kendra's ass."

Capp dried his hands on the back of homies' shirt that stood in the kitchen. "Appreciate that... what's this Amiri?"

If Capp would have said boo, this man would have fucking folded into a box. "Move the fuck out the way!" I yelled.

"According to what I heard, I paid for some shit up in here, so I'm utilizing my new space. Ace took out a loan he didn't pay back, so yeah, this shit is mine until I get my money and a soul or two."

"Fuck," the one sitting next to me whispered as he looked over at his girl, who was doing a terrible fucking job of massaging my shoulders.

"Less knuckles more hand, mamas," I reminded her.

Capp plopped down on the couch, and then looked at Zeke. "Might want to get on the phone with homie and make sure he got my money. Matter fact, go ahead and get out my shit....walk him to the door!" he snapped at the shorty to walk him to the door.

I remember when I used to sit and daydream about who my father was. What kind of man was he? Did he have a cool job or drive a cool car? As I sat across from my pops, I had this immense sense of pride being Cappadonna Delgato's son.

"Throw the controller, pussy."

The one sitting next to me didn't hesitate to give him the controller. "You... sit down right here." He pointed to the chick who had just escorted Zeke out.

She slowly sat down, unsure of what was going on. "Now that I have a daughter of my own, I got a soft spot. I'd take a nigga's head off if he brought my daughter to a fucking trap house. You a queen and you need to make these pussies treat you like one."

She was so scared that she was crying. "O...okay."

"How old are you?"

"Eighteen."

"What you do? I mean, besides fucking on nasty ass mattresses in the back of a trap house." Capp took his eyes off the game and looked at her with disgust.

"I'm in college... I attend John Jay."

"You mean to tell me that you in college and fucking with this bum? What he promised? A new purse, some fire dick, and you ran with that?"

"I love him," she said barely above a whisper.

"And you." Capp snapped his fingers. "You serious about her or you fucking other bitches?" I couldn't help but laugh 'cause this nigga was in here holding a group therapy meeting with this girl, while taking over Ace's trap house.

"He mad serious about her...nigga be acting scared of other chicks!" Homie in the kitchen yelled at Capp's back.

"Let me tell you something. If she means anything to you, you don't ever bring her around your shit. I would never bring my woman around where I handle business... she's far removed from this shit. If I came in here shooting, what would have happened?" He turned his attention to her. "Get the fuck out of here and go to school. Matter fact, the next time I see you, and I will see you again, I want a fucking report card. Until Ace pays me my money, you muthafuckas work for me. Whatever money is made, give that shit over here."

Nobody disagreed. Not like they would, because his ass would have been in here fucking them up.

Me: I'm heading over there in a little while. Wrapping shit up now.

Bae: K.

29
ACE

"What the fuck you mean this nigga is in the trap and had some bitch escort you out?" I barked on the phone at Zeke.

Me and Kendra had just come back from Puerto Rico, and this nigga was on the phone talking crazy. I told his ass not to hit me up because I needed time with my wife. Kendra was all talk, but when I surprised her with a wedding on the beach she cried.

I mean, she was crying too much for me and I was starting to think she was crying because she had to marry me. When Capp came over trying to throw his shit around like he could have my bitch, I had to make a move to lock her ass down.

Soon as I turned my phone back on, this nigga had a bunch of voicemails talking like he was in the confessional room on Bad Girls Club. How the fuck he allowed this sick bitch to enter the trap and blow the bathroom up.

"Look, he said you owe him money. Something about Kendra gave you his money and he want the shit back."

"So what? She gave me his fucking money and he ain't

getting the shit ba....arghhhh!" I hollered, punching Kendra in the head. "You bit my dick, bitch!"

She jumped up with this crazed look in her eyes. "So...sorry, baby... I'm sorry." She profusely apologized. "Did you say that Capp knows about the money I gave you?"

"Hell yeah. Why you all scared? I'm gonna protect you."

Kendra shook her head no and climb off the bed. "I'm not doing this... it was cool when it was little beef, but that nigga will kill us both, Ace."

She was damn near hysterical as she stood in the corner of our bedroom. "I'm not fucking scared of that nigga."

"You fucking should be. Cappadonna is fucking crazy and goes far to prove a point." I watched as she started gathering clothes and shit.

"Where you at?" I turned my attention back to Zeke on the phone.

"On the block just chilling."

Kendra's hysterical ass was pissing me off and I needed to get out the house. This nigga Cappadonna had me so fucked up that I couldn't think straight.

"I'm about to come through."

"So you gonna just leave me in the house?" Kendra was on ten and I needed her to come down to a four, before I slapped her ass around.

"I ain't fucking scared of him and you need to stop being scared, too. You got a husband that's gonna handle the shit."

I could tell from her expression that she wasn't convinced. Ignoring her, I pulled on some clothes and was out the crib before she could piss me off even further. She was acting like that nigga was bulletproof or something.

When I pulled onto the block, I got out my whip and got into Zeke's. He was chilling on the block looking stressed as fuck. "We gonna get that shit back."

"He knows where the fuck my grandmother is, bro'." Zeke was never made for this shit, but he was loyal so I always brought him along.

"And you think he gonna walk in the place and murk your grand moms?"

"He fucking might, Ace! You don't know what this nigga is capable of."

"Calm the fuck down. Both you and Kendra starting to piss me the fuck off." I grabbed my phone out of my pocket.

Unknown: Yerr. Your nephew is fucking beautiful. Lil' sis' was doing good, too.

I stared at my phone like it had transformed in my hand.

Me: Who tf is this?

Unknown: Oh shit... my bad. It's Capp. A shame I held your nephew before you. Congrats, bitch.

Aimee had her baby last week and she was home, so what the fuck was he talking about? I hadn't been able to visit her because I had a lot of shit going on, but Aimee knew I was busy. This nigga went to the hospital to see my fucking sister.

Me: Nigga, you went to see my sister?

Unknown: C'mon on now... niggas ain't tell you I'm not to be fucked with. Tighten up, pussy.

Unknown: Look up, Ace... say cheese.

When I finally looked up, I heard the sound of a dirt bike and saw a masked man driving by, slowing up and pulling his trigger and emptying his gun into the driver side window. I opened the car and fell out onto the floor while he continued to empty his clip into the car window.

He then pulled off down the block, hitting a wheelie as he turned the corner. "Zeke... you good?"

I lifted my head, and saw Zeke slumped in the seat with his eyes wide opened dead. My heart was in my ass, as I took off running toward my car, getting the fuck away from the block.

I was tired of Cappadonna treating me like I was a little nigga. As if I couldn't hold my own and like I hadn't been holding my own since I was a teen. I've put in work and earned my respect back home, and now I had to prove the shit all over again with these niggas. This nigga thought he could take over my trap house and workers like he had it like that.

He crossed the line when he held my fucking nephew and then killed Zeke. I didn't know how to explain to Zeke's mom that his ass was fucking dead because of this bitch ass Capp. My mind was on overdrive as I thought about how he was able to touch my sister. I thanked God nothing happened to her and she was still good. I couldn't say the same about fucking Zeke because he was dead.

Since he wanted to show me the type of time he was on, I was about to show him how the fuck I got down. He under estimated me as a little nigga, and I was about to show him that I could bang my shit just like he could.

He wanted to pretend this shit wasn't about Kendra when I knew it was. He was mad that I not only took his bitch, but I also married her, too. Kendra was all scared, not wanting to leave the house because she was afraid that Capp was coming for her. I couldn't have my baby out here scared, and I damn sure couldn't have her out here doubting me as her man.

I was going to make sure that I showed her that I wasn't to be fucked with. Capp walked around like this big bad wolf, and I was gonna show him that I didn't fear his ass at all. Zeke told me the dread head nigga was with him barking orders and playing my fucking PlayStation 5. I thought it was Kincaid, but he told me it was the other nigga, Chubs.

As I sat across the street, I laughed because I saw him helping an older lady with groceries. He thought shit was sweet and I was about to sit back and allow him to keep playing with me. I let that shit at the block party slide, but it was time for Cappadonna to know that I could come for him and his team whenever I wanted.

I left the car running as I slipped out the driver side and walked across the street. His back was turned because the woman had dropped tomato sauce out the bag. "Oh how you doing?" the lady greeted, and Chubs quickly turned around with his hand on his piece.

I already had mine out and aimed that shit right at his chest, pulling the trigger while the woman screamed, holding her chest. "Oh God, Capella...Oh God—" she fell on the stairs beside him still holding her chest.

"Tell Cappadonna I said check mate." I stared down into Chub's eyes before walking back to my car and speeding down the block.

30
KENDRA

I SHOULD HAVE BEEN happy to be married to a man that wanted to marry me. Except, I cried so hard when he planned this romantic elopement. I started to take my chances by jumping in the damn ocean. Ace was so excited that it broke my heart to tell him that I didn't want to marry him. Capp was going to kill his ass soon, so the marriage wouldn't be that long anyway.

That was the logic that helped me get through the ceremony of me lying about vowing to love him forever and a day. I thought I could fake my way through it until we came back and found out that Cappadonna knew I was giving him money.

Ace was so busy trying to get me to believe he would handle it. How the fuck was I supposed to believe he would handle it when this was the same man that slammed his head into a table, then slapped his cheeks up like a child? I was supposed to trust this man with my life when it came to a lunatic like Capp?

I was surprised that I was still breathing after he found out that I hid his son from him, and cheated on him. Now, he found out about the money, I needed to just pick my dress out and get in the coffin.

My phone started ringing again and I rolled my eyes because whoever had been trying to call me was getting on my nerves. When I grabbed my phone, I saw it was Jasmine and she had called me like twelve times.

"Damn, Jas, what do you want?" I still wasn't fucking with her because she told Capella about his father.

Who the fuck gave her ass the right to tell my business?

"Capella was shot in front of my mom's house, and she suffered a heart attack...get to the fucking hospital now, Kendra!" Jas shrieked on the phone and I sat up.

My chest felt tight and my head was spinning. "Text me the address now... did you call Capp?"

"I fucking called him first... just get here and stop with the questions!" she barked in the phone and ended the call.

I ran around the room tossing anything on and grabbing the keys from the front. Jasmine sent the address to the hospital, and I rushed there. My heart was in my ass thinking about both my aunt and my son. I couldn't lose either of them because they were important to me. Capp couldn't lose Capella because he had just found out about him.

He would really hate me and want me dead if we lost our son. I had years with him sporadically, but he was just getting to know him. Soon as I made it to the hospital, I ran in confused on where to go. After talking to the lady at the front she walked me over to where my cousin was sitting.

"What the fuck happened?"

Jasmine was a mess. Her eyes were swollen and she was gripping the hell out of her phone. "Ma's neighbor called me, and she told me that someone walked up on them as he unloaded the groceries and shot him. She heard mom screaming before she grabbed her chest and fell on the stairs beside him."

I had to sit on the chair next to us and process this. "Why the fuck would anybody shoot him?"

I knew when I found out he was running with Cappadonna and Capone it was a bad idea. He thought living the street life was so glamorous when it was anything but that.

"I don't know. Capella is al—" Jasmine stopped mid-sentence and looked past me. I slowly turned my head to see Capp walking into the emergency room.

His eyes were fire as he held hands with a short plus sized woman with a head wrap. He released her hand and came straight for me and Jasmine jumped in front of me.

"You dead to me, bitch... I can promise that I'm gonna slit your throat if my son don't make it."

His voice, the eyes, and the way he pointed his finger at me scared the fuck out of me. "What are you talking about? I had nothing to do with this," I stammered, scared.

He calmly reached over Jasmine and snatched my phone out of my hand. I didn't bother to try and get it back because he was already scrolling through it. I watched as he put it on speaker.

"What's up, baby?" Ace answered.

"You better fucking pray to God that my son pulls through, because I'm coming to fucking collect either way, pussy." He took my phone and launched it at the wall, causing everyone in the waiting room to jump in fear.

I was still paying for that phone and his ass just tossed it to the wall. The chick he came with, pulled his arm. "Come on, baby... relax, please."

"Who the fuc—"

Capp's hand was around my neck with his face inches from

mine. "You might want to stop talking to me before I have you down in the morgue."

"Cappadonna, stop... they're gonna call security." She pulled on him. "Promise... think of Promise."

I should have been more concerned with the fact that his hand was wrapped around my throat, instead I was more concerned with who Promise was and why he should think of her. He released me and I fell to the floor, gasping for air.

"Is Capella alright... what happened?" Aimee ran over with her baby in her arms hysterical.

Jasmine hugged her, taking the baby from her. "They brought him and—"

When Capp turned around, I saw death in his eyes as he looked at the chick. "Allah knew what I needed... I spared you the last time." The chick he arrived with was doing her best to stand in front of him. "I should have killed you both when I had the chance."

"Cappadonna, don't... that's Capella's girlfriend... this is your grandson!" Jasmine screamed, jumping in front of him while holding the baby. "He...He's your grandson."

To Be Continued.

If you like to discuss my books, make sure to join my reader's group on Facebook.

Made in United States
Orlando, FL
22 January 2025